ALIEN™

UNCIVIL WAR

THE COMPLETE ALIEN™ LIBRARY FROM TITAN BOOKS

The Official Movie Novelizations
by Alan Dean Foster
Alien, Aliens™, Alien 3, Alien: Covenant,
Alien: Covenant Origins

Alien: Resurrection by A.C. Crispin

Alien 3: The Unproduced Screenplay
by William Gibson & Pat Cadigan

Alien
Out of the Shadows by Tim Lebbon
Sea of Sorrows by James A. Moore
River of Pain by Christopher Golden
The Cold Forge by Alex White
Isolation by Keith R.A. DeCandido
Prototype by Tim Waggoner
Into Charybdis by Alex White
Colony War by David Barnett
Inferno's Fall by Philippa Ballantine
Enemy of My Enemy by Mary SanGiovanni
Uncivil War by Brendan Deneen

The Rage War
by Tim Lebbon
Predator™: Incursion, Alien: Invasion
Alien vs. Predator™: Armageddon

Aliens
Bug Hunt edited by Jonathan Maberry
Phalanx by Scott Sigler
Infiltrator by Weston Ochse
Vasquez by V. Castro
Bishop by T. R. Napper

The Complete Aliens Omnibus
Volumes 1–7

Aliens vs. Predators
Ultimate Prey edited by Jonathan Maberry &
Bryan Thomas Schmidt
Rift War by Weston Ochse & Yvonne Navarro
The Complete Aliens vs. Predator Omnibus
by Steve Perry & S.D. Perry

Predator
If It Bleeds edited by Bryan Thomas Schmidt
The Predator by Christopher Golden
& Mark Morris
The Predator: Hunters and Hunted
by James A. Moore
Stalking Shadows by James A. Moore
& Mark Morris
Eyes of the Demon edited by
Bryan Thomas Schmidt

The Complete Predator Omnibus
by Nathan Archer & Sandy Scofield

Non-Fiction
AVP: Alien vs. Predator
by Alec Gillis & Tom Woodruff, Jr.
Aliens vs. Predator Requiem:
Inside The Monster Shop
by Alec Gillis & Tom Woodruff, Jr.
Alien: The Illustrated Story
by Archie Goodwin & Walter Simonson
The Art of Alien: Isolation by Andy McVittie
Alien: The Archive
Alien: The Weyland-Yutani Report
by S.D. Perry
Aliens: The Set Photography
by Simon Ward
Alien: The Coloring Book
The Art and Making of Alien: Covenant
by Simon Ward
Alien Covenant: David's Drawings
by Dane Hallett & Matt Hatton
The Predator: The Art and Making
of the Film by James Nolan
The Making of Alien by J.W. Rinzler
Alien: The Blueprints by Graham Langridge
Alien: 40 Years 40 Artists
Alien: The Official Cookbook
by Chris-Rachael Oseland
Aliens: Artbook by Printed In Blood
Find the Xenomorph by Kevin Crossley

ALIEN™
UNCIVIL WAR

A NOVEL BY BRENDAN DENEEN

TITAN BOOKS

A L I E N ™ : U N C I V I L W A R
Print edition ISBN: 9781803366951
E-book edition ISBN: 9781803366968

Published by Titan Books
A division of Titan Publishing Group Ltd
144 Southwark Street, London SE1 0UP
www.titanbooks.com

First edition: July 2024
10 9 8 7 6 5 4 3 2 1

This is a work of fiction. All of the characters, organizations, and events portrayed in this novel are either products of the author's imagination or are used fictitiously. Any resemblance to actual persons, living or dead (except for satirical purposes), is entirely coincidental.

Brendan Deneen asserts the moral right to be identified as the author of this work.

A CIP catalogue record for this title is available from the British Library.

Printed and bound by CPI Group (UK) Ltd, Croydon, CR0 4YY.

Did you enjoy this book?
We love to hear from our readers. Please email us at readerfeedback@titanemail.com or write to us at Reader Feedback at the above address.
www.titanbooks.com

This novel is dedicated to
Ridley Scott, Dan O'Bannon, and Ronald Shusett,
and David Giler and Walter Hill.

Collectively, you created a masterpiece of a film
that contained three essential elements that
spawned a massive franchise.

I'm honored to now be a part of it.

PART 1

GESTATION

1

TRANSPORT SHIP VX-72383
MAY 23, 2381

Another explosion rocked the ship.

Chris Temple glanced over at the corner of his small living quarters, where his two daughters, Jane and Emma, stood with Alicia, who had both arms wrapped around them. Alicia had what seemed like a look of genuine concern in her eyes, but Chris knew that was impossible. She was, after all, an auton—a highly developed synthetic who nonetheless hadn't been programmed with real human emotion.

Then again, she seemed different lately—ever since those men had broken into their house and damaged her shortly before they'd left it for the final time. The home where his girls had spent their entire lives. The ensuing trip to Gateway Station and then quickly boarding this transport vessel were a blur.

"Dad?" Jane said, her voice breaking on the single syllable. Even though Chris always considered his oldest child shockingly wise for her age, she was still only eleven.

Emma, nearly as tall as Jane even though she was three years younger, stared at her father with a shocked look on her face, almost dazed, as if her brain had shut down—a small miracle, perhaps. Even though this was a new experience for his daughters, Chris had been in similar situations many times, and he'd seen people much older and more experienced than his daughters completely break down during emergencies.

But that was in his previous life. He thought he'd left this kind of thing behind him.

War will always find a man like you, his sergeant had said to him, when Chris finally found the courage to quit the military in the days after the USM *Auriga* smashed into the Earth. So much had changed since Chris had joined the service as a younger man—and was still changing—but that disaster, and all its secrets that had been hidden from the public, were the final straw for him. He wanted out—out of *all* of it. He and his daughters needed a fresh start on a new planet.

Chris calmed his nerves. He'd trained for this.

"Everything's going to be okay," he responded, walking over and kneeling in front of his daughters, placing a hand on each of their shoulders. "I'm sure it's just a minor malfunction."

The lie sounded terrible even to his own ears.

"Alicia," he said without looking at the family's android, forcing his voice to remain steady despite his own fear. "Can you hack into the ship and find out what's going on?"

"My protocols do not allow me to connect with any ship's mainframe without prior United Systems Military authorization," she responded in a monotone voice. She got like that when she was quoting the rules.

"I'm giving you that authorization right now," he said, his voice louder, tone suddenly clipped. His daughters' eyes widened. They had never heard their father speak like that before—certainly not since the death of their mother. "Sigma epsilon default seven seven two, protocol unlock."

He hadn't thought of this specific string of words in a long time, not since he'd been promoted to colonel, but they reemerged out of the dark recesses of his mind as if they'd been waiting there, anticipating this exact moment, all along.

Alicia's head twitched slightly as she slipped into the ship's computer, then glanced briefly down at the girls and back up at Chris, staring him directly in the eyes.

"We should evacuate. *Immediately*."

Jane let out a small whimper, but her eyes remained dry. She gently, silently took her younger sister's hand in her own.

Chris knew that there must have been a reason why Alicia wasn't giving him any details in front of the girls. The situation was bad.

Very bad.

"Grab any essentials," he ordered, his voice still hard. "Only what you can carry. You have ten seconds." Jane nodded, clearly afraid but always a good soldier, and pulled her sister along, off to their tiny, shared bedroom.

Chris hated the way he sounded but knew there wasn't any other choice. He'd been in life-and-death situations before, and survival often hinged on seconds, not minutes.

He glanced at Alicia, who stared back without blinking, even though she was programmed to do so, and then dashed to his own quarters, reaching under his bed and grabbing his go-bag. Elizabeth used to make fun of his "over-preparedness."

Elizabeth.

The thought of her sent a wave of pain racing across his body. He had promised on her deathbed that he would always take care of their girls, that nothing bad would ever happen to them. Those words had elicited a smile from her, the last thing she ever did before slipping away. He couldn't fail.

War will always find a man like you.

"*No,*" he said out loud, running into the common area, where Alicia still stood in the exact same spot, her head slightly tilted as if she was listening to a particularly interesting radio drama. She turned to look at Chris again and opened her mouth to speak, perhaps to clue him in to what the hell was going on, when his girls came running in, too.

Nine seconds, Chris thought, his chest filling up with pride. But no, there was no time to be proud.

"Follow me," he ordered. "Stay close and do *exactly* what I say. That includes you, Alicia."

"But…" she started to respond, then stopped herself and nodded.

The interaction caused Chris to hesitate for the slightest moment. Her programming shouldn't have allowed for any kind of active disagreement with him in this kind of situation, but she was clearly fighting against it. Was that even possible? Her face reflected a mix of conflicting emotions, but he didn't have time to investigate her control structures.

Chris moved to the door. He punched in the security code and watched as the two thick metal panels slid open, revealing a hallway full of smoke and strobing lights.

He stepped forward and could hear his girls and Alicia following close behind. A sort of calm washed across his senses, the bizarre but familiar sensation blanketing him for the first time since he'd been an active soldier.

A memory came back to him—his last real battle before the *Auriga* crash. They'd been sent to deal with a large, violent group of Weyland-Yutani cultists who had carried out a series of terrorist attacks against key USM targets.

The incursion had been brutal and bloody. Chris had been forced to do things that still haunted him.

Weyland-Yutani had been out of business for decades, but an almost religious following had risen up in its place, elevating the company's two founders—Peter Weyland and Cullen Yutani—to almost godlike stature. Acolytes of this faction had continued to work in secrecy after their beloved corporation's collapse, allegedly even having moles within the USM, gathering data and stealing equipment for mysterious reasons, an unknown agenda. It was a slow boil of aggression between the two uneven entities, and then the crash of the *Auriga*—and the resulting secrets that came to light—had thrown this shadow war into open chaos. The world descended even further into confusion and violence. People who had the means to escape, did. Including Chris and his girls.

He continued to move forward, keeping as low as possible, listening as distant screams echoed. He had studied the layout of this transport ship for hours once they'd been assigned to it. *You can never be overprepared.*

When he turned right at the corridor's first intersection, towards the transport ship's escape pods, he glanced back, relieved to see his girls and Alicia were still right behind him, faces stoic and determined. He couldn't wait to hold them close, tell them how proud he was, if… *when* they got out of here.

They continued on. Chris was surprised, and concerned, by the lack of people they came across. Yes, a large percentage of the civilians on board had elected to enter hypersleep chambers almost immediately after takeoff. A few had decided to stay awake for part of the trip, even though they would age at a regular rate during that time. Jane and Emma hadn't been ready to enter one of those intimidating devices for the first time, and Chris decided to let them choose when the time was right.

All awake civilians on board had been instructed to shelter in place during an emergency but that didn't explain where all the guards and other non-civilians were—like the scientists he had seen scurrying around during their months-long journey so far.

He'd heard the rumors—and had done his best to ignore them.

Rumors of genetic materials being shipped with them to their new host planet. Rumors of experiments being conducted during the journey itself in anticipation of their eventual arrival. Even rumors of active cloning. And one name—a name that sent literal shivers up and down his spine every time he heard it.

Ripley.

That name meant nothing to the masses, but his rank within the military had allowed him access to information that would have given pause to even the most seasoned of soldiers.

But no, that was insane. It couldn't be anything more than a ridiculous rumor, spread by people who trucked in conspiracy theories and fantasy. Because if what he'd heard was actually true, if the kind of situation that had doomed the *Nostromo* and the *Auriga* and so many others was playing out in any kind of fashion on this ostensibly non-military mission...

A gurgling sound down a hallway to their left interrupted Chris's thoughts as he and his family continued to hustle forward.

He knew he should keep moving, knew that curiosity was often a death knell in combat situations. But he hesitated, and looked, and then wished he hadn't.

Down the hallway, through the haze of smoke, he saw a security guard who seemed to be floating. The man's arms were outstretched as if in religious ecstasy, but there was nothing religious or ecstatic about the look on his face. His eyes and mouth were wide in soundless agony, his body convulsing in time to some rhythm that no one could hear.

Chris focused his eyes, tried to make out what was happening, and that's when he saw that something was jutting straight through the guard's midsection—in through the front and out the back, with blood gushing down onto the floor, pooling there and reflecting the red strobe of the emergency lights. At first it looked like some kind of black weapon that had impaled him, but the end of it was swaying gently, like a tree branch in the wind.

Or a tail.

The smoke cleared for a moment and Chris finally saw what the black 'weapon' was attached to—something he had read about in military journals, had even seen on grainy, terrifying video footage after his last promotion, but had never actually witnessed in real life. Very few people had.

It was a Xenomorph.

The creature was taller than Chris expected, and its long, ridged tail had skewered the guard while the monster stood staring curiously at the suffering man, as if trying to understand what it had wrought, what it was witnessing.

Its head was a long, glinting slope, coming together at its forefront with a silver jaw of teeth which opened and closed as it observed its prey. Four large ridges extended out of its upper back and its six-fingered claws seemed to be shivering with excitement. Chris had read that the creatures were like animals, that they took no pleasure in slaughter, they were simply acting on pure instinct.

A descriptive term from one of the classified military manuals dedicated to the Xenomorphs suddenly flashed in his mind.

Perfect killing machines.

At that moment, Emma let loose with a scream that almost caused Chris to literally jump. She had clearly caught her first glimpse of the monster. And he couldn't blame her for yelling.

The creature's elongated cranium turned towards them, the skewered guard letting out a final, wet gasp before going completely limp.

Chris had taken notice of the guards during the time they'd been traveling on this ship. They definitely weren't USM officers, retired or otherwise, which wasn't altogether surprising. The chaos that had erupted on Earth after the crash of the *Auriga*, and from the general discontent from the world populace about the heavily polluted, damaged planet, had seen a number of soldiers go AWOL. It wasn't easy to find experienced officers for a long-term, low-paying mission.

He had briefly thought about volunteering to help guard the transport ship, but Chris had pushed the idea away as quickly as it appeared. His daughters had already been through enough. They didn't need their father to be gone for hours at a time, even during an 'uneventful' trip to their new home.

But the current situation was clear enough: the guards on this ship weren't prepared to deal with an emergency of this magnitude.

Chris and his girls were on their own.

He barked a single word—"Go!"—and watched as Alicia surged forward, grabbing each of his daughters by the hand. In situations where an enemy is behind you, the most capable soldier always takes rear position.

Backing up as quickly as he could, hearing Jane, Emma, and their cybernetic caretaker sprinting forward behind him, Chris observed as the Xenomorph quickly withdrew its tail from the dead guard, a final burst of blood exploding from the corpse's stomach before it collapsed on the ground, face first.

The Xenomorph seemed to be staring at Chris, though he couldn't see the creature's eyes, and it bared its teeth at him, saliva dripping from its dark jaw. Then the monster took a single step in his direction, its claws slowly closing into what seemed like purposeful fists.

That was all Chris needed to see. He turned and sprinted after Alicia and his girls.

His vision tunneled. He had never been in this particular section of the ship, had never needed to journey down here. He knew the escape pods were off limits to civilians unless orders were given otherwise, but he didn't care about protocols at this given moment. The commanding officers of this vessel were either dead or very bad at their jobs. No instructions had been given over the loudspeakers, which meant Chris was free to create his own mission parameters, as far as he was concerned. He was getting his daughters off this damn ship.

Alive.

Chris caught up with Alicia and they glanced at each other, the auton smiling slightly, a look of deep compassion in her eyes as she continued to shepherd the girls along to potential safety. He had never seen the family's android like this. If he hadn't been in pure protection and survival mode, he would have been deeply perplexed.

"I remain connected to the ship's central database," she said. At first, he was surprised that she didn't sound winded by the run, but then remembered that she didn't actually have lungs. He wasn't thinking straight. "Despite multiple systems failures, it is rerouting for the closest inhabited planet, LV-1213. There is a colony there—Mining Outpost Omega Seven Tango. There is a twenty-eight percent chance it will be able to reach its destination intact. However, the escape pods are currently unaffected by the power outages."

"How close?" he managed to respond.

She narrowed her eyes almost playfully at his question, what he took as confusion, not an emotion she normally expressed.

"Two minutes until we reach the escape pod. Approximately five hundred thousand miles to the outpost," she said succinctly, answering whichever question he had meant to ask.

"Daddy, I'm scared," Emma finally cried.

"He's doing his best!" Jane yelled, her own face finally revealing the terror she felt, unleashing it on her sister since she couldn't do so on the situation itself. Still running, Chris scooped his younger daughter into his arms, had to stop himself from bursting into tears as she shoved her face into the space between his shoulder and neck, and she started crying instead, her tiny sobs reaching his ears.

"Girls…" he huffed. "We're almost there. We're going to be okay."

A noise suddenly sounded behind them—a skittering that caused goosebumps to run along Chris's flesh. He knew *exactly* what it was. He also knew they were out of time. There was no way they could make it.

"I'm sorry," he whispered. To no one. To all of them. To Elizabeth.

As he started to turn around, ready to go down fighting, Chris was surprised by a blur of motion in the corner of his vision. The Xenomorph exploded out of the smoke right in front of him, its claws heading straight for his face, but Alicia was faster. She tackled the monster at full speed, slamming it into the wall with a concussive force that he could literally feel, and the two of them rolled along the floor in a flash of coiled black muscle and synthetic human limbs.

They vanished back into the smoke.

"Alicia!" Jane screamed, starting to move back towards the family's auton.

Chris grabbed her with his free hand, lifting her slightly off the ground, holding Emma with the other, and pushed forward, drawing from reserves he didn't know he still had.

"No! We have to help her!" his older daughter yelled, fighting him.

"She'll be fine!" Chris lied, and he immediately felt her resistance lessen, but her exertions were still slowing him down. "Jane. Please."

She went completely slack in his grip, and he let go, dropping her to the floor as gently as he could while still moving forward, and she continued to run next to him without missing a beat, keeping an impressive pace. Within moments, they reached the escape pods. The area was depressingly empty. No one else had made it here in the short time since the explosions had begun.

Chris ran to the console on the wall and quickly entered command codes that no normal passenger would know. The doors to the multiple escape pods immediately hissed open and he sprinted for the closest one, still holding a shivering Emma, his other arm now wrapped around Jane's small shoulders and pushing her forward with him.

The pod was smaller than he expected, but he didn't give a damn. He quickly got each girl situated in one of the four seats—a number that broke his heart for multiple reasons. He thought of Elizabeth, part of him glad that she didn't have to experience this, a larger part of him still missing her desperately. And he thought of Alicia, most likely being ripped limb from limb by the Xenomorph at this very moment. He shook the images from his mind and focused on saving his daughters.

The girls now buckled in, Chris shimmied to the front of the pod and collapsed into the pilot seat, hitting buttons on the computer console as fast as he could. The transport ship shuddered violently as another explosion sounded in the distance and his girls screamed behind him. They were both openly weeping now.

Jane hadn't cried since Elizabeth's funeral, and the gentle sound broke Chris's heart.

He strapped himself in, set his jaw against the noise, and finished punching in the launch codes, remembering what his superior officers had taught him: *Emotions get soldiers killed.*

The escape pod door began to shut just as the Xenomorph burst out of the smoke down the hallway, a bone-chilling screech emanating from its gaping, razor-lined mouth. There was no sign of Alicia.

"Don't look!" Chris screamed at his girls, looking around for his go-bag, inside of which was the pistol he'd smuggled onto the transport ship. As he quickly surveyed the pod, he realized they had all dropped their bags while fleeing from the monster. They only had the clothes on their backs at this point.

It didn't matter. Even if they managed to get free of the

transport ship, they still needed to somehow make it to LV-1213.

Panicking, Chris looked over his left shoulder. The door was still closing, slowly, while the Xenomorph got closer and closer. Its speed was astonishing.

Just as the door was about to seal shut, the metal came to a screeching halt, leaving a small opening. Even that slight gap was enough to stop them from ejecting. And the opening might just be big enough for the large but clearly dexterous creature to slip in and slaughter them.

Without hesitating, Chris unbuckled and bolted forward, gripping the metal and pulling down as hard as he could. He told himself not to look through the door's small window, but he couldn't help himself.

The creature was only a few feet away, its claws outstretched towards his face. It almost looked like the monster was smiling.

"Dad!" Jane screamed, but he couldn't respond. His entire being was focused on getting the damn door closed, on rescuing his daughters.

The metal began to move beneath the weight of his exertions, and he said a silent prayer to whatever deity was paying attention to his plight. In the distance, he heard more explosions, but didn't care.

He slammed the door shut just as the Xenomorph reached it, and he heard the creature slashing at the half foot of metal and reinforced glass that separated them, could feel the violent vibrations against his palms.

"Launch protocols engaged," the computer intoned, and then they were blasting away from the main ship, and his daughters were both screaming, and he was flying through the cabin, and his head smashed into something hard, and Chris Temple instantly succumbed to an all-encompassing, undeniable blackness.

2

THREE MONTHS EARLIER
SAN FRANCISCO, CA, EARTH

"Your father will be home soon."

Alicia folded Jane's shirt and placed it in the travel bag, smiling at the girl as she did so. Emma was off in her own room, talking to herself and shoving far too many items into her own luggage. Alicia would need to go in there soon and help her sort through her belongings, figure out the most important things to take—and leave the rest.

"Are you sure?"

Alicia could hear the fear in Jane's voice, but her sub-routines instructed her not to mention it. Humans didn't always like to have their emotions pointed out, especially the 'negative' ones, though it was often difficult to decipher which were positive, and which were not. And sometimes, the values flip-flopped. It was hard to compute, impossible to predict. So, Alicia remained silent on the matter, and instead placed her hand gently on the girl's shoulder.

"Yes. He sent me a message an hour ago that he was on his way."

Jane looked up into Alicia's face, her eyes asking questions that her mouth couldn't seem to quite verbalize, then went back to going through her belongings. She was considering each object as if she was an archeologist, attempting to pinpoint the value of every artifact she held, then either putting it into the bag, or placing it gently into the discard pile.

Although Alicia didn't experience human emotions, something about the care the girl was taking with each decision made her circuitry almost physically hurt. She couldn't quite understand the intricacies of what she was witnessing, no matter how hard she tried. So, she shunted the images to one of her many sub-processors, would attempt to comprehend them again later, when circumstances weren't so tumultuous.

"Do you think the colony will be nice?" Jane murmured, holding two stuffed animals, looking back and forth at them quizzically, weighing their individual merits, knowing that only one would be deemed worthy to be chosen.

"Based on the records and the images to which I have access," Alicia responded, "I believe it will be more than adequate for our needs."

"Yeah, I know," Jane said, looking up. "But do you... you know... Do you think we'll *like* it?"

Alicia contemplated the question, tilting her head slightly—it was an affectation that she couldn't control, a glitch in her programming. None of the other domestic autons she had met did this. It bothered her. Chris said he liked it, but Alicia considered it a personal failing, and often wished that he would authorize a diagnostic to fix the error. But she didn't verbalize this, decided that such a request would cause inconvenience for the Temple family.

"I do not know. I certainly hope so," she responded after a moment.

"Are you... definitely coming with us?" Jane asked, looking away from Alicia, keeping her eyes focused on the pair of pants that she was now folding.

"Of course," Alicia said quickly, the speed of her response surprising even her. She tended to compute answers to her humans' questions very carefully, running through any number of options and variables. But this time, she had spoken before processing, something she couldn't recall ever doing before. "If you and your sister and your father still want me to, that is," she added—a more calculated addendum to her initial, spontaneous answer.

"I do," Jane responded softly, then looked up, directly into Alicia's eyes. "I love you and I want you to come with us. Very badly."

Alicia opened her mouth to speak but her various operating systems seemed to be at odds with each other. Since the moment she had been switched on at the factory, no one had ever said that they loved her. It wasn't something she expected to hear, if she was being truly honest with herself, and even though her central processing unit always formulated dozens of acceptable conversational responses within milliseconds, she now found herself unable to speak.

"It's okay," Jane said, turning her eyes back to her work. "You don't have to say it back. Dad has trouble saying it sometimes, too, since Mom died. But I love you, Alicia. And so does Emma. She told me yesterday. We both want you to come with us and be with us forever."

"Jane, I—" Alicia started to say, having settled on an answer that her programming indicated was gentle and honest. However, the sound of smashing glass downstairs interrupted her words and caused Alicia to raise a hand, instantly stilling the girl's movements.

With her heightened hearing, she listened as Emma's footsteps padded down the hallway, soft but urgent, and the small girl burst into the room a moment later, her eyes wide with fear.

"Did you… Did you hear that?" she asked, barely more than a whisper.

"I did," Alicia answered, standing smoothly and heading towards the hall. "I want you both to stay here and lock the door after I leave. I am sure it is nothing serious, but I will make sure and come right back. No matter what, I will not let anything happen to you."

Jane nodded, swallowing nervously, while Emma sat down on the bed next to her older sister, shimmying in close. It was something Jane wouldn't normally allow but she didn't seem to mind the proximity at this particular moment.

Alicia exited the room and shut the door behind her as quietly as she could. After a moment, she heard the lock click. *Good girl*, she thought. Based on the sound of the footsteps and the weight on the floorboards beneath them, it was Jane. To Alicia's surprise, the girl's words— *I love you*—replayed in her mainframe but she bypassed those memory circuits and focused on the task at hand. She would process what she'd heard later. Right now, she needed to investigate what was happening on the first floor of the house. She couldn't hear precisely what was occurring down there, but she knew someone was inside. Possibly more than one person.

She descended the stairs in utter silence. Despite the carpet, they were wooden and old enough that they creaked with nearly every step when Chris or his two girls went up and down them. Alicia, however, knew every inch of the stairs, could avoid any part of them that would make even the tiniest amount of noise.

Alicia saw them first—two huge men who were rummaging through drawers, shoving random items into backpacks. They whispered to each other, determined to keep their conversation to themselves, but she could hear every word. They were thieves, pure and simple. Break-ins, muggings, and robberies had increased 876 percent in the past year alone—just one of the reasons Chris was taking his family off this planet.

She caught a glimpse of one man's profile and ran his face through her database. It had become increasingly difficult to get reliable information as the worldwide information network attempted to stabilize amidst global chaos, but information about this criminal downloaded almost immediately into her mainframe.

He had been incarcerated for larceny. Assault. Murder. And was supposed to still be in prison. But had escaped, along with another dangerous inmate. Presumably the other man currently pilfering Elizabeth's jewelry.

Alicia watched them for moment, her head tilting. She recognized that humans had created a society that was inherently unfair, where people suffered while others flourished, sometimes outlandishly so. But she couldn't compute this kind of desperation, or the decision to hurt others in order to prosper. It was especially difficult for her to comprehend because the Temple home was modest by most standards. Then again, there were many things about humans that she found impossible to understand. Like how Jane and Emma would sometimes tickle their father until he literally cried.

The second man, slightly smaller but still significantly taller and broader than Alicia, turned and noticed her. He looked alarmed for a brief moment but then looked her up and down, and a nasty smile spread like liquid silver across his stubbled face.

"Yo," he said, elbowing the other man in the ribs. "Check out what we got here."

The larger thief turned as well and instantly showcased a similar grin.

"Ooooh, bonus," he growled, then licked his lips and took a step forward.

He grabbed at her, but she deftly sidestepped his lunge, clocking the other man in her peripheral vision as he flanked her. She thought about grabbing and smashing them together, putting a quick end to this, but her behavioral inhibitor was switched on, which meant it was impossible for her to harm, or by omission of action allow to be harmed, any human.

"She's a fast little bitch," the taller one said, then grabbed at her again, quicker this time. But it was slow to her, and she slapped his hand away, a little harder than she'd intended. The discrepancy between intent and action was curious, and shouldn't have happened. She would have to run a self-analysis once this situation was handled.

"Please leave this home immediately," she said without emotion. "It is a private residence, and you are trespassing, which is a violation of United Systems Military law."

"Look at that, Terrence," the larger man said, circling her, zipping up the half-full backpack and dropping it onto the floor. Alicia could hear his heart rate increasing. He was excited, ready for violence. "She's quotin' the rules at us."

"Hot," the other man responded, also circling her now, twin orbits ready to crash into her at any given moment. She could only keep her cybernetic eyes on one of them at a time, but her other senses were far more expansive than a human's, so she could inherently 'see' both of them at the same time. Terrence's heart rate was more controlled, as was his breathing, which she took to mean that he was the more dangerous of the two, even though he was smaller.

And sure enough, Terrence lunged forward, an impressive display of speed for an organic, and jabbed a punch at her face. She dodged it but the other man tackled her from behind at the same moment. His surprised grunt when she didn't fall made it clear that he had no idea what he was up against.

"The fuck?" he grunted, his arms still around her, legs straining, trying to knock her over. "Hit her!"

Terrence threw another punch, but she moved her head at the last second and his knuckles passed millimeters from her nose. "I'm trying, Mackie!" he practically screamed.

Alicia attempted to redirect her sub-routines so she could lash out and attack these two men, but her protocols were too deeply ingrained in her programming. She could avoid their blows, even defend herself within a certain set of confines, but she was unable to hurt them. Even if she believed, on some level, that they deserved it.

Mackie let go and the two men faced off with her again. Terrence withdrew a large knife from within his long leather jacket, and a large smile appeared on his face.

"I like when they play hard to get," he murmured, and then lashed out with shocking speed once again while Mackie also feigned an attack at the same time. Their simultaneous movements, combined with Alicia's internal battle against her own programming, caused her to hesitate just long enough for the knife to connect along her arm, splitting the silicone skin and revealing an epidermis of metal and silver circuitry. A small burst of electricity resulted, and two of her fingers instantly went dead. Milky white liquid oozed from the cut.

The two criminals stared at the wound, at what was revealed within.

"She's a robot, man!" Mackie shouted. "Let's fucking *ice* her!"

The larger man withdrew a knife, too, and Alicia doubted herself for the first time since the start of this encounter. Her programming put her at a distinct disadvantage here. She could defend herself, yes, but without being able to press an attack, there was a significant probability that the two men would eventually overpower her. She backed up a step, running through options. After less than a second, she resolved that discretion was the better part of valor and decided to connect with local law enforcement—even though there were many reports lately of calls for help that had gone unanswered.

Still, it was what she should have done initially. Why hadn't she? Another aspect of her programming to investigate when she had time to run that analysis.

As the men began to advance on her again and her digital call for help was silently sent, a voice cut through everything.

"Alicia?"

Her head snapped to the right and she looked over her shoulder, even though she knew exactly who it was.

Jane stood on the steps, still in her pajamas, eyes huge and confused and concerned.

The two men also stared at the young girl, and now Terrence's heartbeat increased for the first time since Alicia had encountered him. He stepped towards the stairs, knife raised, and at that moment Alicia's programming clicked into a different mode. Jane was in danger.

Or by omission of action allow a human to be harmed.

Alicia moved faster than she ever had since the moment she'd been activated. Terrence was several steps from reaching Jane, but Alicia caught his forearm, snapping it backwards and breaking it before the man even knew what was happening. For a moment, he stared at the appendage as it flopped lifelessly, and then he started screaming, a high-pitched noise that sounded like the cry of a newborn human.

She heard Jane's sudden intake of breath at the shocking violence from the family's auton, but before Alicia could say anything to help assure the girl, to calm her, Mackie was on the android, grabbing her from behind and driving his knife deep into her back, more white fluid exploding out from the wound and all over his hand and arm. Luckily, the blade missed any of Alicia's vital systems, but it was still a curious sensation. She lost control of eighteen percent of her left leg as a result of the incision but in relation to the violent encounter in which she was engaged, it was not a significant disadvantage.

She let go of Terrence's arm and the man immediately slumped to the ground, his scream having been replaced with a jagged whimper. Mackie was shockingly strong for a human and shoved the blade deeper into her frame, causing her left leg to buckle further, down another twelve percent. She titled her head slightly as she attempted to move that leg, wasn't completely successful. She had never been damaged like this.

"I'm gonna fuckin' kill you," the man whispered harshly into her ear. "And then it'll be that little bitch's turn."

Something about the man's words caused her sensors to go slightly fuzzy, and while the man began to raise the knife up along her back, causing further damage and more milky fluid to gush out, she reached back and grabbed hold of his neck, squeezing with more strength than she had ever applied to a human before. She felt the skin and muscles immediately give underneath her grip, and the man screamed. She didn't care.

She flipped him over her head, smashing him hard against the bottom of the stairs. The knife went flying out of his hand and the breath exploded out of his mouth, eyes going wide in pain. Blinking rapidly, he looked at her with confusion, wordlessly asking for mercy as she pulled her fist back.

Alicia was not merciful.

The impact to his face broke nose, teeth, and one eye socket, rendering Mackie instantly unconscious. She brought her bloody fist back, ready to deliver a second blow, but she waited a moment, her sensors determining that he wouldn't be waking up for quite some time. Terrence had passed out, too. His readings indicated that he would be unconscious for a significant duration as well, and his arm would never regain normal function.

Alicia attempted again to contact local law enforcement. She reached them after thirty-six seconds and explained the situation without having to say a word out loud. Based on her interactions with the USM system, she knew that help would arrive within six to ten minutes. Neither man would be awake by then.

As she looked up and took a step forward, she stumbled slightly, surprised by how much her leg had been impacted by Mackie's attack. To Alicia's surprise, Jane was there, moving more quickly than the auton could have anticipated, helping the family's android regain her balance.

"Are you okay?" Jane whispered, heart beating rapidly within her small chest.

"I am operating within acceptable parameters," Alicia responded, running another diagnostic. Overnight self-repairs would be more than sufficient to handle her wounds.

"Alicia, no," Jane insisted, looking into her auton's eyes. "Are you *okay*?"

Alicia tilted her head at the question, one she had already answered. She checked her database, attempting to delineate the difference in the exact same question, and then settled on an answer that seemed appropriate.

"It was an unsettling experience, Jane. But I am very glad that you and Emma are safe."

The girl smiled at the answer and then wrapped her arms around Alicia, hugging her tightly. Alicia replicated the movement, hugging back. They stayed like that for a while. Emma came running down the stairs a moment later and joined the embrace. The house was quiet, other than the labored breathing of the two injured men.

At length, the two girls pulled away from Alicia. Jane stared at the android, then slowly tucked an errant piece of hair behind the auton's ear.

"You do love us, don't you?" Jane said slowly, quietly, eyes large with emotion.

Alicia ran the question through her sub-processors. Love was a concept that androids had been programmed to avoid at all costs—human history proved that it was too dangerous to engage in the matter. Therefore, autons were discouraged from discussing it, and never permitted to express the emotion, to a human or otherwise.

Still, she wanted to say the words to them. On some level, Alicia felt the girls deserved to hear them from her, especially after the death of their mother. And maybe she... *felt* that way, too? But no, that was impossible. Synthetic beings had no emotion, not *real* emotion anyway. Any errant electric impulses her servers were expressing at this moment were clearly because of the damage that had been caused by the two criminals. She would repair herself, diagnose any internal problems as needed and fix them, and do her job, just as she had been created to do.

In response to Jane's question, Alicia simply nodded. She wasn't saying the words—so no programming ethics had been breached. And clearly the gesture was enough, because Jane hugged her again, even stronger this time, and Emma did the same.

"I love you," Jane whispered.

"I love you," Emma whispered, too.

Alicia fought to respond, to say what they wanted to hear, but her program wouldn't allow it, so she simply continued to nod. Over and over again.

3

MINING OUTPOST OMEGA SEVEN TANGO

Chris Temple shot up, screaming.

He was sitting on a small bed in a dark, unfamiliar room. There was a single window to his right, but it was covered by a cloth shade, and there was no light emanating from behind it. It was night. Or simulated night, if he was on a ship. But this didn't look like any ship he'd ever been on.

There was a door across the room, so he quickly stood up, nearly lost his balance as his head swam, but powered forward, placing a hand along the smooth, painted wall as he headed towards the room's only seeming exit. He didn't know where he was or what was happening, but he needed to find Jane and Emma.

Just as he was about to reach it, the door burst open and several people rushed in, surrounding him and grabbing at his arms. They were talking all at once, but his head was spinning, and his mind went white as his training kicked in instinctively.

Chris grabbed the closest person and pulled him forward, using the man's height against him, then flipped him over and slammed his large frame against the floor. A gush of pained breath exploded out of his first adversary's lungs, and the man didn't get up right away, just rolled onto his side and groaned.

One down.

Before the other two could react, Chris threw a vicious uppercut into his second adversary's chin, connecting with a nasty crack, throwing the man violently against the wall, his head snapping back against it. He slumped to the ground in a disheveled pile, arms and legs a tangled mess.

Chris whirled on the third and final enemy. It was a woman and she stared at him with fear but held up two fists, clearly ready to fight. He advanced on her, jaw set, studying her posture, ready to take her apart and get the hell out of there. Wherever he was. He still couldn't clear his mind, couldn't piece together his last memories before the gaping maw of darkness in his mind. And then they came to him in a rush.

The ship. The Xenomorph. The escape pod.

Just as he grabbed the woman by her green shirt and drew back his fist, a familiar voice instantly froze him in his tracks.

"Dad! Stop!"

Chris's head snapped over his left shoulder and all the fight instantly went out of him. Jane and Emma were standing there, staring at him with shock on their faces. He didn't recognize their clothes and their hair was pulled back in twin, braided ponytails, something he hadn't seen since Elizabeth had died. But he didn't care. They were unhurt. They were *alive*.

He rushed forward and fell to his knees as he reached them, wrapping his arms around their small bodies, fighting back tears of relief and confusion. His thoughts were still so hazy, but he just closed his eyes against the buzzing in his mind and pressed his face into the small space between his daughters, feeling their warmth on both sides of his head.

"Are you okay?" Jane asked, quietly.

The tenor of her voice snapped him out of his momentary fog. He pulled back and blinked several times, looking up into their eyes, smiling despite his bewilderment, and then stood up, glanced around.

The three people he'd just been fighting were slowly getting their bearings, rising to their feet, and they regarded at him with a mix of abject anger and fear. He stared at them more closely, the heat of battle fading away, and realized they were all wearing scrubs.

"Oh my god," he said, taking a half step towards them. The medical professionals all tensed, raising their hands slightly as if a new fight was about to break out. "I'm so sorry."

"Mr Temple?" a new voice said. He turned back around and saw a woman standing behind Jane and Emma. She was tall, almost as tall as him, and had dark hair that was pulled back into the same braided ponytail that his daughters were currently sporting. He glanced down at his girls, smiled sadly, then stepped forward and looked directly into the woman's eyes.

"Where am I? What's happening?"

"I'm sure you're confused, and I'm sorry about that. We were hoping to be with you when you woke up, but our doctors assured us you'd be unconscious for a lot longer. I guess you're a bit stronger than they anticipated."

She laughed slightly but he just watched her, waiting for answers.

"My name is Lexa Phelan. I've been watching your girls while you were unconscious. They were really worried about you."

"You didn't answer my question," Chris said, trying to keep his voice calm. He had no idea what was going on, had no idea if he and his daughters were in danger, but he needed to get as much information as possible while concurrently scoping out his surroundings for potential exit routes and weapons. Exactly as he'd been trained to do. "Where are we?"

"This is Mining Outpost Omega Seven Tango. You and your lovely daughters crash-landed here. But you're safe. Everything's going to be fine now."

Emma suddenly rushed forward and hugged Chris's legs. She was breathing fast, and she squeezed harder when he gently placed his palm on the top of her head.

"I'm so glad you're okay, Daddy," came her muffled voice.

Chris looked at Jane and she beamed at him, clearly happy as well.

"We were really worried," she confirmed.

"You're okay, too?" he asked.

"They've been taking really good care of us," Jane responded, glancing up at the woman, who was still staring at Chris.

"Are you hungry? Or thirsty?" Lexa asked, then gestured to her right. "We have a small cafeteria down the hall. I mean, it's not very fancy, but it has some basic provisions. And we could talk. Catch you up on what you missed while you were napping." She smiled again and he suddenly realized how beautiful she was.

At that moment, the three nurses moved past Chris as they headed out of the room. "Sorry again," he mumbled but they didn't look at him, just kept moving forward. As they made their way around his girls and Lexa, Chris attempted to lick his lips and realized that his mouth was bone dry. He couldn't even swallow.

"Yeah," he said. "I'm very thirsty."

Emma suddenly looked up at him, her eyes huge and glimmering.

"Come on, Daddy," she said, grinning her gap-toothed smile at him. "I actually think the cafeteria is *really* fancy. And the food here is yummy."

Chris reached down and lifted her up, placing her in the crook of his left arm, like he'd been doing since she was a toddler.

"Oh yeah?" he asked, feeling his entire body relax slightly. "Well, if you say it's fancy, it must be *very* fancy. Let's go check it out."

A jealous scowl darkened Jane's face for a second and then she reached out and took her dad's free hand, led him through the door and away from the hospital room. Lexa followed them, not saying anything, clearly wanting the small family to reconnect before she explained the situation.

"I'm not sure if I'd call it fancy," Jane countered, and a smile crept across Chris's face. This kind of petty bickering between his girls was sometimes annoying but right now, it filled him with happiness. "But she's right—the food *is* really good. Last night, Lexa gave us these fried potato things that are crazy delicious."

"Oh yeah, so good!" Emma echoed. As his daughters chattered, Chris held Emma a little closer, squeezed Jane's hand a little tighter, and listened to every single word they said to him.

"Tell me everything."

Chris and Lexa were sitting at a table against the wall of the nearly empty cafeteria, several windows dotting the walls with their shades drawn. Chris had just finished drinking a giant glass of water without saying a single word, and Lexa had simply watched, letting him finish the entire thing in a few gulps and then catch his breath. Jane and Emma, the only other people in the room, ran around the tables and chairs, loudly playing tag as if everything was normal. Their exuberant behavior after the events on the ship, memories that were still coming together in Chris's mind, comforted and disturbed him in equal measure.

"Our long-range sensors detected your escape pod before you even hit the atmosphere," Lexa said. "We were able to track your descent and luckily you landed a few miles away from us. There was some debate about what to do, but ultimately, we sent a party out to check for survivors... or recover parts if there were none. Of course, we had *no* idea what we were going to find. We don't get a lot of visitors out here, to say the least. I'm just glad that you landed during daylight—the nights last an extremely long time on LV-1213. And then it gets *very* dangerous out there."

The mention of danger jogged his memory further—the Xenomorph's claws, its dripping teeth. He felt his stomach tighten.

"Did the transport ship make it?" he asked.

At that moment, Emma came sprinting up and held out a rations bar in front of her father's face. "Hungry, Daddy?" she asked, a huge smile on her face, eyes giant circles.

He wasn't. Not even vaguely.

"I am, sweetie." He took hold of the bar and tousled her hair. "Thank you."

"You're welcome," she said sweetly, and then her face got serious as she watched her sister speeding around the tables, and Emma took off after her.

"Completely destroyed," Lexa intoned once the girls were out of earshot.

"Are you sure?"

"Very," she responded quickly. She leaned in closer, spoke in a clipped whisper. Her eyes were locked on his. They were hazel and extremely intelligent. Chris was coming to realize that she was highly capable, very confident. "Most of the ship burned up in the atmosphere—I'm assuming its shields failed completely—and what *did* make it to the surface shattered on impact. The main impact was only a few miles away from where you touched down—a minor miracle, really. But there wasn't much left. No one could have survived that, unfortunately."

Chris closed his eyes. The monster was dead—he and his girls were safe. But that also meant…

Alicia.

When she had first shown up at their home, he had only thought of her as a piece of machinery, the exact way the military had taught him to consider the androids who sometimes accompanied them on missions. But over time, she had become a part of the family, and he knew that his girls absolutely loved her. Realizing that she was gone forever, Chris felt sick to his stomach, had a hard time catching his breath.

Yet another loss.

"Can I see the wreckage?" he asked, opening his eyes.

"Well…" she said. "After we salvaged any metal that was worth anything—and there wasn't much of that—our team shipped the rest out to our scrapyard, which is miles away across pretty rough terrain. We do make a monthly trip out there to dump garbage, and you can go with the refuse team then, if you really want to. But it won't be for another few weeks, and I'm telling you, there was nothing left worth seeing. I wish there was. I'm sorry if you lost any valuable personal belongings. I know that's not fun."

"No," he agreed. "It's not."

"In the meantime, you're here and you're safe. And your girls seem to be doing okay, especially considering everything that happened to them. They stayed with me the last couple of days but they were very concerned about you. Had trouble sleeping, wanted to keep coming back here and see if you were awake."

"I should have thanked you right away," he said, smiling slightly at her but inwardly annoyed with himself. He'd fallen back into his pre-retirement personality for a moment—a personality that had led to a number of problems in his personal life. "For watching them while I was unconscious. I take that kind of thing very seriously. I appreciate it."

"It was honestly my pleasure. They're sweet girls," she replied, smiling too, and looking at Jane and Emma, who now sat at one of the tables and were having their own hushed conversation. The serious looks were unintentionally comic on their small, cute faces.

"So, this is a mining colony?" Chris asked, trying to keep his tone light. "What exactly are you mining out here? Are you in charge? And where is everyone?"

"That's… a lot of questions," she laughed. "I mean, not that I blame you. I'd have a lot of questions, too. But it might be easier to show you than tell you. Especially since the day is just starting." Lexa stood up, taking hold of a string connected to the top of the window above them and pulling. The shade raised up, letting in a swath of light.

Jane and Emma came sprinting over.

"Daddy!" they both shouted.

"You're gonna love this!" Emma continued.

"It's *so* cool," Jane confirmed.

Chris squinted against the growing luminescence. The fluorescent bulbs used in the hospital weren't particularly bright, perhaps to make patients feel more comfortable as they recovered from illnesses and injuries, so the light streaming in from outside was nearly blinding. He held up a hand as his eyes adjusted. Finally, he lowered his arm and blinked as the view outside the window came into focus.

"Wow," he said.

Dawn broke across the sky in a brilliant display of colors.

Chris and his daughters walked down the street, small, intermittent trees covering them periodically in shadow as they traveled. "I can't get over this," Chris said, looking around. "It's incredible."

They were following Lexa down a small, paved avenue away from the hospital. They passed a few houses as they moved along, squat one-story structures ringed by grass.

Chris caught movement in the corner of his eye and saw an older man fixing a broken windowsill. Inside the house, through the glass, Chris caught sight of a German Shepherd wearing a collar, its tongue lolling out of its mouth. When the man noticed Chris staring, he raised a hand in greeting, grinned in a friendly manner, and then got back to work.

As they continued on, taking a left onto a slightly larger street, his girls talking excitedly to Lexa, Chris looked up and saw that the mostly blue sky was full of ethereal white clouds and a single sun cast its brilliance down upon them. He shook his head as he glanced back down.

It was like something out of a dream.

And just as hard to believe.

"Lexa," he said, and she slowed down, then matched his pace. The girls continued ahead of them, caught up in their own conversation, pointing at things as they went. "The sky. There's something… *off* about it."

"Very observant, Chris," she said, clearly impressed. "That's not actually LV-1213's sky. We're covered by a dome and have multiple atmosphere processors at work— the only way to survive long-term with this planet's inhospitable conditions. But no one wanted to look at storm clouds and lightning all the time, so the dome's been fitted with hundreds of digital panels that allow us to program whatever we want along its surface. So, every day is sunny. And every night sky is filled with stars—*our* stars… the Big Dipper, Orion, all of them. You can even catch a shooting star now and then, if you're lucky."

"Interesting," he said simply, following his daughters as they ran forward even faster, yelling excitedly. They were entering a wider open space surrounded by a semicircle of buildings that were clearly not homes. A handful of people were entering and exiting the structures, nodding to each other as they did so. In the middle of the area, there was a large rock surrounded by benches. "What's this?"

"This is our town center," Lexa responded. "We modeled this entire community after late nineteenth- and early twentieth-century America. I guess you could say the founders of this colony were a nostalgic group. And can you blame them? There's just something about that era that's... I don't know. Romantic? Simple? Something like that."

He glanced over at her and saw that she was staring at him, smiling. He realized again how attractive she was but pushed the thought out of his mind. There was still so much that he needed to learn about this planet, and about ways off of it.

She started pointing at buildings as they made their way around the town square. Jane and Emma were playing on the grass at the center, laughing. The sound filled Chris with an almost overwhelming feeling of relief and joy, despite his physical pain and lingering confusion and suspicion.

"We have a pharmacy, a restaurant, a small grocery store, a bakery that has great coffee... even a movie theater."

As Chris turned around in a circle and tried to take it all in, as he noticed that people were starting to stop and stare, his mind began to spin and his vision blurred slightly. He lost his balance, but Lexa was there, supporting him with an arm around his shoulder.

"Whoa. You okay, Chris?"

"Just… just a little dizzy," he responded, trying to clear his mind. His girls ran to him, stared up with concern.

"What's the matter, Dad?" Jane said. She always reverted to calling him 'Dad' when she felt she needed to sound more like an adult. He both loved and hated it.

"I'm fine," he lied, smiling at them. They scrutinized his face, and he realized that they often knew when he wasn't telling them the truth.

"This is my fault," Lexa said, shaking her head. "I pushed you too hard. You probably needed more time in the hospital. We should get you back there right away."

"No. I just need a minute to get my bearings and then figure out our next steps. We were on our way to our new home." He thought of Elizabeth again. Their wedding rings both had the word *home* etched into the inside of the metal. And those rings were in his go-bag. Which was now gone forever.

"There will be plenty of time for that, Chris," Lexa replied, quietly, her voice calm. "But in the meantime, if you don't want to go back to the hospital, I can take you to your house."

"My… *house*?" he said. He was desperately trying to clear his head, but his wooziness was getting worse, not better, and now he was feeling a little nauseous, too.

"We have a house, Lexa?" Emma said, her eyes huge and hopeful.

"Yes," the woman responded, still bearing a significant amount of Chris's weight with no difficulty. "As soon as we got word that there were survivors from the crash, we had one of our empty homes prepared for you. It's not very luxurious, but there's hot water and towels, and even some canned goods, and milk and fruit from our farm waiting for you."

"Wow," Emma said, a big smile appearing beneath her excited eyes.

"Can we check it out, Dad?" Jane said, staring up at her father.

Chris hesitated for a moment. He had been trained to question every situation, to assume danger was around every corner. But he was hurting. He was exhausted. And his girls *needed* some peace and quiet. Even if just for a few hours while he figured out exactly what the hell had happened on the transport ship. And what was happening here.

"Yes, of course," he said to his older daughter, touching her cheek gently.

Chris glanced over at Lexa, who still had her arm around him. They stared at each other for a moment, and then she laughed, shook her head, and pulled away. He couldn't tell but it almost looked like she was blushing. Maybe he was, too.

"Thank you," he said quickly. "I don't feel great, but I think a little bit of rest would do wonders for me. And then maybe we can talk. I'd love to find out more about your operation here. It's… really impressive. You must be a very good leader."

Lexa laughed and flashed that dazzling smile. "Oh, I'm not the leader, even if I have to tell people what to do sometimes. We're run by a small executive board, and we decide everything together. It's great. No egos here—we all just want to do our jobs, treat each other respectfully, and maybe have a little bit of fun once in a while."

He nodded, his head swimming slightly again, which she seemed to notice.

"Look at me babbling while you're not feeling well," she said, stepping away, back towards the street down which they'd just traveled. "Come on, I'll show you the house. I think you're really going to love it."

Jane and Emma closed ranks around their dad, sensing that he needed them, physically and emotionally, and the small family unit trailed after their host, the fake sunlight streaming down on them, the gentle sounds of an awakening town reaching their ears and fading as they headed to a house that was theirs, but that they'd never actually seen.

4

"This is really nice," Chris said, looking around the small home, shocked at how quiet it was inside the freshly painted walls.

The girls were already scampering around, choosing rooms, testing furniture, opening every cabinet they could find.

Still standing by the door, Lexa handed Chris a key and took a step back outside. "Okay. I'll leave you to it. Take as much time as you need. I'm going to try and find you a spare walkie-talkie, and then you can call me anytime you need. If I'm in range, of course. The electrical storms, that you can't actually see, sometimes wreak havoc with our communication. It's... kind of nice sometimes. Very annoying at others. When there's work to be done."

Chris grinned and then turned serious.

"Lexa, I still don't understand everything that's happened

here. I'll have a lot of questions after some sleep and about four hundred cups of coffee. But in the meantime, thank you. For taking care of my girls while I was out. It means more than I can ever properly express."

"Like I said, they're very sweet girls. And you're obviously a fantastic dad. I'll talk to you soon."

And with that, she turned and headed down the walkway with purpose, pulling the radio off her belt and talking into it quietly. Chris closed the door.

"Girls!" he said loudly. "Kitchen table. Family meeting."

He listened with a grin as two sets of feet scrambled along the wooden floors and his daughters appeared in the kitchen as he sat down at the small but sturdy table. Sitting down had literally never felt so good.

Jane sat down directly across from Chris and waited, staring at him. Emma stood behind one of the chairs, but her eyes darted towards the fridge.

"Go ahead," Chris said, fighting back a smile. Jane stayed in place, but he saw one of her eyes twitch slightly. "You, too, soldier."

Jane moved faster than he thought possible, almost beating Emma there despite the smaller girl's sizable head start. They jockeyed for position until Chris cleared his throat, an unspoken signal that Jane knew well. She stood down, let her younger sister open the refrigerator door.

Both girls emerged moments later with hands full of fruit: apples, strawberries, and blueberries. A few of the latter fell through Emma's fingers as she delicately walked back towards the table and she hesitated for a moment, unsure how to proceed.

"Leave 'em," Chris intoned. "We'll pick 'em up later. Wash 'em. Eat 'em."

A huge smile reappeared on her face. Back on Earth, food that fell on the floor usually went into the composter.

They had only left their home months ago, but it seemed more like years. Chris wondered what was happening back there. If society was able to right itself, or if it had collapsed completely. He shook his head. He couldn't dwell on it. At least not right now. He'd get answers soon enough.

Both girls settled into their chairs and Emma gently handed her father an apple. He took it with a grin, and then they all bit into the fruit, silent, appreciative. Back home, back when Elizabeth was still alive, they would never eat fruit—when they could find it—without washing it first, but that was then. And this was now.

Chris had never tasted an apple this good. The juice rolled down his chin and he laughed, not even bothering to wipe it away, just took another huge bite.

"Daddy!" Emma said, laughing too.

Jane just shook her head, stood up, and walked over to the far counter, returning with a cloth napkin. He lowered the fruit from his face and wiped the juice away.

"Gross," she said, but she was smiling.

"Sorry," he replied but he wasn't, and he knew she didn't think it was gross either.

They ate in silence for several minutes, reveling in the taste, in being together.

Finally, all the fruit that the girls had delivered was gone. Emma looked at the fridge again, but Chris stopped her with a glance.

"No. First, we talk."

And talk they did. For a long time. Chris listened, mostly, asked a few questions here and there, choosing his words carefully. He knew these two girls better than he knew anyone in the universe. They often spoke with movement, with half-uttered sentences. This time was no different.

They talked about being rescued, about watching their father's unconscious body being transported with them from the crashed pod and across the windy, rocky landscape to the dome. About how kind everyone had been to them, especially Lexa. They talked about how impressed they were by this colony. How happy they were that their dad was okay. How devastated they were by the loss of Alicia.

At length, Emma started to yawn, and then Jane did, too, even though it was only the middle of the day. When the younger girl's head began to fall forward, Chris quickly stood up, even though he himself was exhausted, and lifted her into his arms again. He was reminded of holding her like this back on the doomed transport ship, when they were running away from the Xenomorph. He shook the images away, focused on the present, and walked an already sleeping Emma to her new room. Placing her gently down, he then pulled the blanket over her small body and watched for a moment. She murmured gently in her slumber.

Chris thought about closing her door to keep the light out but decided against it. He didn't love not sleeping in the same room with her right now, but she'd be fine. He was only going to sleep a couple of hours anyway.

Jane was waiting for him in the hallway, looking like she was going to collapse at any moment. Without even thinking about it, he picked her up into his arms and held her close, too, something he hadn't done in a long time. Something she would have told anyone that she had outgrown. Instead, she wrapped her hands around her father and squeezed.

"I love you, Daddy," she whispered.

Tears sprung to his eyes as he walked her into another bedroom, laid her down just as he had done with Emma. Jane looked up at him, her lids heavy. She looked so much like Elizabeth when she was tired. It somehow broke his heart and healed it simultaneously.

"Are we going to be okay?" she asked, eyes starting to close.

He thought about lying but then decided against it. She was old enough to hear the truth.

"I don't know," he responded. "I hope so. But I will do everything in my power to keep you and Emma safe. Okay?"

Jane didn't respond. Couldn't. She was fast asleep, already snoring slightly.

Chris covered her with a blanket, too, but she kicked it violently away, then turned over and snored even louder. He chuckled as he made his way out of the room, leaving her door open as well.

He thought about heading to the third and final bedroom, but despite hurting almost everywhere on his body, he now felt wired, especially after everything his girls had told him. He needed to process it all, or at least some of it, so he headed back to the kitchen, went straight to the fridge.

He glanced at the fruit and vegetables and the bottled milk, but his eyes were drawn to another clear glass bottle in the back. Glancing around like a sneaky teenager, then laughing at his own paranoia, he took hold of it and popped the cork that had been unceremoniously shoved into its top.

Chris knew exactly what it was.

It smelled awful. And it was just what he wanted at this moment.

He grabbed a glass from one of cabinets, sat down, and poured a couple of fingers. It burned going down, a terrible sensation, an amazing one.

So, they brewed their own moonshine on Mining Outpost Omega Seven Tango.

Chris sat back and considered the drink in his hand, his mind going back to the story his two girls had finished telling him just a few minutes earlier.

They had been incredibly lucky. But he never fully trusted luck.

Letting out a long sigh, he finished his drink in a gulp, and then poured another.

The sound of a faint knocking pulled Chris out of the worst nightmare he'd ever experienced.

In it, he was trapped beneath a mound of wet dirt, and claws were coming up through the earth beneath him. He dug frantically at the muck above as the unseen creature raked his skin, but he was trapped, the talons digging deeper and deeper into his flesh. There was no way out.

He sat up with a gasp, sucking in a huge breath of air. Looking around, he realized that he'd fallen asleep at the kitchen table in this strange but admittedly comfortable house, the bottle of homemade alcohol and the empty glass still perched in front of him, a painful reminder of the day before. He had slept a *long* time. Had clearly needed the rest.

Even though he had a crick in his neck from sleeping on the hard wood of the table, and could feel the start of a hangover, Chris felt significantly better than when he'd woken up in the hospital. Daylight streamed through the windows, and he blinked against it.

No. Not daylight. *Fake* light. Digital manipulation. A reminder not to get too comfortable here.

As if responding to his slightly paranoid waking thoughts, the gentle knocking came again, and he stood up, moving toward the front door. Then he stopped, headed back to the table, and put the bottle of moonshine back into the fridge. He quickly checked in on the girls and found they were both sound asleep. Clearly needing a lot of sleep, too.

When he opened the door, blinking against the morning, he was pleasantly unsurprised to see that it was Lexa. She was holding two ceramic cups with lids, and he could immediately smell what was inside.

"Is that coffee?" he asked, feeling better already.

"It is. First of the four hundred. I didn't wake you up, did I?"

"Of course not," he lied. "But the girls are still asleep, so…"

"Oh," she said, deflating slightly. "Of course. Here, just take this, and I'll talk to you later."

"No, sorry, that's not what I meant," he responded, taking the offered cup and smiling at her. He indicated the two chairs on the front porch. "Do you want to stay for a little bit? I'd love to ask you some more questions, if you don't mind."

She matched his smile.

"Sounds great."

They sipped at their coffee within the shade of the covered porch, avoiding eye contact.

Finally, Lexa cleared her throat and said, "Did you sleep okay?"

"Um..." he replied, formulating an answer in his mind. He thought about telling her that the bed had been amazing, that he'd crashed as soon as she'd left the night before, but he liked Lexa, already respected her. "No. I fell asleep sitting at the kitchen table. I may or may not have discovered the moonshine in the fridge."

She laughed and shook her head, looking at him with a mischievous glint in her eyes. "No judgements here. I've had my fair share of that devil's brew myself over the last few years. The restaurant manager makes it in her bathtub. This colony started dry... but that didn't last very long. It's not the most subtle of drinks, but it gets the job done."

"That it does," he concurred. There was another moment of silence, but he was already feeling more comfortable with her, so he pushed forward. "Look, Lexa, like I said, I have a lot of questions for you. But first, I want to talk about the transport ship. I know you said it was completely destroyed, but I just need to confirm. To know one hundred percent that nothing could have survived."

"Because of Alicia?" she asked.

"What?" he responded, surprised that she already knew about the family's auton. Then again, his girls weren't known for keeping information close to the vest.

"Chris," Lexa said, leaning forward and looking into his eyes. "Nothing survived the impact. *Nothing*. I'm sorry."

He looked into her eyes, which were full of empathy. "Why are you sorry?"

Lexa took another sip of coffee. "Jane and Emma told me about Alicia while you were unconscious. I know she was only an android, but it sounds like your girls really cared about her."

His mind whipped through memories of Alicia taking care of his girls. She had been a part of the family. Especially after Elizabeth's death. "They did. We *all* did."

Lexa simply nodded and they continued to drink their coffee, enjoying the silence of the morning. After a few moments, Chris heard a fast-approaching noise coming from his left, and he tensed up, looked over, ready to act. A paunchy man with a beard walked quickly towards them, raising his hand in greeting. He was wearing what looked like some kind of worker's uniform—drab but showcasing a geometric design that Chris figured designated the man as a miner.

"Mornin'!" he called out.

Chris half-raised his own hand, forcing his body to relax.

"Good morning, Tom," Lexa responded, standing up.

The man stopped at the bottom of the porch steps, so Chris stood too, and took a step forward. He reached out a hand and the man did the same, and they shook. Locking eyes, sizing each other up.

"You're the guy from the crash, right?" Tom asked.

"I guess I am," Chris answered, letting go of the guy's grip, and a moment of silence hovered.

"Tom is one of our miners. The lifeblood of the OST."

"The what?" Chris asked, glancing over.

"Sorry. Mining Colony Omega Seven Tango. OST. It's just a moniker that someone came up with when we first got here. And it kind of stuck."

"Fair enough," Chris said.

"You comin' to Delilah's tonight?" Tom asked, squinting up at them. The 'sun' was bright as it rose into the morning sky. Chris marveled at how quickly he came to believe the falsehood of the hours in this place. He wondered what the actual sky looked like on this planet at this moment—and then realized he didn't care. Perhaps he had earned a little bit of perceptual subterfuge. Even if just for a day. And if *he* hadn't, his girls certainly had.

"Where?" he asked.

"Delilah's," Lexa responded, stepping nearer to Chris. She was standing so close to him now, he could feel her warmth. He wasn't sure if he liked it or not. "It's the bar that's part of the restaurant I showed you yesterday. Named for the woman who makes the moonshine. She throws a kind of party once a week, and that night is tonight. You and the girls should come. There's usually some other kids there... should be a good time. If you're up for it."

"You should totally come," Tom nearly shouted before Chris even had a chance to contemplate the idea. "It's a blast. It's Friday... I mean, for us. Who knows how time really works on this planet." He barked a laugh. "And all us miners need to cut loose a little. There's some food, a little live music, and plenty of Delilah's hootch."

"I'll definitely think about it," Chris said, shifting his coffee cup from one hand to the other. In the distance, he noticed other miners leaving their homes and heading towards the dome's primary exit, all wearing the same uniform that Tom was sporting.

"Looks like it's time to punch in," Lexa said, her voice taking on a slightly more authoritarian tone. Tom noticed.

"Right. Of course," he responded. "Great to meet you, Chris." And then he was moving away, whistling as he walked.

Chris hadn't introduced himself, had never mentioned his name.

He and Lexa sat back down and continued to sip at their coffees. Despite the somewhat awkward encounter, the liquid still tasted amazing and the quiet sounds of the town waking up filled Chris with a pleasant quietude.

"Sorry about that," Lexa finally said. "He's a little overeager at times. But a nice guy."

"I'm sure," Chris mused, watching as the group of miners headed down the street and out of sight. There was a couple dozen of them, men and women. They moved as one, almost like soldiers. "How long have you all been here? And how many of you are there?"

"Solid openers," she teased, then turned serious. "The terraformers got here about fifty years ago and worked for a generation. It wasn't easy. This planet isn't particularly friendly to humans, so even though the air is breathable... barely... the atmosphere processors had their work cut out for them. But LV-1213 just happens to produce a particular ore that's found in only a very few key places—and has sped up our space travel capabilities significantly."

"Quadromite," Chris murmured.

"Exactly," Lexa said, staring at him appraisingly. "I'm impressed. You know your stuff."

"I know a few things about a few things," he said, flashing her a smile.

"The miners and their families, and some executive officers to run things, like me, arrived once this dome had been built around the terraformed section. Just about... five years ago. Wow. I can't believe it's been that long. Seems like five days sometimes."

She stared out at the street, lost in her own thoughts.

"I totally get that," Chris said. "Even our time on the transport ship seems like a million years ago. So, how many people live here in the OST?"

She grinned at him. "See? I told you it was catchy." He laughed slightly. She wasn't wrong. "Let me see," she continued, "I can never remember the exact number, but I think we're just south of a hundred people, altogether."

"And does the USM send supply ships? Do you swap out personnel?" Chris continued, trying to keep his tone light. He had dozens of questions rattling around in his brain but didn't want to make it sound like he was interrogating her.

"We get an occasional supply run from home, though things have certainly become more sporadic after the Lacerta Plague and since the *Auriga*."

"Of course."

"Mostly, things just stay the same here. We're kind of our own little bubble. I guess literally. The terraforming, of this section of the planet at least, was highly successful, so we've been able to farm and grow most of our own food. We have a scientist, Margaret Livingston, who figured out a way to speed up tree growth, which really adds a lot to this place. And we brought some animals. Besides, we have a lot of vegetarians here. Myself included."

"Roger that," Chris said, putting his coffee onto the ground. Although it tasted good, it was turning sour in his stomach—he was suddenly ravenous, hadn't eaten anything other than several pieces of fruit since escaping from the transport ship. Still, he had a lot more questions. He decided to ask the most important one.

"Can I send a message to the USM? I need to figure out our next steps."

"Absolutely," Lexa answered, leaning towards him, staring him right in the eyes. "I'm sure you're eager to get your voyage back on track. I realize that you and your girls are between homes right now. That's never easy."

"Exactly," he responded.

"We did send a message as soon as we discovered your escape pod, when we realized there were survivors. Communications take a bit of time to reach Earth and come back, so as soon as we hear something, we'll put you in direct contact with the USM, and they can help you decide how best to proceed."

"I appreciate that."

"Of course," she said, smiling at him again. There was something about her smile that put him at ease, and he felt his entire body relax. He still had more questions, but right at this moment, he couldn't think of any. They both enjoyed the morning sounds for a moment, and then she spoke again.

"May I ask *you* a few questions?"

"Absolutely," he said, turning towards her slightly.

"Nothing too invasive, I promise." She laughed a little, smiled again. "I have to admit that I looked you up after your girls told me your names. It was part protocol but also curiosity. We don't get many surprise visitors here, so everyone knows about you, was asking questions. I didn't have any answers—and I'm the kind of person who likes to have answers."

"Same," Chris said.

"I figured," she replied. "The USM database pulled up your information right away—at least, as much as I was allowed to see. Chris Temple. Retired United Systems Military colonel. The recipient of multiple honors and medals, and the leader of a host of highly impressive missions. Despite finding out about all of that, I was shocked to discover how much I *wasn't* allowed to see. A lot of top-secret information about you in the system, Chris."

"I'm mysterious," he responded, feeling his guards go back up but keeping his tone light again.

"Don't get me wrong," she said, holding up a hand, her eyes getting wide. "I'm not asking you to divulge any state secrets. I'm just impressed, to be honest. I never expected that the guy we pulled out of the smoking wreckage was a war hero."

"I am *not* a hero," he said darkly, and silence abruptly asserted itself on the porch.

He was about to apologize when the door burst open, and Emma came barreling onto the porch.

"I'm starving!" she shouted, jumping onto her dad's lap.

"Oof!" Chris said, watching as Jane followed after her sister, still rubbing the sleep out of her eyes. "Morning, sunshine."

Jane muttered something, and then noticed that they had a visitor.

"Lexa!" she said, her mood brightening. Chris clocked this with interest. It was rare for anything to pull his older daughter out of her morning grumpiness.

"Good morning, Jane," Lexa responded. "Sleep okay?"

"Pretty good," she said. "But I'm hungry, too, Dad."

"Yeah, me three," Chris agreed. "Not sure fruit is going to cut it, no matter how delicious it was."

"Come on," Lexa suggested, standing up. "I can take you over to Delilah's. They open early for the miners. The menu isn't huge, but the scrambled eggs are to die for."

The idea of a fresh, hot breakfast after months of the transport ship's packaged food, not to mention everything that had happened in the last couple of days, instantly made Chris's stomach growl loudly.

"Ew. Gross, Dad," Jane said, rolling her eyes.

"Sorry," Chris muttered, embarrassed.

"It's okay, Daddy!" Emma said, taking his hand.

Chris's and Lexa's eyes met again, and she grinned at him.

"Come on. Let's get you three fed. Then I can continue pestering your dad with a million questions."

"You can ask me questions, too!" Emma shouted as the four walked down the porch steps and headed towards the center of town.

"Okay," Lexa said. "What's your favorite color?"

"Turquoise," the eight-year-old said without hesitation.

"Mine's red," Jane volunteered.

A half step behind them, Chris watched as Lexa asked his daughters a series of questions, eliciting excited answers and laughter. He closed his eyes for a moment as he walked. He wasn't sure what his next move was, how he would get his family back on track. But right now, in this exact moment?

He almost felt happy.

5

After the best breakfast Chris could remember eating, Lexa showed the three of them around town again, introducing them to various townspeople, most of whom were married to the miners who were outside the dome for the day, drilling for quadromite, or people who had other functions within the OST.

Shortly after noon, they went to see a movie and ate popcorn and dried fruit for their lunch. Lexa left the theater once the movie started, citing a need to get some work done, and Emma crawled into her dad's lap, falling asleep almost instantly despite having slept so many hours the day and night before.

The movie was short and animated, and honestly not very good, but Chris glanced over at one point while Jane was laughing at some onscreen antics and saw the absolute joy on his older daughter's face. Neither of his girls had ever experienced a movie inside an old-fashioned theater before, and Chris had only done so once, decades earlier while on leave after a particularly bad mission.

Just as the credits started to roll, Lexa reappeared. When Chris stood, awkwardly, Emma woke up and slid down onto her feet, a little wobbly.

"Did you like it?" Lexa asked as they walked up the aisle, through the lobby, and out the theater door, the faux sunlight nearly blinding the three of them.

"I loved it," Jane said assuredly, looking as if she was replaying the events of the film in her mind.

"Me too!" Emma lied.

"It was terrible," Chris murmured, leaning in close to Lexa's ear so his girls wouldn't hear his critique.

"I know," she whispered back. "Sorry."

The two shared a laugh and then Lexa walked them home. The digital sun had passed its apex and was heading towards the horizon. Lexa stopped on the sidewalk outside their house.

"I still have some work to do, at least until the miners come back," she said as the girls ran up the walkway to the porch. Chris lingered, tried to figure out the right thing to say to this kind stranger.

"Of course," he said. "Thank you so much for spending part of your day with us. I know how busy you must be."

"I am pretty busy, not going to lie," she said. "But I've really been enjoying your company." She paused as they looked at each other. "You and the girls, I mean."

"We appreciate it. Great breakfasts and terrible entertainment. It almost feels... normal."

"Good," she replied, starting to turn away, then stopping herself, looking back at Chris. "Hey, if you're up for it, I'd love to take you three to dinner tonight. Unfortunately, we only have the one restaurant, but it's a lot more lively for dinner than it was for breakfast. Especially tonight. Like Tom said, the moonshine will be flowing. If you can handle more of it."

"I think I can handle it," he said, then raised his eyebrows as he considered the notion a little further. "Maybe."

Lexa laughed. It was a wonderful sound.

"We'll be there," he said, then turned and followed his daughters up the path to the house.

"I look forward to it, Chris Temple," Lexa said.

He was tempted to look back but fought against it, and instead walked up the few steps onto the porch, unlocked the front door, and walked with his girls into a house that was already feeling shockingly comfortable.

The fistfight broke out over five words.

Dinner had been a raucous, delicious affair. Just as Tom and Lexa had intimated, the nighttime vibe at Delilah's was very different than morning. While breakfast was quiet and serene, the evening meal was full of incessant chatter, a handful of kids running around tables like their lives depended on it, increasingly drunk miners congregating along the long bar, and platters of food passed around tables like everyone was one, giant family.

Chris was introduced to more people than he could keep track of, but he drank only water, despite many offers of the moonshine. Throngs like this made him nervous—no doubt a result of years dealing with crowd control and insurgents who would sometimes come flying out of a mob with a weapon, attempting to make their point against the USM.

Lexa sat close to him, and while this kind of closeness to a virtual stranger would normally have made him uncomfortable, she was the person he knew best on LV-1213, other than his daughters—of whom he only caught the slightest glimpses as they sped around tables, chairs, and other patrons. Their laughter rose up and over the din, reaching his ears, and he couldn't remember the last time he had heard or seen them so happy.

"Having fun?" Lexa asked, leaning in even closer to his ear.

Earlier, Chris had fallen asleep as soon as they'd entered the house, crashing onto the unmade bed without even taking off his shoes. He couldn't remember the last time he'd slept that soundly, but he awoke with a start, feeling like he'd left himself and his daughters in serious peril by allowing himself such a deep slumber.

He sprang up and rushed out of the bedroom, only to find both of his girls sitting on the couch, reading books. Actual, physical books.

Emma looked up and saw him, a huge smile spreading across her face.

"Daddy, will you read this to me?" she asked, holding the book up in her tiny hand.

"Absolutely," Chris responded, moving forward and settling in between the two of them. As he read, he felt both girls snuggling in closer. It was a moment of utter satisfaction—the first in recent memory.

And now, sitting next to Lexa, equally close, on a bench in a booming dinner hall, his stomach full of food, he felt equally satisfied.

"I am," he said, looking into Lexa's eyes. "I'm having a lot of fun."

A wave of guilt washed over him. Not only because of Elizabeth but also because of Alicia, and everyone else who had perished on the transport ship. Eight hundred and sixty-two souls. And here he was, eating and drinking and laughing a couple of days later like nothing had even happened.

"Excuse me," he said, standing and placing the cloth napkin down on his vacated seat.

"Are you okay?" Lexa asked, starting to rise, too.

"I'm fine," he said quickly, placing his hand on her shoulder. "No need to get up. I'm just gonna go to the bathroom. Be right back."

Lexa nodded. The look in her eyes made it clear that she understood it was more than just that, but she didn't press him. He appreciated that. She was an extremely kind woman. Smart. Great with his girls.

These thoughts were pushed out of his head as he passed through the horde of miners at the bar. Two of them were arguing, loudly. He realized that violence was lingering just below the surface. He'd been involved in countless altercations, most involving weapons but plenty that boiled down to humans with nothing more than their fists.

He knew something bad was about to happen. And then he heard those five words.

"We shouldn't have done it," one of the miners said, a big dude with a red beard and a black beanie on his head.

The guy he was arguing with, taller but not as wide, sporting a dark buzzcut and a salt-and-pepper goatee, threw a punch so fast that Chris barely even saw it. Red Beard clearly didn't either. It connected with a shocking amount of force, throwing the man back into a group of other miners, who roared their disapproval at being unceremoniously knocked into.

A brawl broke out almost instantaneously, with Chris unintentionally at its center. Everything else around him fell away, and without even having to make a conscious decision, he felt his brain click back into the Chris Temple that had retired from the military at the top of his game. All his training reasserted itself, as if it had simply been waiting to once again be called upon.

Another miner, muscular and with a nasty scowl on his face, saw Chris and there was a glint in the man's eye, almost as if he was elated that the newbie had ended up in the middle of the melee. He threw a fist towards Chris's cheek, just as fast as the punch that had knocked Red Beard out.

But Chris was much faster than Red Beard. And faster than this guy, too.

Using his left forearm, he blocked the blow easily and responded with his own punch, driving his right fist into the man's unprepared gut. He doubled over, a surprised grunt emanating from his mouth, and then Chris brought his knee up, connecting with the man's face, blood exploding from nostrils, and he collapsed to the ground.

Two of the guy's friends approached Chris, anger creasing their faces. They were both muscular, too, clearly miners. The woman swung first, her lips lifting in a snarl. Chris wanted this to be over, fast, but he also didn't want to really hurt anyone else, especially with his daughters watching.

He dodged the woman's wild punch, let her own momentum work against her, and threw out a foot, causing her to trip and crash to the ground. Their drunkenness wasn't doing them any favors. Regardless, he wouldn't want to go up against several of these miners during daylight hours—they were all strong and fast, spent hours each day unintentionally honing themselves into perfect physical specimens.

The other man landed a punch across Chris's face, though he managed to roll with it slightly so it didn't hurt as badly as it might have. Still, he tasted blood, and then his mind went white. He forgot about his girls, about where he was, about everything that had happened over the last couple of days.

When his thoughts cleared, Lexa was pulling him back and several miners were splayed out at his feet. Everyone else had stopped fighting and was staring at Chris—scared or impressed, he couldn't tell. Maybe both.

"I... I'm sorry," he said, wiping his bloody mouth on the back of his hand.

"There's no need for you to apologize," Lexa responded. She turned to the tall man with the buzzcut and goatee, the one who had started the fight. He was leaning against the bar, staring at Chris and Lexa with something that resembled jealousy. "Cosgrove! I want you out of here. Now! We will discuss this at HQ in the morning."

Cosgrove looked hurt for a moment, surprised. He opened his mouth, about to say something, but then shut it, clenched his jaw, and headed for the exit.

Lexa led a dazed Chris back to their table. "I saw everything," she said quietly as they sat down. "You were just defending yourself. But I wanted to get you out of there before you embarrassed anyone else. I don't think they're used to dealing with a real opponent."

And sure enough, all the miners seemed to be getting along fine now, laughing and toasting, helping their hurt comrades up off the floor. After another moment, Jane and Emma came running up to Chris, grabbing at him, eyes wide.

"Dad, are you okay?" Jane said, her voice sounding so much like her mother's.

"I'm fine," he responded. "And I'm sorry you had to see that. I was just trying to go to the bathroom."

"Daddy… That. Was. *Awesome!*" Emma said, raising her tiny fists and shadowboxing the air in front of her.

"It really wasn't," Chris responded, gently lowering her hands. "Violence is never the answer, unless you're trying to protect yourself. Which I was," he hastened to add.

A few other kids suddenly appeared and pulled his daughters away in a frenzy of noise and activity. Jane and Emma had barely touched their food and he thought to call them back, then let it go. They were having the time of their lives. They could eat later.

"I mean, she's not wrong," Lexa said, smiling slyly at Chris. "It *was* pretty awesome. Where'd you learn to fight like that? Not every USM officer is that good at hand-to-hand."

"I took a lot of classes when I was younger. Just wanted to be prepared for anything, you know?"

"Well, it shows," Lexa said, taking a sip of her moonshine. Her eyes sparkled while she looked at him. The live music had started again after pausing briefly during the brawl and the entire atmosphere in the restaurant seemed to have kicked up a notch after the end of the fight.

"Right before that first punch, the guy with the red beard said, 'We shouldn't have done it.' Any idea what he meant by that?" Chris asked. He noticed that someone had placed a cup of the moonshine in front of him, and he decided to take a sip. His mouth hurt from where he'd been punched, though he'd certainly taken worse before.

Lexa considered Chris's words, a look of confusion sweeping across her face, and then shook her head. "No idea. But the miners spend eight hours a day underground, sometimes longer, cracking open this planet and trying to earn their keep. Tempers tend to flare every once in a while, unfortunately. But we generally let it go. If we prosecuted every miner who started a fight, we'd have no miners. That being said, if you'd like to bring a charge against the guy who hit you..."

"No," Chris said, taking another sip. "Absolutely not. I'd rather just sit here and talk with you, and watch my girls absolutely lose their minds."

And sure enough, the small group of kids continued to circle the restaurant in a blur of laughter and flailing limbs, and Chris watched, feeling Lexa next to him, deeply appreciative for all of it despite the dull ache in his jaw.

The four of them walked home in silence.

Emma was asleep on Chris's arm and Jane held his other hand, though he considered it a miracle that she was still walking. Her eyes were barely open, and she was dragging her feet like the undead. Lexa walked on the other side of him, quiet, a bemused smile on her face.

They had closed Delilah's down and by the end, it was like the fight had never even happened. Lexa introduced Chris to practically every single person in the bar, which meant he'd met almost every single person in the OST. Even the miners with whom he'd been brawling were completely different people by the end of the night, clapping him on the back and welcoming him to town, as if they hadn't bloodied each other's faces a few hours earlier.

But Chris had seen this kind of thing before, both within the military and at other bars back on Earth. Humans sometimes had incredible capacities for forgiveness. And for violence, too, of course. It was a strange dichotomy that Chris had spent his entire life trying to understand, especially growing up as the only child of a highly decorated USM officer. He'd worked hard to impress his mother. His father had died of cancer when he was only an infant. She had been hard on him—some people said too hard, but even as his exterior toughened over the years, he quietly fought to protect that soft, hidden part inside his soul. Elizabeth and their daughters had helped ensure that the kernel his mother had unintentionally almost destroyed was still there.

When his wife died, Chris thought that part of him had perished, too. But almost losing his daughters to a Xenomorph on a doomed transport ship had made him realize that it still existed. And that it was more important to him than ever.

Just as his arm was starting to go numb, Chris and the others reached the house and Emma suddenly woke up, eyes wide, and scrambled out of her dad's arms.

"I'm awake, I'm not tired," she insisted, answering a question no one had asked. Jane grabbed her sister's arm and dragged her inside. Chris lingered on the sidewalk for a moment, turning to Lexa.

"That was... interesting," he said, smiling slightly. He'd only had a couple of glasses of the moonshine over several hours, plus more food than he'd eaten in a long time, but he still felt slightly tipsy. In the distance, he could hear a few other citizens of the OST making their way home, shouting good-naturedly, singing, laughing. They were good sounds. Almost completely foreign to him at this point.

"I know you told me to stop apologizing, but I'm sorry," she said sheepishly. Even though she wasn't the town's leader, she had berated each of the offending miners quietly during the night, thinking Chris couldn't hear. She was tough and concise, attributes he appreciated, and the miners seemed to respect that, too, because they bowed their heads while she spoke, grumbled their own apologies when she was done talking.

"Seriously, Lexa, it's fine," he responded, still aware of the ache in his mouth. Weirdly enough, it felt good. A reminder that he was still alive. "And honestly? I've been in way worse fights than that."

"Oh yeah?" she said, taking a half step forward. "Do tell."

"Well, there was the time that a bunch of USM cadets went AWOL during shore leave on Korari. I was ordered to lead a small contingent of soldiers to bring them back. It got... uhh... ugly, to say the least."

Before Chris realized what was happening, Lexa's lips were on his, her arms wrapping around him. For a moment, he gave in to it. She felt and tasted and smelled so good. But the moment quickly passed, and he felt his guard going up, fast. He gently took hold of her shoulders and pushed her away. She had a surprised, then crestfallen look on her face.

"I shouldn't have done that," she said, then turned to walk away. He took hold of her shoulder again, still gentle, and turned her back to face him.

"Lexa, no, I…" he started to say, and fumbled for the words. He had never been the best at expressing himself, had worked hard to get better at it when Elizabeth called him out on that particular failing. "I like you. A lot. You're intelligent and gorgeous and clearly a bad-ass."

She laughed, looked up into his eyes. "I don't know about that."

"Yes, you do," he countered. "And that's impressive, too. Your confidence. I see the way people look at you, the way they talk to you. I'm honestly surprised that you're single. There seem to be plenty of people in this colony who would love to be with you." *Like Cosgrove*, he almost added.

"Maybe," she said. "But I've never been interested in that. I took this assignment because I believed in what this colony had to offer. A new world. I haven't been interested in a serious relationship. Don't have time for it. But there's something about you, Chris Temple. I don't know what it is."

"My wife... Jane and Emma's mom... she's been gone for a year, but I still miss her. And every time I've even thought about anyone else, I've been wracked with guilt. And then everything went to hell on Earth—the plague, the riots, the *Auriga*, the panic. And of course... what happened on the transport ship."

She waited, eyes widening, clearly hoping he would elaborate.

"Anyway," he continued, "I'm very flattered. And I'm not... I'm not saying no. I just need some time to figure this out. Figure *myself* out. Can we take our time, and be friends, and see what happens?"

"Of course," she responded. "I hope you know that you're welcome here for as long as you'd like. Your girls seem to be loving it, and maybe I could find a job for someone like you. Even with your redacted file, I know you've got a pretty killer skill set."

"I'm open to discussing that," he said.

His mind raced through all his and his girls' possible futures. Could they even get to the colony they'd been heading towards before the Xenomorph had derailed their plans while also killing hundreds of other people? How long would it take for another transport ship to arrive? Were there any transport ships even left? They had managed to catch one of the last ones off Earth before the latest round of martial laws were being instated.

Maybe staying here, on the OST, wasn't such a bad idea. Lexa was right: his girls seemed happy here. *Very* happy.

Why risk something good for a greater unknown?

"Good night, Chris. I'm sorry your transport ship was destroyed by something you refuse to discuss with me—but I'm very glad you ended up here," Lexa said, then turned again and walked away.

He watched her go, feeling a conflicting tug of emotions, then walked into the house. All was still inside, dark, but comforting. He locked the door and headed to the girls' rooms. Neither was there.

Chris panicked and sprinted to his own bedroom, then laughed when he got there. Jane and Emma were both asleep, sprawled out like two starfish, already snoring and drooling. They looked absolutely content. He just watched them for several minutes, reveling in the quietude.

At length, he headed to Jane's room and settled down into the bed, realizing just how exhausted he really was. Despite his performance and what he'd told Lexa, he hadn't been in a fistfight in a long time, and he felt this fact in every muscle in his body. He closed his eyes and was confident that sleep would come immediately.

He was wrong.

His mind raced. The day had been a series of clearly delineated occurrences—breakfast and lunch, the movie, dinner and drinks and the brawl... and Lexa's kiss. But even though they all felt like exceedingly separate events, it all blurred together in a confusing mishmash of emotional highs and lows. But Lexa's mouth on his was easily the most perplexing.

Especially since it wasn't Lexa that he was now thinking about.

It was Alicia.

He couldn't get the image of her face out of his mind. Even when Lexa had kissed him, it was Alicia to whom his brain had immediately gone. But that made no sense. Not only had Alicia been destroyed but she was also only a machine.

As he lay there, desperate for sleep, memories of the auton swept over him. Time spent with her and his daughters; late nights where Alicia would listen to his concerns about the growing chaos on Earth; how she had selflessly sacrificed herself to save them from the Xenomorph.

He had never told her how important she was to his family.

And to him.

The minutes clicked by, and he forced Alicia out of his mind, and instead took refuge in the amazing day he'd just had. The kind of day he wanted Jane and Emma to experience again and again.

And then he heard that echo again. The five words. They had been niggling at the back of his mind all night, though he had been ignoring them as the noise of the crowd, and the closeness of Lexa, distracted him.

We shouldn't have done it.

Lexa's vague explanation made sense, on some level, but Chris prided himself on reading people—it was an attribute that had served him well as an officer of the USM. There was something else going on there. The look in the red-bearded man's eyes betrayed something larger, and Chris was too curious by nature to ignore it.

Standing up, feeling wide awake despite his deep-seeded exhaustion, he quietly walked around the house and checked all the windows again. They were locked and it wouldn't be easy for anyone to break in without smashing the glass. He wrestled with his next move, and then made a decision. He was conflicted, but knew it was the right call.

Besides, he wouldn't be gone long. Just wanted to poke around a little bit. This wasn't a prison planet, after all. He was allowed to go for a nighttime walk.

Chris Temple slipped out of the front door, silently, locking the door behind him, then moved into the shadows like he'd been born to them.

6

The streets were quiet.

Chris kept to the darkness, even though no one was out. It was probably well after three o'clock in the morning—or at least *simulated* three o'clock. The fake nightscape showcased a sliver of a moon and several clouds that lazily arced across the expanse overhead. He had to remind himself that none of it was real. The digital projection hid the truth of LV-1213's real sky. Hell, for all he knew, it was daylight out in the real world, or the middle of a raging storm, or perhaps it really was nighttime.

His mind kept replaying those five words, over and over again.

We shouldn't have done it.

Elizabeth had accused him of being obsessive at times, as had his commanding officers. It was part of what had made him such a good soldier. He didn't take things at face value, always checked and rechecked every nook and cranny of any given situation. But it had caused friction in his relationships at times. Pushing too hard when it wasn't necessary. Demanding perfection when such a thing was impossible. It had been the root of more than one fight with Elizabeth when she'd been alive.

Chris walked along the periphery of the town square, avoiding its streetlamps, and headed to the back of the stores, an area he hadn't seen during Lexa's tours of the OST. It was dark back here, unremarkable, but as he continued on, he saw a distant line of trees. Lexa had talked about the colony's ability to grow them at an accelerated rate—the work of a scientist named Margaret Livingston—but seeing them in such number, even in the darkness, was nothing short of stunning.

After glancing behind him, and seeing no one, Chris entered the makeshift forest.

It was quiet here, even more so than the rest of the town, and he marveled at the tree trunks as he walked deeper amongst them, placing his hand on several, reveling in the rough bark against his skin. He found himself falling into the same kind of fugue state that he'd experienced a few times during combat, but rarely during 'regular' life. It was a disquieting realization, and he wondered if he was fully recovered from the blow to the head he'd received when the escape pod had jettisoned from the transport ship.

Just as he was about to turn around and head back to his girls—he had been gone longer than he'd wanted—a noise in the distance caught his attention. He paused for a second, faltering, but then pushed ahead.

The noise was peculiar—a grating of metal followed by hushed, shouting voices. Not the kind of thing you would expect to hear at three o'clock in the morning in a sleepy mining colony.

Sinking even farther into the shadow of the trees, Chris headed towards where he thought the noise had originated, though it had grown completely silent now. Just as he started to doubt his own ears, he made out a large structure beyond the emerging end of the forest—easily the largest building he had seen so far in the OST. When he reached the final line of trees, he stopped, remaining in the deep darkness of the branches, and waited while his eyes adjusted to the light that was coming from the sole edifice.

It was a warehouse—made of wood and painted a very dark color, either dark blue or brown or black; it was impossible to say in the murky darkness of manufactured night. There didn't seem to be anything particularly interesting about the building, other than the fact that it stood alone in a clearing away from everything else he'd seen of this colony so far, but there was probably a lot about this place that he didn't know. Still, the sounds he'd heard had triggered something deep in the back of his mind. Even if it wasn't anything to be worried about, he was still curious.

After several minutes, confident that no one was around, Chris headed out of the shadows and into the relative brightness of the faux moonlight. The air was what he considered the perfect temperature, and he recalled Lexa telling him earlier in the night, at the bar, that they had calibrated the climate within the dome to the most comfortable for the average human, and made it so the temps fluctuated as closely as possible to a 'perfect' Earth day. He approached the warehouse, moving farther into the luminescence of both the moon and the warehouse's external lights.

Once again, his mind drifted as he slowly walked towards the looming edifice. The ideal temperature was just one more example of the larger perfection of this place. The sound of his daughters' laughter earlier at the restaurant, as they ran around with wild abandon, replayed in his mind. And the taste of Lexa's mouth on his. He hadn't kissed or been kissed by another woman since Elizabeth died, and he was wracked with conflicting waves of emotions.

He didn't feel like he'd betrayed his wife, but at the same time, he wasn't sure if he was actually attracted to Lexa. Yes, she was beautiful and smart and strong, but there was also something guarded about her—perhaps a function of her job, being one of the leaders on a USM outpost. Despite the idyllic nature of this colony, they were still on a hunk of rock that apparently sported constant, horrendous storms, no matter what the digital sky showcased.

Chris let out a long breath, the tactical side of his brain completely at odds with his feelings. He often found that he could think like a soldier, or think like a dad, but almost never at the same time. In fact, since Elizabeth's death, the person he'd frequently received the best advice from was Alicia.

Just the thought of her sent another stab of regret searing through his gut. He had memories of being slightly too harsh to her at times, treating her as less than human, and he regretted that now. He wished he could apologize.

"Hey!" a voice suddenly called out, pulling him out of his reverie. "You're not supposed to be here!"

Chris cursed himself as he looked over and saw a man silhouetted by one of the warehouse's spotlights. He'd allowed his mind to wander and gotten careless. If this had been a combat situation, he'd be dead right now.

Instinctually, he held up his hands and squinted into the lights. The man had stopped moving and his right hand was on his hip. Was there a weapon holstered there? Chris wasn't sure. But it was possible, so he kept his breathing calm, forced a smile onto his face.

"Just out for a walk," he said as innocently as possible. Now he was even more curious. A warehouse that needed twenty-four-hour security on a mining colony? Maybe they were protecting the quadromite that they mined each day.

Maybe.

"No one's allowed in this part of the OST—day or night. You should know that," the man said, disdain dripping from his words.

"I'm new around here," Chris said, keeping his voice friendly. This guy was already rubbing him the wrong way.

He knew the type. A man given an ounce of power who suddenly felt like it was his obligation to lord it over anyone he could. "Maybe you heard about it? My daughters and I crash-landed a couple days ago."

"Oh yeah?" the guy said, feigning genuine interest. "Well, I don't give a shit. You're still in a *restricted* zone. So, go run home to where you belong, with the other little girls."

Chris knew he should do exactly that. Apologize, turn around, and walk back to the house that this colony had so kindly provided for him. Get some sleep, wake up the next morning, and start a new day—maybe even figure out a plan for a life on the OST.

Instead:

"What'd you say to me?"

The man strode forward, emboldened by Chris's response, and his features were revealed as he did. He was the same height as Chris but younger, probably in his late twenties, clean shaven, with a buzzcut like Cosgrove's—either a former soldier himself or a wannabe. The sneer on his face looked almost permanent.

"You're not allowed to be here." He jabbed his finger into Chris's chest as he said his next two words. "*Go. Home.*"

For a second time, a distant part of Chris's mind told him to walk away, that he gained nothing by giving this man what he wanted. But he'd often had trouble walking away from conflict, something that had sometimes called his promotions into question, or so he'd been told.

"Make me," he responded, quietly.

The guy was faster than the miners in the bar, Chris had to admit, as the fist hit him square in the cheek, rocking him back slightly. But this kid was weak, soft, all bluster. Like so many people he'd squared off against in his life. He'd been hit harder many times, and on many different planets.

Despite the pain from the rumble earlier in the evening, he replied with his own display of speed, hitting the guy's chin with an uppercut the kid never saw coming. He was knocked back more than just slightly, stumbling, confused that his feet weren't obeying his brain's commands, and then collapsed into a discombobulated heap.

Chris stepped forward, ready to press his attack. The man had insulted him, had thrown the first punch. And that kind of thing simply would not stand. He had been through too much. The last couple of days, yes, but also the last few years as well. He had lost so much. *Too* much. And damn if he was going to let some overzealous bully push him around.

As he grabbed the guy's shirt and lifted him up, cocking his fist back, a shouting voice nearby stopped him in his tracks.

"Hey!"

Chris let go instantly, his mind clearing, shame instantly washing over him. Getting a better look at the guard on the ground beneath him, he saw the fear on the man's face. His tough veneer had crumbled after a single blow. Chris sighed, annoyed with himself. Sure, the guy had been an obnoxious jerk, but he was just doing his job.

Like Chris used to do.

Cosgrove was approaching from the warehouse, one hand resting on his sidearm. They were approximately the same age, he surmised, but Chris felt like a teen who'd been caught stealing.

"Cosgrove. Look, I—" Chris started but the man interrupted, walking past him and grabbing the young guard, pulling him to his feet.

"Is that how you treat our guests, Milliken?" he snarled, eyes narrowing as he spoke.

"I... I mean..." the younger man sputtered, eyes going back and forth between his boss and Chris.

"Apologize," Cosgrove demanded, staring down into Milliken's face, like a teacher scolding a child who had crossed a line at recess.

Milliken's cheeks went red for a moment, and Chris could see his internal struggle playing out on his face. Then, finally:

"I'm sorry," he mumbled, turning and walking back towards the warehouse, head hanging low.

After a moment, Cosgrove turned to Chris, a grim smile on his face.

"You okay?" he asked, pulling a small metal box out of his pocket and withdrawing a hand-rolled cigarette from within.

"I'm fine. I've been hit harder than that before," he said, still watching Milliken walk away in a slow sulk.

"I'm sure," Cosgrove responded, holding out the cigarettes. Chris contemplated them and then shook his head. He'd tried one before, back when he was a grunt, and immediately decided the habit wasn't for him. Breathing was hard enough as it was out in the field. "Fair enough," the man said, eyeballing Chris like he was the first person to ever turn down a cigarette from him, then shoved the small box back into his pocket.

Cosgrove held out his hand, kept his eyes locked on Chris's.

"I'm sorry about what went down at Delilah's. I had a bit too much of her hooch, wasn't thinking straight. I'd like to start over, if that's okay with you. I get the feeling that you and me might have a lot in common."

Chris contemplated the man for a second, and then shook.

"USM?" he asked, noticing for the first time a long scar along the back of Cosgrove's hand.

"Yep. Six years keeping the peace before I decided to bounce. A few years before the *Auriga*. When I heard about a job on the OST, I jumped at the opportunity. A chance to start over... you know how it goes."

"I do," Chris murmured.

"I bet we could trade some war stories," Cosgrove stated, taking a long puff of his cigarette, and then letting out a slow exhale after a moment of enjoying the smoke in his lungs.

"I bet we could," Chris responded, distracted by Milliken punching a code into a panel on the warehouse wall, then opening a door that he hadn't even noticed was there.

"What are you guys hiding in there?" he asked, looking back at Cosgrove.

"Ha!" the larger man barked, switching his cigarette from one hand to the other. "Not much to hide on this planet. Nah, we're storing some radioactive waste in there… one of Margaret's energy experiments gone wrong. Just trying to keep our citizens safe. If one of these drunk miners stumbled in there and died a few days later from radiation poisoning, the USM would be all over us. Better to just be safe and keep people clear."

"Hm," was all Chris offered as a response.

Cosgrove eyed him again, took another long drag.

"If you fill out some paperwork, I can probably get you a tour. I'm sure Lexa can help push it through all the red tape. But honestly? It's pretty boring in there. You're probably destined for better things on the OST. If you and your girls are staying, that is."

Chris looked over Cosgrove's shoulder again. Milliken stood at the open door of the warehouse, talking to another guard who had appeared from within, a tall woman with red hair pulled back into a ponytail. After a second, they both looked over at them.

"Maybe," Chris said.

Cosgrove shifted, blocking Chris's view of the warehouse, rubbed his chin.

"We should grab a drink sometime. On a night when everyone isn't getting wasted and punching each other. I can tell you the ins and outs of this place, and you can tell me all about the fun you had with the USM. I heard your files are redacted like a motherfucker. I'm betting my service years were a lot more boring than yours."

Chris considered the offer, thought about conversations he'd had with Elizabeth over the years, back when she was alive. There had been couples they'd hang out with, a few here and there at different points in their relationship, but he couldn't recall ever having a friend during their marriage. In fact, the last time he'd had a male best friend was when he'd been a teenager, before he joined the military. After that, he'd basically only had two relationships: Elizabeth, and the USM. His wife would gently mock him for not having any of his own friends, and he'd roll his eyes, say he was too busy, but he was keenly aware that it was something missing in his life.

Maybe this was a chance to finally turn that around.

Or maybe Cosgrove was playing an angle, something Chris suspected the longer he stared into the man's eyes.

"Sounds good," he responded. A moment of awkward silence ensued, and part of Chris now regretted the entire exchange. He could tell that the man just wanted Chris away from this warehouse as soon as possible. "Anyway, I should head back. I don't want the girls to wake up and wonder where I am."

"Of course," Cosgrove said. "Get some sleep and then let's chat tomorrow, if you're up for it. Or the next day. Whatever you prefer."

Chris turned and walked away. He felt completely exposed, turning his back on virtual strangers in the dead of night, but maybe he was being paranoid.

Despite his urge to turn around, to see if Cosgrove was watching him, Chris kept going. He thought about Jane and Emma, silently prayed that they hadn't woken up. He had a vision of them searching the house, crying—confused and angry—and hastened his retreat from the warehouse.

Just as he was about to enter the shadows of the trees through which he'd come, he finally relented, giving in to his own insatiable curiosity, and glanced back.

Cosgrove now stood near the warehouse door with the two other colonists, and all three were watching Chris. The silence of the entire scene was almost palpable, and Chris stopped for a moment, surprised by their stare.

After a moment, Cosgrove raised his hand, and Chris did the same, but otherwise the trio didn't move, didn't head into the warehouse despite the darkness and the late hour.

Chris finally broke the silent standoff and turned back around, walking into the shadows thrown through the branches and onto the ground from a moon that continued its arc across a false sky.

PART 2

EMERGENCE

7

Captain James Taggert stared at the readout in front of him, frowning at what he saw.

Most of his crew was still in hyper-sleep but he preferred to wake up before his marines when he was sent on potentially dangerous missions like this. He'd heard of crews who all woke up together, like it was some kind of camaraderie badge of honor. He thought it was ridiculous.

Why should he wake up after a long bout of inactivity at the same time as the soldiers under his command? He had a hell of a lot more on his mind than they did, and he'd rather work through the complexities of a mission with as little background noise as possible. There was nothing he hated more than a bunch of jittery USM soldiers gearing up for a mission after the long sleep. It was the worst possible mix of aggression, nerves, and excitement.

No. Taggert preferred to do his deepest thinking when

the majority of his subordinates were fast asleep. And there was a lot to think about.

The beginning of this mission had been a whirlwind, as were the days leading up to it. He wondered how many of these events were coincidental, and how much of everything was interlocked from tip to tail.

As someone who had been serving in the military since he was eighteen, he didn't believe in coincidences. Nothing happened in a vacuum, not even in space.

Taggert looked away from the readout, blinking. He had a bad habit of obsessing over data, examining it from every angle possible. He believed in being prepared, in life, yes, but especially during missions, and while it had helped him excel in the USM, it had come at a cost. He had no spouse, no real friends. USM was his life. And honestly? When he really thought about it? He was fine with that. He had purpose, he was helping people. Even when they sometimes didn't realize they needed help.

But things had become more complicated lately.

He shook his head. Weyland-fucking-Yutani. Like they always had, that ridiculous company—and its tenacious remnants—constantly made things more difficult, for everyone. Now more than ever, in some ways.

Back when he'd first started out as a grunt, things had been simpler. Mega-corporations like Weyland-Yutani had been outlawed in 2349 following decades of increasing social, financial, and political pressure. People were sick of these companies' power and influence. This was underscored when the Nu Indi colony sued for independence from Weyland-Yutani and, to everyone's surprise, won.

And to add injury to injury, the corporate behemoth failed to secure a USM contract for faster-than-light drives, losing to a rival company, Ridton. Weyland-Yutani started circling the gutter faster and faster. After centuries of ascendant power, history had finally caught up to them. And they deserved it. They had made many questionable decisions over the years, and had always managed to litigate their way out of any real consequences.

But the court of public opinion had rendered its verdict and nothing these massive companies did could change what was happening. Once the too-powerful conglomerates were outlawed, armies of lawyers and politicians taking them apart little by little on paper, despite seemingly endless appeals, the companies were literally stripped down. Weyland-Yutani, the largest manufacturer of weapons on the planet, was formally dissolved, and the majority of their research and physical assets were taken over by none other than the United Systems Military.

And that was that. Young soldiers like Taggert were actively recruited and told this was their chance to better a world that the corporations had nearly destroyed with their greed and self-serving desire for power. Taggert believed it then, and he believed it now.

He had fulfilled his mission over his career. Helping people, stopping those who would hurt society and its innocent citizens, obeying commands even when he didn't completely understand them. His commanding officers in the USM saw the bigger picture, and when he was promoted, again and again, he expected his subordinates to follow him the way he had followed his own mentors over the years.

But Weyland-Yutani wasn't completely dead.

Of course it wasn't.

When you kill a single cockroach in your kitchen, only a fool would think that the job is done. The shadows hide the true size and scope of your enemy. And Taggert had been taught how to scour those shadows, how to shed the righteous light of justice into the dark.

During the years since the fall of Weyland-Yutani, Taggert and his fellow USM officers learned of loyal agents of the demolished corporation who were working quietly behind the scenes to help raise the company from the ashes. And in order to do so, they needed to strike back at the USM, who they felt had used and betrayed them.

At first, it had been simple. Track the intel, often collected through espionage or more direct, painful means, and wipe out Weyland-Yutani cult-like cells as they sprang up. But when Taggert had been poring through data one night, even after he had been told to go home and get some rest, and discovered that Weyland-Yutani had infiltrated the ranks of the USM itself, he knew that the fight was far from over. In fact, it had become much, much deadlier.

The moles within his own organization hid their tracks incredibly well, and the few times he managed to flush them out, they never spoke, never gave up any info—no matter what he did to them.

And he started to see the effects of these spies, with USM missions suddenly, inexplicably failing. Equipment malfunctions, enemies seeming to be aware of their plans before they could even enact them, sensitive information being disseminated to the public.

Even though the sides were not exactly even, this was clearly a war. A war in which Taggert was happy to engage.

He believed in the principles of the USM, especially after the corporate recklessness of Weyland-Yutani and its ilk, both on Earth and on all the other worlds where humans now lived and worked. For them, it was about profit over all other considerations, no matter who got hurt, or how many lives were destroyed as a result.

He had heard the rumors about this cult that had risen up in the mammoth corporation's place, people who subscribed to the 'original' intentions of Peter Weyland and Cullen Yutani—a belief in bettering the human condition through the concurrent ascension of consciousness and technology, allowing these two disparate things to evolve together in a natural melding of the organic and the technologic.

In other words, total horseshit.

Taggert lived in the real world where actions had consequences, and heady philosophies didn't put food on the table or pay the rent. He believed in right and wrong, and the feel of a weapon in his hands.

Not much else mattered, as far as he was concerned.

And now he'd been sent on his latest mission. A very clear-cut case of right vs wrong, and he would do his job. Take care of the problem. And then head back home, wait for his next set of orders. Simple. The way he liked it.

He heard two pairs of footsteps approaching and he pulled himself out of his reverie. He'd been staring at the data for a few minutes without absorbing anything, had allowed his mind to wander.

First Lieutenant Riya Ashraf and Second Lieutenant Douglas Parsons entered the bridge, nodding at him and taking their respective seats. Taggert switched off the data stream. Even though there was no way his officers could read it from their vantage points, it still contained confidential information, and Taggert followed the rules, no matter what.

"How was the inspection?" Taggert asked, looking at Ashraf.

"All quiet, Captain," she responded, punching data into the computer console at her station.

"Yep, the jarheads are still sleeping like babies," Parsons added, lowering himself into his seat, letting out a long breath and tossing his signature stress ball into the air, catching it without even really looking. Taggert found the habit highly annoying, wouldn't allow most of his officers that kind of indulgence, but it seemed to center the younger man, and Parsons brought a lot to the table. He wasn't the brightest, necessarily, but he was the best marksman Taggert had ever met and the large man could more than handle himself in a hand-to-hand combat situation. "They should be nice and rested and ready to kick some ass by the time they wake up."

"Outstanding," Taggert said. He liked when things went nice and smooth. And today was no exception. "We can wake them up as soon as you both finish your final diagnostics."

After a few minutes of quiet work, Ashraf said, "Huh."

"I don't like the sound of that, Lieutenant," Taggert replied, standing up and walking over to her station.

"It's nothing to worry about," she continued, her eyes running over the lines of data that were streaming in. It was moving so fast that Taggert was surprised she could even understand what it said. But she was smart—the smartest officer with whom he'd ever worked. They'd grown incredibly close over the years. He knew that she'd have her own command eventually, but for now, he appreciated having her work under him. And he'd hold onto her as long as he could.

"Is that... an SOS?" he asked, trying to decipher the information that was flying past on the screen at an astonishing rate.

"It is," she confirmed, punching buttons on another console without looking while still reading the messages that were flashing on her main screen. Parsons appeared next to Taggert, looking over his commanding officer's shoulder at the data that Ashraf was collating. He was squeezing the stress ball in his large left hand, which resulted in a slight, rhythmic squeaking sound. Taggert glanced down at it, annoyed, and Parsons noticed, stopping the activity immediately. The ball disappeared into the man's uniform pocket.

Taggert waited for Ashraf to say more but his XO was clearly lost in the data stream, what almost looked like a smile playing out on her face. He knew how much she loved attempting to decipher technological mysteries—the harder, the better. If synthetics weren't banned from the USM, he would almost suspect that she wasn't human at all, just a bunch of wires and electrical impulses.

"Well…?" he said, no longer able to wait for her analysis.

"It's pretty garbled," she responded, glancing up at him for a brief moment, then looking back down, tapping at the keyboard in front of her. "Difficult to make sense of it, and it looks like the distressed ship was comprised of several different sections, and they were all saying *very* different things."

"Can you break it down for us?" Parsons asked, a confused look on his face. He clearly had no idea what Ashraf was talking about.

She smiled again, that slight crooked grin that Taggert secretly loved. A distant part of his mind wondered if he loved more than just that. A part of his mind that he actively shut down whenever it piped up.

"Absolutely," she responded, turning around in her seat as the lines of information continued to run across the screen behind her. She stared up at the two men for a moment, enjoying their anticipation. Then, finally: "The messages are a couple of days old—took some time to travel to us, of course. But the bottom line? A colony transport ship was in trouble. Some kind of serious problem broke out on board, and the situation escalated quickly."

"What kind of problem?" Taggert asked, glancing at the screen behind Ashraf, still having trouble deciphering what it was saying.

"That's the weird part," she answered, shaking her head as if she'd been presented with a particularly annoying riddle. "A large portion of the captain's SOS message was redacted by another section of the ship before it was broadcast."

"That shouldn't be possible," Taggert said, cocking his head, confused by what his XO was saying.

"Exactly," she confirmed.

"I don't get it," Parsons admitted, the squeaking noise suddenly emanating from his pocket, where his hand continued to work furiously. Taggert rolled his eyes but only Ashraf saw it, and she smiled at him. It was a secret smile, the kind they often shared during missions, when something happened that only they understood.

"An SOS message coming from the bridge is completely secure. No one has access to it other than the captain, or whoever's sending it if the captain is incapacitated," Taggert explained.

"In theory," Ashraf countered. "But all systems are hackable. And they're especially vulnerable from within the ship." She turned around and pointed at a line of code that neither man could translate. "Another section of the ship was aware of the captain's SOS as he was recording it. Which in and of itself shouldn't have been possible. Even more troubling, in the few seconds between the recording of the message and the sending of it through all channels, someone actively garbled certain sections of it."

"Weird," Parsons offered.

"To say the least," Ashraf agreed.

"Which section did it?" Taggert asked, leaning closer as the data stream started over again.

"That's what I'm trying to figure out," she responded, punching in a series of commands, causing the data to reconfigure. "They were smart. Hid their tracks very well."

"Smarter than you?" Taggert challenged.

In response, she simply smiled again and increased the speed of her typing. The data flew by at an even faster rate, and Parsons laughed almost silently, impressed and also thoroughly confused. Taggert tried to keep up but couldn't.

Finally, Ashraf stopped. "Huh," she said again.

"Is that better or worse than the first 'huh'?" Taggert asked.

"Worse, I think," she responded. "It looks like the transport ship had an additional science lab on board that the captain didn't even know about. Some seriously top-secret stuff was going on in there."

"Can you find out what?"

"Nope. Thus, my second 'huh.' I should be able to access it through a backdoor sub-routine, but they clearly prepared to block any attempts to access whatever it was they were doing. I've never seen security overrides like this on a USM vessel."

"Interesting," Taggert said, standing up straight, his tone shifting back into command mode. "But not our problem. We have a mission. Once we finish it, we can see if they still need help. For now, we have our orders."

"Of course," Ashraf answered, clearly having heard the change in his voice. She shut down the data stream, turned around. "I found it more curious than anything else. Something to research after our mission, maybe. Based on the messages I was able to download, from the captain and others, it was a very bad situation. I doubt the ship survived, unfortunately."

"How many civilians?" Parsons asked quietly. He had a wife and three kids back on Earth. Despite being a beast on the battlefield, Taggert knew that the kid had a gentle heart.

"Over eight hundred," Ashraf answered just as quietly. She had a tactical mind and found great pleasure in solving complex equations, and silently berated herself for losing sight of the very real potential human loss behind the SOS.

Taggert shook his head and headed back to his command seat. There was nothing to say to that. The loss of innocent life was always a tragedy. And it sounded like this particular accident had been avoidable—but then again, they only had half the information. If that. And it wasn't a part of their mission. He forced it out of his mind and unlocked the small hatch that had been built into his chair. A hatch that remained closed except for one instance during each mission. Parsons noticed what he was doing.

"Is it time?" he asked, a slight smile appearing on his face.

"It is," Taggert confirmed.

The captain withdrew a bottle and three small glasses from the compartment. His two top officers walked closer to him and waited. After a moment of considering the bottle, he looked up and grinned, too. It wasn't a smile of mirth or excitement but one of grim anticipation. The three of them had been here many times. It was never easy, but they each took great comfort in facing the missions as a team.

Taggert handed each of them a shot glass and uncorked the bottle.

"What do we have this time?" Ashraf asked. It was different every time.

"A 2356 Glaswegian whisky. Almost impossible to find. But I know a guy who knows a guy," Taggert said, winking at his XO.

She laughed and held out her glass, which he filled a quarter of the way. Sometimes they just took a sip or two, sometimes they drank it all. Depended on the mood and the mission. The point wasn't really the alcohol. It was a tradition. A moment of quiet appreciation before a dangerous assignment.

Taggert poured some into Parsons' glass, then his own. Last, of course.

They each considered the brown liquid.

"Who's up?" Ashraf asked.

"I went first last time, so it's Parsons," Taggert responded.

"I hate going first," the third-in-command sighed, then squinted and looked at the ceiling, wracking his brain for a toast. After another moment, he held up his glass. "Here's to an easy mission and a quick return home."

"You stole my line," Ashraf faux-fumed, giving her comrade the evil eye.

"I guess you shoulda gone first then," Parsons countered.

"Fair," the XO responded. "Okay. Fine. I'll come up with a new one." She swirled the whisky in the small glass for a moment, seemed to delight in the alcohol almost sloshing out over the lip but staying within its spherical confines. Taggert mused that this was her personality in a nutshell: push everything to the edge but stay within your boundaries no matter what. "Here's to the best damn unit in the entire USM. There's no one else I'd rather have my back than the two of you."

"And the dozen marines asleep on the other side of this ship," Parsons added.

"And the dozen marines asleep on the other side of this ship," Ashraf confirmed.

They both laughed and nodded at each other. Despite being so different, the two officers genuinely liked one another. They never spent time together outside of their training and missions, probably never would have met if not for the USM, but they made for solid teammates.

After a moment, they turned their attention to the captain of the USS *Weaver*.

He was staring off into the distance, lost in thought. They gave him the time he needed.

Finally, he shook his head slightly and caught sight of his two lieutenants staring at him. He chuckled quietly, raised up his glass.

"Sorry about that," he said quietly. "Your toasts were both great and got me thinking."

"No worries, Cap," Parsons said. Ashraf kept her eyes on her boss's.

"Here," Taggert said, licking his lips, raising the glass slightly higher, "is to the USM. Rising out of the ashes of a corrupt corporate system, the United Systems Military, even with its imperfections, strives to bring order to a universe that has been drowning in chaos."

"To order," Ashraf said in a strong voice.

"To order," Parsons echoed, and the three of them clinked glasses, and downed the shots.

Parsons' face scrunched up, like it always did when they drank the whole thing, while Taggert and Ashraf enjoyed the burn as the liquid ran down their throats.

"Blech," the third-in-command said, shaking his head as if the act could somehow ward off the aftertaste.

"You're crazy," Taggert said. "That stuff is delicious."

"Can confirm," Ashraf commented, handing her glass back to Taggert with another small nod. Their eye contact lasted a second longer than it needed to, and then she turned and headed back to her station, began punching in data.

Parsons gave his glass to his captain as well and let out a long sigh. "I guess I'm just more of a beer fella."

"Sit-rep?" Taggert said after stowing the glasses and bottle back into their compartment.

"We'll be arriving to our target's orbit in approximately ninety hours," Ashraf answered immediately, as if she'd been anticipating the question.

Parsons hurried over to his station as well and tapped away at his own computer terminal. "All systems are running at maximum efficiency. We are looking good for immediate exfil on arrival. With extreme prejudice, as needed."

"Excellent," Taggert said, impressed as always by his top two team members. He let the moment sink in for a moment, and then stood up. "Okay. Shall we wake everyone else up?"

8

MINING OUTPOST OMEGA SEVEN TANGO

Tommy Travers was tired of being yelled at all the time.

Yeah, he messed up once in a while, that was true. But who didn't? And they were all dealing with extremely unusual circumstances, further complicated by the arrival of Chris Temple and his two kids.

And what was left of the doomed transport ship.

As dawn was breaking across the 'sky,' Travers swiped his security badge and entered the warehouse, letting out a frustrated sigh. He'd been instructed to continue the secondary, more detailed survey of the ship—or what was left of it after it had crashed a few miles away from their dome.

The residents of the OST had been lucky, everyone knew that. If the ship had landed on the outpost itself, who knew how many people would have died. But it had crashed close enough that they'd been able to haul its sizable remaining shell inside and hide it inside the warehouse before Temple was aware. It was imperative that they keep this quiet. There was way too much on the line. Even a lower-level worker like Tommy Travers knew that much.

But right now, as he made his way deeper into the building, he took little comfort in any of those truths. He was exhausted and had been shouted at constantly during his previous shift.

Stop wandering around the ship!

Stop touching stuff!

Stop being such an idiot!

Stop drinking on the job!

He was *so* sick of Milliken. Sick of the way he looked at him, the way he talked to him. One of these days, when his superior officer was least expecting it, Travers was going to *accidentally* slip a knife into the man's back.

Oops, how did that get there?

Travers laughed at the thought as he approached the remains of the transport ship. It was in better shape than he would have initially expected, which had made its transfer into the dome, and then the warehouse, much easier than it would have been otherwise. Unfortunately, everyone on board had died during the crash, but Travers hadn't been part of that clean-up crew, thankfully. He didn't do so well around blood.

No, he much preferred his current job—make his way through the twisted remains of the ship and catalog everything that the primary team had missed during their first sweep. Make Milliken aware of anything useful he found. Especially weapons or communications systems. Just *don't touch them*. And he wouldn't. He didn't feel like getting yelled at anymore. He would just do his job. Keep a low profile. Maybe get that raise Lexa had promised him when he'd recently been 'promoted.'

Lexa.

Just the thought of her sent shivers of pleasure up his spine. It was surreal to have a crush at his age, but there was no question that Lexa Phelan made him feel like the schoolboy he had once been, all those years ago on Earth.

He knew she didn't think of him like that, at least not yet. But that didn't mean she wouldn't someday. In fact, maybe if he made some great discovery on the transport ship and told her about it directly—instead of going to Milliken or even Cosgrove—she would see Tommy with new eyes.

She would get to know him. Realize how much he had to offer.

Then again, he'd noticed the way Lexa had been looking at Temple since the man's arrival. The memories made the butterflies in Travers' stomach turn to acid.

Chris Temple.

He didn't belong here, was only making things worse. Maybe that same knife would accidentally end up in Temple's back, too. Then Travers and Lexa could raise those cute little girls themselves. A perfect family.

Travers smiled at the idea as he made his way into the transport ship, slipping through one of the many huge cracks in its exterior. The ship had clearly landed with incredible force, smashing open like an egg dropped to the ground.

He'd been inside this spooky ship longer than anyone else on the OST. Had even volunteered for extra hours—both for the additional rations it accorded him, but also to impress Lexa. It was true that she had seemed to become more aware of him during the past few weeks, but that awareness already seemed to be fading. Temple's fault, most likely. Another reason to get rid of the guy as soon as possible.

Tommy carefully made his way deeper into the bowels of the mangled ship. It might take a while but everyone on this rock would eventually realize how valuable he was. He and his twin brother Francis had originally been hired as glorified custodians but had been promoted recently—no real titles, admittedly, and no pay rise, but they'd been told that they would be more involved now. *Especially* now.

And helping scour this half-destroyed hunk of junk was part of that.

Sure, the bigwigs had already taken all the good stuff out immediately after the ship had been dragged into the warehouse. But the Travers twins were in charge of finding anything good that their bosses had overlooked. That was a big deal. *Tommy* was a big deal. And better than his obnoxious brother. They worked separate shifts since they fought when they spent too much time together. Always had. Even as little kids.

Yep, the solo work suited Tommy just fine. One more way to differentiate himself from his twin. One more way to impress Lexa.

Admittedly, Tommy hadn't found much yet—a few items here and there that Milliken seemed happy about. Well, maybe not *happy*, but satisfied enough not to yell at Tommy for once. He'd take it.

Besides, his gut told him that eventually he was going to find something amazing in this hunk of trash. And maybe today was that day.

"What are you doing in here?!" a loud voice shouted from a nearby shadow. Tommy jumped, whirling, ready to get yelled at by one of his bosses again. But the words were followed by a familiar cackle, and his brother stepped out of the darkness, a big dumb smile plastered on his face.

"Made you jump," Francis mocked. Even though they were technically identical twins, Francis was taller, had more angular features, and generally had his shit together more than his younger—by eighteen minutes—brother. At least according to *some* people.

"You asshole," Tommy hissed. "What are you even doing here? I thought you were off today."

"Milliken wanted me to help you out," his brother answered. "Things are moving slower than him and Lexa want."

"I don't need help!" Tommy shouted, annoyed at how easily his brother was able to get under his skin.

Francis shrugged. "Just doing what Boss Man told me.

Besides, it'll be fun. We haven't hung out much since we got promoted. You're always at Delilah's with your new friends lately."

"Yeah, cuz they *respect* me," Tommy replied, then worked to calm his breathing. His older brother had been doing this their entire lives—overshadowing him, making him feel like a loser—but deep down he still liked him. Maybe even loved him, he would admit, if drunk enough. "Anyway, come on. Let's go find something and then maybe *you and me* can celebrate at Delilah's."

"Sounds good to me, little bro. You know this ship better than I do, so I'll follow your lead."

Francis made a sweeping gesture with his arm and waited. Tommy laughed despite himself and headed farther into the ship. He heard his brother following and reflected that it was kind of nice to have the company. Something he'd never say out loud.

After several minutes of squeezing around now-familiar crash-created corners, Tommy eased himself down through a rip in the floor into a lower level of the ship, followed a moment later by his brother. Tommy hadn't been down here yet and it was much darker than the section above, none of the warehouse's ultra-bright fluorescents piercing the layers of flayed metal. It was disquieting but also kind of comforting, too. The type of silence that Tommy liked. He withdrew the small flashlight from his pocket, clicked it on, and continued making his way down the shadowy corridor. Francis did the same, the twin lights arcing out and crisscrossing each other as the two brothers walked along the highly damaged corridor.

There was a lot more debris down here and Tommy forced himself to look away from a particularly disturbing splotch of blood and who-knew-what-else sprayed across one of the walls. He didn't know exactly how many people had died on this ship, and he didn't want to know. It was the kind of thing that would haunt his dreams if he knew too many details. His mother had often called him *too sensitive*, as opposed to his more composed brother, and Tommy hated when she said that.

He missed her. She'd died when he and Francis were young, and they had never known their father, but Tommy's memories of his mother were mostly good, except for the times she hit him. Maybe too hard. Maybe too often. But he knew she loved him, even if she didn't say it very often. He could just tell. She hit Francis, too, but not as much. Not nearly as much.

Maybe if she hadn't died in that accident, the Travers twins wouldn't have been forced to enlist. Their whole lives could have been different.

Tommy's mind resettled on Lexa, on the way she had looked at him once or twice in the past couple of weeks. She hadn't said much, but there was something in her eyes. Probably admiration. He could read her eyes the way he had been able to read his mother's.

As he lost himself to his memories and slowly made his way deeper and deeper into the ship with Francis next to him, their weak light bouncing off the cracked walls, a distant noise suddenly stopped them in their tracks.

"What the hell...?" Francis said, a rare look of fear on his face.

In a subtle display that was just as rare, Tommy smiled. Maybe this was it. Maybe he was about to find something that was going to turn his life around. That was going to make Lexa Phelan really notice him.

Tommy quickened his pace and his brother hustled to keep up.

"Maybe we should—" Francis started to say but Tommy stopped short, and his twin nearly crashed right into him. "What's wrong with you?!"

Tommy ignored him, strained to listen to the sounds of the destroyed ship, and swore under his breath when he realized that the strange noise had vanished. Maybe he had just imagined it? It wouldn't be the first time he'd heard something that was only in his head. But no, Francis had heard it, too. There had definitely been a sound, a real-life one, almost like a tapping. And he was going to find whatever it was. He sped back up, teeth clenched, determined. Behind him, Francis swore, but followed.

Tommy's enthusiasm waned a few minutes later as they approached what looked like an unnatural, bent metal wall in the middle of the hallway. Halting his momentum once again, he and Francis shined their lights around the obstruction.

"Looks like another part of the ship came through here during the crash," Francis murmured, morbid fascination in his voice. "Maybe a wall... or part of a floor. Jeeeezus."

Tommy ignored his brother. It didn't matter what it was, or where it came from, it completely blocked them from the other side—and whatever treasures might be hidden there.

No. Not completely.

Looking closer, Tommy noticed there was a sizable crack near the top of the blockage, possibly big enough for him and Francis to slip through. For once, the twins' relative smallness might actually work out in their favor. Milliken would certainly never be able to fit through there!

Tommy chuckled at the thought of his boss clambering up there and getting stuck in the hole, calling for help, Cosgrove finding and berating him. Instead, Tommy and Francis would be the ones to make it through to a section of this damaged transport ship that no one else had managed to investigate.

Excited, he looked closer and found several cracks in the makeshift wall that led to the larger one near the top. Placing the flashlight in his mouth, he dug his fingers into two of them, and glanced back. "Gimme a boost," he commanded, Francis looking surprised at his younger brother's display of confidence.

After getting about halfway up a few times and sliding back down into his brother, both swearing louder each time, Tommy finally reached the larger opening at the top.

His trembling fingers strained as he pulled his full weight up, into, and through the hole. Before he realized what was happening, he tipped forward and fell into darkness, the flashlight popping out of his mouth and clanking off into the distance, its illumination immediately blinking out of existence.

Tommy landed on his back on the other side of the divide, hard. The breath was instantly slammed out of his body, and he struggled to draw any oxygen into his lungs, felt himself starting to panic. Was he dying?

Then, after a moment, his body adjusted, and he drew in a massive gulp of air.

"What happened, you moron?" Francis's voice called out.

"I made it through, didn't I?" Tommy shouted back.

"Be right there!" Francis said, and Tommy listened as his twin attempted to scramble up the wall.

"There's no way," Tommy mumbled, ready to move on alone, but a moment later, his brother gracefully dropped down next to him.

"Did it without any help," Francis bragged, smiling.

"Whatever," Tommy replied. "Help me find my light."

Moving forward slowly, squinting his eyes, lit by the thin line of Francis's beam, Tommy searched for his flashlight. Based on the earlier sound, he had a general idea of where it had gone, but damn if it wasn't especially dark down here.

Tommy heard the tapping noise again and stopped moving in response. The sound ceased at the same time.

"Maybe it's some kind of echo," Francis said. "This might be a total waste of time."

"*No*," Tommy said angrily. "There's something down here."

Finally, just as he was getting frustrated and debating the idea of agreeing with Francis and giving up, Tommy's foot connected with the small metal cylinder and sent it clattering across the floor. He sprinted forward, following it based on the tinny sound along the metal floor, ignoring his brother's laughter, and managed to grab it just as its motion was ceasing.

"Got you, ya little bastard," he muttered, grinning at his success. He clicked the flashlight, momentarily blinding himself, and then turned the device away from his face, his grin morphing into a litany of curses. He blinked furiously until the white dots faded from his vision.

Tommy looked around the large room he'd inadvertently entered.

It was a laboratory. Or it had been. But enough of the machinery and devices had survived the devastating crash to make it clear that this area had been used for scientific experiments. Not that he really recognized anything specific—but Tommy Travers knew a lab when he saw one.

"Francis! Get in here!"

As Tommy ran the light over the cluttered contents of the room, his eyes widened and his imagination soared. This stuff would be very valuable to Lexa. Once he went back and told her about this personally, he would be a hero.

This was going to change *everything* for him.

Francis appeared next to him, slightly out of breath. "Daaaaaamn," he whispered as he shined his light around the room as well. "Nice work, little brother."

Tommy's moment of pride was interrupted by that strange sound again, closer this time. Louder. Like a mouse trying to get into a pantry. But that was impossible. Everyone said that *nothing* could have survived that crash. And the leaders of this colony had been *very* careful about what non-human creatures made it on, and off, the original transport ship, back when this colony was in its infancy. They had prided themselves on not allowing a single rodent to step a single paw onto the surface of the OST. Not like those old stories of sea ships that had led to infestations in countries all over Earth. No, the only animals on this planet were the ones that had been painstakingly chosen for the optimal life of the colony. For food and companionship. That was it.

So, this wasn't a stray mouse here on this broken-down ship—it was something else. Something that might be highly valuable. Some kind of experiment that would change Tommy's life forever, and maybe Lexa's, too.

Silence again.

"Let's take a look," Tommy said, then moved around the cavernous, battered room. Francis headed to the other side of the large laboratory.

Tommy peered into glass containers, a few full of brackish liquid, most shattered and empty. Masses of tubes were strewn across tables and the floor like dozens of snakes, coiled and ready to strike. Metal containers were flattened against walls and littered in corners as if blown there by a particularly bad storm. Thick wires hung from the ceiling, either purposefully or not, connected to bizarre apparatuses that almost looked like torture devices.

And then Tommy's light fell upon several thick plastic cases that were still intact, and inside were strange objects— they almost looked like large, oblong leather balls.

Something in the back of his mind told him that he had found the treasure. This was it. The opportunity that had eluded him for his entire life. He wondered if he could somehow keep this secret from Francis and then realized how ridiculous that idea was. Still, he would take full credit when they told Lexa about this discovery.

He stepped closer, shining his light fully on the cases, and the noise occurred again, as well as movement inside one of the leathery objects. There was something in there. And it wanted to get out. Maybe it was dying.

Tommy hesitated. The rational part of his mind, admittedly something he generally ignored, flashed a warning: he had no idea what this was, and no one knew they were all the way down here. He and Francis could simply head back, crawl through that opening again, and return with Milliken, get his read on the situation.

But the other part of his mind, the one that usually spoke loudest, painted another scenario.

By the time they got back, whatever might be inside these objects could be dead. His imagination formed a scene where Lexa stood in this exact spot, holding a dead creature in her hands, looking at Tommy with recrimination and disappointment.

How could you? her eyes would say. *If you had only moved faster, been smarter, everything would have been different. We could have been something different.*

No. He wouldn't allow that to happen. Whatever was inside there looked small. How much damage could it really do?

"Francis!" he said in a strained whisper. "Get over here!"

Just to be safe, he glanced over and saw a long shard of metal strewn on a table, and he grabbed it, feeling its weight in his hand. If this creature tried anything, it would find out just how dangerous of an enemy Tommy Travers could be.

Francis arrived and his mouth gaped as he stared at the containers in front of his brother.

"What the hell are *those*?"

"Shut up," Tommy responded. "Keep your light on this one." Putting his own flashlight in his pocket, he gripped the top of the plastic case and pried its lid open—the crash had damaged the frame a bit, but not so much that he couldn't force the damn thing to reveal its contents.

The light behind him shifted off the container and he glanced over, shocked to see that his brother was opening one of the containers, too.

"What the hell are you *doing*?" he demanded.

"You're not the only one who's gonna get extra credits!" Francis hissed, and Tommy just shook his head. *Typical*, he thought, and looked back down at his own container, at what lay inside.

The creature within the egg slowed its movements and then grew still entirely.

Aww, Tommy thought. *It's probably just a baby and totally terrified.*

Placing his makeshift weapon on the floor by his feet, close enough so he could grab it in the unlikely event he was threatened, Tommy reached into the case and carefully ran his hands along the object. It felt moist and rough against his palms, and he snorted a quick burst of laughter through his nose. If his mom could only see him now! She would be so proud. Finally.

He knelt next to it, squinting at its sides, trying to see if the creature inside was still alive.

"Think we should go get Milliken?" Francis ventured.

"No!" Tommy almost shouted, annoyed. "Then he'll take all the credit."

"Yeah, true," Francis agreed.

At the sound of their voices, the creatures inside both objects moved, and the tops of the two eggs began to shudder. Hearing Francis suck in an excited breath, Tommy rose higher on his knees, not even looking at the weapon as his fingers curled back around it.

After a moment, the quivering ceased and then the

objects opened at exactly the same time, their four flaps unfurling like a flower. Tommy's jaw dropped open in amazement. He had never seen anything like this in his entire life.

"Whoa," Francis said.

"Right?" Tommy responded. Despite how much they fought, it was kind of thrilling to be doing this together.

Inside the egg, pulsating slightly, was a pinkish mass, wet and veiny, and Tommy thought it looked like a hunk of chicken meat, ready to be put into an oven before a big holiday meal. He laughed quietly at the thought. How could he have been even vaguely afraid of this thing? It was just a blob. He'd scoop it out, find something to stick it in, and head back. He couldn't wait to show this to Lexa.

The strange mass suddenly shuddered again, and Tommy leaned in even closer, examining it, trying to figure out the best way to reach in and extract it without hurting the poor thing.

"Yours acting weird, too?" Francis asked, also staring down at his quivering mass.

"Yeah," Tommy said. "Maybe we can—"

Before he could finish his sentence, the thing inside the egg flipped over and burst up towards his face and took hold, something that felt like long fingers wrapping around both sides of his face. He fell back, screaming, immediately dropping and forgetting about the piece of metal that he'd thought would save his life in case of danger.

He could hear Francis struggling next to him, too.

Tommy's scream was cut short as something entered his mouth and shoved its way down his throat. Blind, choking, he fell backwards, smashing into already-broken equipment, pulling at the thing on his face, but it was no use. Its grip was incredibly strong, and he was already starting to see stars as oxygen was denied to him.

The two alien organisms deposited their cargo down through the twin brothers' esophagi, fulfilling their biological duties almost simultaneously, Francis and Tommy writhing under their weight.

Soon, the destroyed laboratory grew entirely silent, except for the gentle rising and falling of the creatures' multiple lungs.

9

Chris scratched the cow's head, smiling, as a large cloud rolled lazily across the sun.

Fake cloud, he reminded himself. *Fake sun.*

But damn if it didn't feel good. There even seemed to be a breeze, though he was probably just imagining that part. He was wearing a fresh set of clothes, including a pair of boots that fit perfectly. He had no idea where they'd come from—but several boxes of clothes had appeared as if by magic on their porch that morning. Back on Earth, money had gotten tight after Elizabeth's medical expenses and the funeral, and then he'd quit the USM. Plus, it hadn't been exactly inexpensive to book passage off the planet. It would have been cheaper if only he and his girls had gone but there was no way he was leaving Alicia behind. Jane and Emma adored her.

He looked around, surveying the farm. Even the scent of animal shit smelled good after months of being cooped up in a tin can hurtling through outer space. Numerous crops grew in even lines over a large patch of dirt, and a small grouping of long tents protected one plant in particular—tobacco, Chris reasoned.

Across the dirt road that bisected the property, inside a paddock, a bespectacled man named John Wilkins was giving Emma and Jane riding lessons on ponies. He could see both of their huge smiles even from where he was standing. They'd never been on horses before—Chris wasn't even sure if they'd ever seen an actual horse in their entire lives.

Other animals milled in and out of the large barn, including a surprising number of dogs that roamed the property in small packs, sometimes co-mingling in a playful manner, sometimes nipping at each other and growling. There seemed to be a whole dog subculture on this farm, Chris thought with a smile. And unlike the German Shepherd he'd glanced, and a few others he had seen the colonists walking, these dogs weren't wearing collars.

The barn was painted a bright red, like something out of an ancient painting. Bales of hay were stacked in meticulous columns along one of the structure's exterior walls, and a small house sat about a thousand yards up the dirt road, painted a darker shade of red, a single-story affair with quaint, green wooden shutters.

He heard movement to his left and turned, happy to see Lexa approaching. She seemed more relaxed here, and maybe he was more relaxed, too. Perhaps there was something about being on a farm that necessitated a certain kind of slowing down. He remembered visiting one when he was a kid, with his mother—who didn't seem thrilled to be taking time off from work—but the memory was vague, fuzzy on the edges.

"Cute, isn't she?" Lexa said, joining him along the fence.

"Very," Chris responded, gently patting the cow on her head again before she moseyed off and began munching on some nearby hay.

"I sometimes forget that we're basically inside a box— that we're surrounded by constant, violent storms. It can be so peaceful here," she murmured, staring off into the distance, a bemused look on her face.

"It really is pretty incredible," Chris said, looking at her profile. "You have a lot to be proud of, Lexa."

She smiled and looked at him, her eyes focusing as she took in his features. "I wish I could take full credit. But a lot of people spent a lot of time getting us where we are today. And it hasn't always been easy. The early years, when I first got here, were hard. *Very* hard."

"I guess that's always true of terraforming," Chris agreed. "I thought about going into that line of work when I was in school."

"Really?"

"Well, for about thirty seconds," he laughed. "And then my mom pointed me to some more information about what it was really like, and it honestly just sounded awful. So, I gave up on that idea pretty quickly."

"Well, it's not like the military is a picnic," she countered.

"True," he said. There was a moment of silence, and he could tell that she was waiting for him to expound further about his time in the service, but he couldn't bring himself to say anything else. He had trouble understanding how he felt about it himself.

"Your girls are having fun," Lexa said after a moment, shielding her eyes from the suddenly increased digital brightness of the sun as it cleared the cloud, looking over at the paddock as Jane and Emma laughed, their horses circling each other.

"It's honestly incredible," he repeated, following her gaze. Tears sprang up in his eyes, surprising him. Lexa noticed but didn't say anything. He appreciated that. "I don't think I've ever seen them this happy. Certainly not since…"

"It's okay," Lexa said quickly. "You don't have to."

"No, it's fine. Since their mom died. Elizabeth. It's not easy for me to talk about her… but it's not as hard as it used to be. She would be so happy to see them like this."

"I'm sure."

"I don't mean to be weird," Chris blurted out suddenly. "About the USM. I just… I haven't really opened up about it since I quit. With anyone."

"Chris," she said, placing her hand on his arm. "Again. You really don't have to."

He looked down at her hand. It felt so good. But it also didn't. He was more confused than ever. After a second, she withdrew it, and he appreciated that, too.

"You're very kind. But you also make me want to talk about things—which is a pretty impressive trait. If this whole mining colony thing doesn't work out, you should look into being a therapist."

"Ha!" she barked. "I don't think so. Trust me, once you get to know me, you'll find my constant pushing and probing super annoying."

"I have a hard time imagining anything about you that would be annoying," he said softly.

She smiled but said nothing, and they enjoyed the silence for a moment, watched the girls as they continued their horseplay. Emma yawned and then looked around, clearly hoping that no one had noticed. Chris took a deep breath, then spoke.

"My mom was a legend in the USM. She was really tough on me, so growing up in that household was extremely hard at times. But there was never really any question about what I was going to do with my life. It was just understood. So, I joined the military right out of high school." Chris rubbed a hand across his face. It felt awful and amazing to be talking about this.

Lexa didn't say anything, but he could tell she was listening intently. Which was fine. Throughout his adult life, people had often asked him about his life with the USM, and he had constantly disappointed them. He and Elizabeth would be at dinner parties and some drunk husband would ask him how many people he had killed during his career, and he'd just smile and nod, feeling his wife's fingers wrap around his arm. A silent plea not to kill *this* dumb jerk.

"I was all in at first," Chris continued, his eyes watching his daughters but his mind casting back into the past, so much of it crystal clear in his recollection—even the things he wished he could no longer remember. "I told myself I would never be swayed by mindless propaganda, but I honestly believed in the mission. After so many years of corporations rolling over human rights, putting profits over all other considerations, the USM's philosophies just made so much sense, you know? Get back to the basics. Community. Family. Law. Tradition. Order. Those are the kinds of things my mom stressed constantly, and it just felt… right."

Lexa listened intently. She wasn't even looking at the girls anymore. Chris had her full attention.

"Some parts of it… weren't fun. I don't like hurting people. I never have. But I was sometimes put in a position where I had to—to keep myself safe—but more importantly, to keep my fellow soldiers safe. I never fired first. Ever. But once the fighting did start, I was just… really, really good at it." He took another deep breath, lost in memories that caused him physical pain, his gut twisting. He pushed them out of his mind, focused back on Lexa's eyes. "And then, as time went on, it just got harder and harder."

"Which part?" she asked quietly.

"All of it," he answered after a moment. "All of it. I still believe in the USM, I guess, but it doesn't seem as clear cut as it did when I was eighteen. I mean, what does?"

"I'll drink to that," she said, smiling.

"This stuff is really hard for me to talk about, and I'm barely scratching the surface, but this is more than I've told almost anyone. As I got promoted and saw more and more behind the curtain—and especially after Elizabeth died—I just couldn't be an active part of it anymore, you know? I had to be a dad first. Everything else at that point was secondary."

"I understand," Lexa said, though he suspected there was no way she really could. She still worked for the USM, after all, even if it was from a great distance.

"I'm sorry," he said. "I know I'm bad-mouthing your bosses."

"Stop," she laughed. "I'm just a cog in the machine."

"I sincerely doubt that," he responded, chuckling too. In the distance, Jane was getting down from her horse, but Emma was still going full tilt, probably pushing the poor little pony a little harder than she should have been. When she set her mind to it, she would do the same activity for hours on end until Chris physically barred her from it. It had been the source of more than one meltdown.

"We're our own little world out here, Chris," Lexa said. "We've created something that feels timeless. I don't think anything like this exists anywhere in the universe, not even back on Earth. I'm... *We're* all very proud of it."

"You should be," he answered, watching as Jane starting walking towards them, that big smile still plastered on her face. He could tell she was trying, and failing, to tamp it down.

"But it takes a lot of work," Lexa continued. "And the right kind of people. Not everyone is cut out to live and work here. But maybe you could be...?"

Before Chris could answer, Jane was within earshot. He glanced at Lexa with a quizzical look, and she raised her eyes as if to say, *The ball's in your court, buddy.*

"Hey, you," he said to his older daughter, resisting an urge to hug her. He knew she would recoil from the gesture, especially in front of Lexa. "Did you have fun?"

"I guess," she demurred, but the look on her face said otherwise. Chris just nodded, let her have her way on the matter.

"If you'll both excuse me," he said, "I need to use the latrine."

Jane rolled her eyes. "Geez, Dad, just say bathroom like every other human in the universe."

"Fine. I'm going to the *bathroom*," he responded, elongating the final word in a comical, and clearly annoying, manner.

"Ugh," Jane retorted as her father ambled awkwardly away, like some kind of confused cowboy.

Lexa laughed as she watched Chris walk towards the farmhouse.

"My dad used to drive me crazy, too. I have this one very specific memory of him getting into a fistfight with one of my teachers at pick-up. I don't even remember what they were fighting about, but I do remember all the kids and parents staring at them, and at me, of course. The next day was *brutal*."

"Really?" Jane said, looking up with big eyes.

"Yep," Lexa confirmed. "He was a teacher himself, and he took education very seriously. Maybe too seriously. He was *tough*. Your father is very, very different. You're lucky."

Jane considered this as she watched Chris walk up the steps of the house. "Huh," was all she offered up as an answer to Lexa's appraisal.

In the distance, Emma whooped as her pony continued to circle the paddock, at one point even taking both of her hands off the bridle, like someone on a rollercoaster in one of the old-timey photos that Lexa had once seen in a museum. Those didn't exist anymore, but they looked fun—a lot had been lost in the name of progress, she surmised silently and not for the first time.

"Are you enjoying your stay in the OST so far?" Lexa asked after a long moment of silence. "I mean, I know your arrival wasn't exactly planned, and the way you got here... wasn't fun." She cringed inwardly at her words. She really liked Chris's daughters, but she had never spent a ton of time with kids, was never sure of the right tone to take with them.

"I feel bad..." Jane started to say, and then paused, her face screwing up as she searched for her own words. Lexa prepared for the worst. *I hate it*, or some variation thereof. "But I love it here. And so does Emma. She says she wants to stay forever."

"Oh. Wow," Lexa said, a surprising feeling of warmth filling her chest.

"Yeah," the girl said, as if it was shocking to her, too. "We didn't really want to leave our house—you know, on Earth. But Dad said it was getting dangerous, and we knew he was right. Some really scary guys broke into our house right before we left."

"Really?"

"It was fine," Jane responded quickly, looking up at Lexa. "Alicia took care of them."

"That was your family's android that you were telling me about, right?" Lexa saw Jane's body tense and realized immediately that she had phrased that incorrectly. "Your dad told me how much she meant to your whole family," she quickly added.

"Yeah," Jane said quietly, turning and putting her arms on top of the fence, her chin on her arms. "I miss her."

Lexa let the moment stretch a bit. Recalibrated.

"But you do like it here," she said, placing her own arms on the fence, mirroring the momentarily somber girl next to her.

Something passed across Jane's face, and she perked up, lifting her head and turning back towards Lexa. "I really do. The transport ship was *so* boring. And we saw pictures of the place we were heading—the colony—and it looked… fine? I guess? But the OST is way better. I mean, the movie theater and the restaurant and this farm and our house and…" Her words trailed off and she suddenly looked embarrassed. "I mean, I know it's not *our* house. Me and Emma just really like it. When my dad was asleep, we like went through the entire place and like named stuff and found all kinds of cool things, and I'm sorry, I didn't mean to say it was ours."

Lexa smiled kindly and placed her hand on the girl's shoulder. She was surprised to see that Jane was trembling slightly.

"Jane. It's fine. That house *is* yours if you want it."

"It is?"

"Absolutely," Lexa confirmed, placing an errant strand of hair behind the girl's ear. "That's a secret between you and me for now, okay?" Jane nodded. "I still need to talk to your dad. But I really like you. All of you. And I'm hoping that you stay."

"I hope the same thing," Jane said in a small, excited voice.

They both looked over as a high-pitched scream reached them. Emma was sprinting in their direction, arms flailing, that same huge smile stretched on her face.

"I like talking to you," Lexa said, amazed that she mostly meant it.

"I like talking to you, too," Jane responded, peering up shyly. And then her entire personality shifted as she looked away. "Oh my God, Emma, be quiet! Why do you have to be so loud?!"

Lexa smiled as the two girls began bickering, loudly, and Chris came bounding out of the house, an annoyed and embarrassed looking creasing his face as he witnessed the prepubescent fight breaking out in front of him.

Dealing with kids was something that Lexa would need to continue working on. But it was certainly getting easier.

Chris and Lexa walked behind the girls, watching them as they made huge, looping zigzags across the road, laughing as they did so.

The digital sun was heading towards the horizon, and in the distance, they could hear the miners returning from another day of dealing with the actual conditions of LV-1213.

"Are you sure it's okay that you're missing so much work?" Chris said, finally breaking the silence that had descended on both of them. Chris could tell that Lexa had something she wanted to say to him—she would glance over and then quickly away when he met her eyes. She generally wasn't shy, and he liked that about her. But she was acting very different now than she had been at any point in their admittedly short friendship.

"Well, I should probably get back to HQ tomorrow," she admitted, smiling at him. "But I'm kind of the unofficial welcome wagon at the OST, and we don't get visitors very often."

"Or ever?" Chris suggested.

"Or ever," she confirmed. "And actually, I guess you could kind of consider the last few days work-related."

He felt his stomach tense and he immediately knew

what was coming next. But he didn't want to interrupt her or voice assumptions. But still, he knew.

"How so?" was all he said instead.

She stopped walking and faced him. He did the same. The girls continued to run and shout in absolute pleasure.

"I get the feeling you know exactly what I mean, Chris," she answered, studying his face. "But that's fine, I appreciate you letting me get it out into the open in my own way." He nodded, waited. Lexa let out a breath. Was she... nervous? "We're still waiting to hear back from the USM about getting you off this planet, but I've been thinking, and talking with the rest of the executive board, and we'd like to offer you a job."

"What kind of job?"

"That's up for discussion. You can shadow some of our people, pick your own thing. Maybe work at the movie theater." He laughed, loud, and she laughed a little, too. "Kidding, kidding. But I was thinking, something like... a sheriff?"

"A *sheriff*?" he said, incredulous. *That* he had not expected.

"It's not the right term," she quickly added. "But it kind of... *is*. I don't want to say policeman, because that's too strong. But we've all noticed how well you can handle yourself. I obviously don't have full access to your USM records, but from what I *have* been able to read, you are way more qualified at the whole 'law and order' thing than anyone else on this entire planet. And honestly?" She paused, seemingly struggling to find the right words.

"What?" he asked. Despite his confidence in knowing what she would say only moments earlier, he now had absolutely no idea what was going to come next.

"You're incredibly human," she added. "Not very USM at all. The way you are with your girls, with the people in town, with that cow." They both laughed again but she quickly grew serious. "With me."

He nodded, then looked away, unable to maintain her intense eye contact. His girls continued to run and laugh. It was the greatest sound in the world. On any world.

He started walking again, and so did Lexa.

"Can I think about it?"

"Of course," she said quickly. "Take as much time as you want. But there's a home here for you, and your girls, if you want it."

"Thank you, Lexa," he said, and he meant it. "It's an amazing offer. Very tempting. But I need to really consider it, talk about it with Jane and Emma. And I promise I won't take too long. I just need a day or two. Okay?"

"Sounds good, Sheriff Temple," she said, smiling, and then ran forward, joining the girls in their crazy loop-de-loops. Chris shook his head at the sight, laughed in absolute wonder, and then sprinted forward, joining in, losing himself to the moment completely and with abandon.

10

Cosgrove looked down at his watch, shook his head, scoffed in frustration.

"Where the hell are those idiot twins?" he barked at Milliken.

"I've been looking but can't find them," the young guard said. "Probably drunk in the barn again."

"They better not be," Cosgrove responded, entering data into his computer console, frustrated at the speed—or lack thereof—that a full accounting and diagnostic of the crashed transport ship had been taking. There were still secrets inside this vessel, he was sure of it. They didn't have time to waste looking for a loser like Tommy Travers and his only slightly less moronic brother Francis.

Cosgrove glanced around his section of the warehouse— the largest and most top secret of the building's various sub-structures. He had recently been promoted and initially had been nervous about assuming this kind of responsibility, but now found that he liked it. The position suited him. His unexpected advancement had capped a series of events that he hadn't anticipated when he'd arrived at the OST, but he wasn't about to let this kind of opportunity go to waste.

He punched in a series of commands, then looked around. No one was watching. Then he hit a final key command, and their USM-backed database took form on the screen in front of him. He tapped in a name and cursed under his breath, again. Temple's file was still mostly redacted. Their attempts to unlock the command protocols continued to be unsuccessful.

Cosgrove shook his head in frustration and switched off the screen, clenching his jaw and letting his vision go fuzzy as he tried to concentrate, tried to figure out his next steps. Lexa seemed intent on bringing this stranger into their inner circle, but a deep gnawing in Cosgrove's stomach told him that it was a bad idea. They needed more information about Temple's past before they could be sure that he wouldn't fuck up everything they had worked so hard to achieve. In the meantime, Cosgrove would pretend to be friendly to this interloper for as long as necessary. After that...

"Commander!" Milliken yelled, pulling Cosgrove from his thoughts. He looked over and was shocked to see the Travers twins stumbling out of the transport ship.

"What the hell?!" he yelled, standing and storming over to the disheveled brothers.

Milliken had grabbed Tommy Travers by the arm and was pulling him towards their commanding officer. Francis stumbled behind, his eyes as glassy and confused as his brother's.

When they got within a few feet of Cosgrove, Milliken let go and stood behind the dazed subordinates, arms crossed, eyes dark buttons beneath a furrowed brow.

"Where have you been?" Cosgrove said, his voice almost a whisper. He fought an urge to backhand Tommy, to slap some sense into him. "We've been looking for you. For both of you."

"I..." Tommy began, his eyes darting rapidly around the warehouse as if he'd never been inside it before. He wiped his mouth with the back of his hand, then stared up into Cosgrove's face. "I don't remember."

"Bullshit," Milliken growled, shoving Tommy slightly. If the smaller man noticed the contact, he gave no indication of it. Francis just stared forward, not seeming to actually see anything. "You were in there getting hammered, weren't you?"

Cosgrove warned Milliken off with a glance.

"What were you two doing in the ship? Last I heard, you were cataloging any new items for our database. And then... what? You brought a bottle with you, took a little break, lost track of time?"

"I don't know," Tommy whined, eyes huge and emotional. Cosgrove couldn't smell any liquor on his breath but that didn't mean anything.

Francis finally spoke, his voice as ragged as his twin's. "I'm not feeling so good. My stomach hurts."

"Mine, too," Tommy said.

"Fine," the commanding officer responded, turning away and heading back to his station. "I'm docking you today's salary and writing you up. This is your *final* warning."

To everyone's surprise, Tommy didn't protest, just huddled closer to his brother and headed towards the exit, both men clearly forcing one foot in front of the other. Cosgrove looked over at a confused Milliken, raising his eyebrows. Francis wasn't a complainer, no matter what happened, but in the past, whenever Tommy had lost a single credit due to behavior issues, he would complain until the breath left his body. Watching him plod towards the exit without saying a word was completely out of character. And honestly kind of nice.

Milliken walked up to Cosgrove as the older man sat down, shaking his head, ready to get back to work.

"What the hell was that?" Milliken asked.

"I don't know," Cosgrove muttered, "And I don't care. I'm going to fire them tomorrow. They can go back to cleaning toilets at HQ for all I care. I told Lexa it was a mistake to promote them. They're a couple of drunks. And we have way too much at stake right now to have any weak links. You read me, Milliken?"

"Yes, sir," the younger guard responded, standing up straighter. "I'll take over cataloging the ship."

"Good man."

Milliken collected the material he needed from his own workstation and headed towards the heavily damaged vessel, a resolute look on his face. Cosgrove watched appraisingly. This was the kind of soldier they needed if they were going to succeed on their current mission. Not people like the Travers twins.

And certainly not someone like Chris Temple.

Tommy and Francis Travers burst into their small home, drawing ragged breaths through aching lungs and grimacing against pounding headaches. Tommy fumbled for the overhead lights.

They'd only been living in this house for a few weeks, had barely unpacked—in truth, they didn't own much. Their sudden promotion had been unexpected, like so many of the recent events on the OST. But they didn't care about any of that right now. Sweat ran down their faces and the backs of their necks as they asked each other truncated questions, trying to remember what had happened on that damn transport ship.

Francis collapsed into one of the two reclining chairs and closed his eyes, a small groan emitting from the back of his throat.

Heading into the kitchen, Tommy pulled open the refrigerator with more force than he intended, the door smashing into the wall and leaving a hole there. He didn't care, barely realized what had happened.

His mind was a muddled mess, strange images bursting to life in his brain and then disappearing just as quickly. He had never had a worse headache in his entire life. And he'd experienced some *epic* hangovers.

The things he was seeing couldn't be real. Could they?

He grabbed the bottle of Delilah's moonshine and brought it to his lips, chugging greedily. It was early afternoon and he and his brother normally waited until at least quitting time before indulging, but he needed it right now. He was convinced it would clear his mind.

Instead, more images pulsated behind his eyes, and he staggered back, as if he was being attacked again.

Again?

He suddenly remembered that there had been a creature down in those shadows. All legs and tail. The memories were coming back to him.

"Francis!" he shouted, lurching out of the kitchen and collapsing into the other reclining chair in the sparse living room, taking another pull from the bottle and wiping the sweat off his forehead with the back of his hand.

"What?" Francis murmured, squinting at his twin.

In response, Tommy handed over the bottle, which his brother took with a grateful look in his eyes. Francis took a long gulp and then handed it back.

"That monster did something to me," Tommy whispered.

"Monster?" Francis responded, incredulous. "You're losing your mind, Tommy boy. Cosgrove was right. We probably got drunk and blacked out. I can't remember anything."

"No, I..." Tommy started but faltered. Maybe he really was losing his mind. Maybe they had snuck a bottle into the ship and gotten wasted. It wouldn't have been the first time.

Still, his stomach had never felt like this. Not back on Earth, and not on the OST.

He should probably go see one of the colony's doctors, but he pushed the thought out of his mind. They would just judge him, like everyone else did. He was an idiot, a drunk. They didn't take him seriously. Not even his own brother did most of the time.

An incredible burst of pain arced out from his abdomen and Tommy gasped in surprise. He thought about eating something but wasn't hungry. A few more sips of the hootch would calm his body down. Then he would sleep again, and when he woke up, everything would be fine. He would track down Lexa, tell her that he'd found something important hidden away in the transport ship, though he wasn't sure exactly what it was. She would hug him, tell him he was a hero.

He smiled at this thought and abruptly realized that the pain in his stomach had faded away. In fact, he was starting to feel a little better. He laughed, took another long gulp of the alcohol, enjoyed the familiar burn as it rolled down his throat. He held it out to his brother again, who drank greedily, then handed it back. They smiled at each other, a new appreciation for one another seeming to dawn after their strange adventure in the ship.

Tommy looked around his house with new eyes. Not very long ago, he and Francis had been sharing a shitty little apartment with some of the roughest miners—the troublemakers. But the twins had worked hard to stand out, had stepped up when they were needed, and now they were stepping up yet again. They had a job, had their own house. Sure, it was small—smaller than Chris Temple's, which was in and of itself ridiculous. Tommy's thoughts turned dark again as he thought about the newest member of the OST.

Thought about the violence he would inflict on the man if he got between Tommy and Lexa.

A sudden burst of pain abruptly radiated out from his stomach, worse than before, and he dropped the bottle, which smashed on the wood floor, its contents spreading out like a living thing.

"Tommy!" Francis shouted, starting to get up, but then screamed in agony, a horrible sound, and collapsed to the floor.

Instead of abating, the pain in Tommy's stomach increased. Tommy wailed, his arms flailing out wildly, back arching against the chair, legs shaking uncontrollably. He tried to breathe but found the act impossible, the air refusing to pull back into his lungs. He attempted to stand but that, too, was not feasible as waves of pain surged through his entire body. Francis writhed on the ground as well, both men's movements mirror images of the other.

Tommy thought about his mother, even though she was only a vague memory, and wished she would somehow appear, hold him, tell him that everything was going to be okay.

Instead, a burst of blood exploded up from his chest, soaking his already sweat-infused shirt. He blinked down at the expanding splotch of crimson, completely confused, shaking his head slightly. The pain was so intense that it almost didn't register anymore. He laughed, his brain swimming. On the floor, a similar burst of red erupted from his brother's chest and Francis screamed, the sound a distant echo in Tommy's ears.

More blood erupted from Tommy's midsection, ripping through his shirt now, and he was finally able to pull some oxygen into his body, and he screamed, too, sounding exactly like his brother, the unimaginable pain reasserting itself, his entire body shaking as if he'd stuck a piece of metal into an electrical outlet. He now remembered the noises inside the transport ship after the creature had covered his face, blinding him. It had sounded like a second monster had attached itself to Francis.

Tommy wished he would just die. But that was a mercy that wouldn't be granted. Not yet.

The agony was unimaginable, a magnitude of pain he would have thought impossible. Feeling his life slip away, his head lolled, and he looked down at the ragged hole in his stomach, shocked to find a small head poking out, jagged teeth bared, a literal nightmare pulling itself out of his rent flesh. The creature emitted a high-pitched scream, followed by a similar scream nearby, as blackness began to consume Tommy's mind.

Although it took a significant amount of effort, and despite everything that was happening, he found himself worried about Francis. Blinking against the huge black dots that were filling his vision, he glanced over and saw that a similar monster had exploded out of his brother's chest as well. Francis stared at his brother, surprise and confusion and torment etched into his features. Tommy wished he could somehow comfort his brother but he couldn't move, couldn't even open his mouth.

Instead, he watched through blurred vision as the twin creatures found each other, then skittered around the small home, breathing new life for the very first time—the final sounds he would ever hear, the gore-covered monsters the last thing he would ever see.

As the aliens slipped into the shadows of the house, of its unopened boxes, Tommy and Francis Travers' bodies shuddered a final time, at almost exactly the same moment, and then went completely silent and still.

Lexa swiped her ID card to gain entry to the warehouse, feeling impatience bubbling up from her stomach.

The security pad beeped, and she threw the door open, storming into the warehouse, nodding at the security guard stationed nearby, and made her way towards Cosgrove's section, entering her hand-picked code into the electronic grid at the next door.

The afternoon was winding on, and the miners would be returning fairly soon. She liked to greet them on their return when she could. They appreciated it, and with all the recent changes, it was more important than ever that they knew she had their backs.

Cosgrove looked up as she approached. He looked stressed, though he was clearly trying to hide it. But she didn't blame him. She was feeling the pressure, too, and she didn't believe in compounding negative emotions with criticism. In her experience, that never helped any situation, no matter how dire.

"Hey," she said, grinning.

"Hey," he repeated, with an obviously forced reciprocated smile that looked almost painful on his face.

"What's wrong?" she asked, stepping up to the tall man and stopping, scanning his features for clues. He looked around as if the answer to her question was somewhere in the shadows of the warehouse, and then settled his eyes back on hers.

"You know, the usual," he answered, clearly choosing his words very carefully. "We're understaffed as it is, and the Travers twins are pulling their typical bullshit."

"What now?"

"Drunk, of course," Cosgrove said, clenching his jaw. "They came stumbling out of the ship a couple hours ago, could barely speak. Looked like they'd just woken up after a bender."

"They *slept* in there?"

"Seemed like it."

"Ugh," she blurted, turning and looking at the shell of the transport ship. Every time she looked at it, it filled her with a strange mix of emotions—sadness, awe, excitement, trepidation. It was unbelievable that Chris and his girls had survived. All the more reason to be impressed by him.

The damage to the ship was incredible, and the human remains they'd found inside were barely recognizable—nearly everyone who had been part of the recovery effort had thrown up, including her. It was a tragedy, there was no doubt about it. But it also represented an unexpected and significant opportunity. It was a game changer for them. Especially one particular item that they'd found.

"What's the latest on our new friend?" she said, turning back to Cosgrove.

"Margaret has been working non-stop for the past eighteen hours. She sent me a message about twenty minutes ago that she'd made a breakthrough. But I was waiting for you before I went in there."

"Let's go," she said, then headed towards one of the several doors in the large room, not waiting to see if Cosgrove was following. She knew he would.

She scanned her badge and the door beeped, then clicked. She felt a rush of butterflies about what was hidden behind this door, then a wave of apprehension. So much had changed lately. It sometimes overwhelmed her, the rapidity of recent events, but she pushed those feelings aside—there was far too much at stake, too many people who were depending on her.

She and Cosgrove entered the room, made their way around the mountains of half-assembled technology. After a few moments, they found Margaret hunched over her latest project—admittedly the most important thing she'd worked on during her time on the OST.

She was a small woman, older than Lexa or Cosgrove, and it seemed like she was perpetually leaned over a project. She and Lexa had met on the journey to the colony, and Margaret was probably one of the kindest people on LV-1213, and the most technologically proficient by far—which was why Lexa had given her this assignment. Considering the extremely delicate nature of the situation, it helped that Margaret was highly trustworthy as well.

A moment stretched out while Lexa waited for Margaret to notice her. But the older woman was entranced by her work on the circuitry that was laid out in front of her, examining it the way a child observes an anthill: enthralled, curious, and just slightly confused by what was transpiring.

Finally, as Cosgrove tensed next to her, probably ready to tap the older woman on the shoulder, Lexa gently cleared her throat and the scientist jumped slightly, dropping her soldering iron, which clattered onto the desk. She whirled, surprised panic in her eyes, then laughed when she saw who it was.

"Sorry," she said, shaking her head at herself. "I was lost in my work. This is… pretty fascinating."

"How's it going?" Lexa inquired. Part of her wanted to ask Margaret how she was doing—they had spent more than one night at Delilah's, especially recently, talking about their lives, about their hopes and dreams for the OST. In some ways, Margaret was the mother Lexa had been yearning for ever since her own had died in the accident that claimed both her parents' lives.

Margaret had led an incredible life, had spent decades working on Earth before taking this job, and was the only person Lexa had ever met who had been offered jobs by both Weyland-Yutani *and* the USM—and had turned down both. She never seemed to tire of Lexa's questions, especially about the former. Margaret had a near photographic memory, so she knew more about that corporation than anyone on this colony, and perhaps more than anyone in the entire universe.

She also never seemed to tire of giving Lexa wide-ranging life advice, counseling her on everything from her complex on-again off-again relationship with Cosgrove to the complicated and recently explosive politics of the OST. They had closed down Delilah's on more than one occasion, laughing deep into the night, and sometimes crying, too.

But right now, Lexa Phelan was all business with her mentor.

"Honestly?" the scientist responded. "I've been wanting to work on one of these new models but never had the chance. And they're surprisingly different to their older counterparts. I mean, some of the rudimentary mechanics are the same, but there are subtle differences that are breathtaking, for lack of a better term. I'd love to talk to the team that—"

"Get to the point," Cosgrove barked and the older woman flinched, looked down at the floor.

Lexa glanced at the man and narrowed her eyes, annoyed with his unnecessary brusqueness. She knew as well as he did that Margaret's work could change everything for them, especially in a moment when there was so much at stake for so many people. But she also knew that Margaret, like every genius Lexa had ever met, was overly sensitive to outbursts and criticism. Even when it was frustrating, Lexa handled the scientist with care. She was currently the most important person in the colony.

Cosgrove's face softened under Lexa's glare and he took a half-step back, ceding the floor to her. In response, Lexa moved forward and placed her hand on Margaret's shoulder. The scientist looked up, an appreciative look in her eyes.

"Margaret, I know how stressful things have been lately, how hard you've been working. I think we're all just under a lot of pressure. But we're moving this colony in the right direction. And this project you're working on could accelerate that considerably. Have you had any luck turning it on?"

The scientist's eyes flickered and her scientific mode reasserted herself, her entire demeanor filling with more confidence as she turned to her computer and began punching in data. Schematics filled the screen, multiple views of the inert subject on the table next to them flashing by as Margaret surveyed the data.

"Not yet but I think I'm almost there. It's a remarkable piece of machinery. The fact that it survived the crash is in and of itself highly impressive. It's almost as if it reacted to the impact in a way that would most likely ensure its survival."

"Survival?" Cosgrove sneered.

"Wrong word," Margaret hastened to correct. "My apologies. It's easy to start thinking of it as a living thing. I've had to keep reminding myself that that's not the case as I've worked on it."

"Can you try again now?" Lexa asked, tampering down her furthering annoyance with Cosgrove. This was exactly the kind of behavior that made him increasingly unattractive to her. Unlike Chris Temple. Her mind began to wander as she thought about the new man in her life. She found it hard to keep him out of her thoughts but now wasn't the time. "To wake it up? Since we're here."

"I *have* made a lot of progress in the last few hours, which is why I called Cosgrove, but I don't want to get your hopes up," the scientist said, doubt clouding her face. Despite the woman's response, Lexa knew that Margaret loved a challenge, thrived under pressure. She and Cosgrove waited in silence as the scientist worked, mumbling to herself as she picked up her fallen instrument and began to solder wires, plugging them into the object on the table, withdrawing them, entering data into her computer, and then trying again.

Finally, after what felt like hours but was actually only minutes, she sat back in her chair, sweat dotting her forehead. She glanced up at Lexa, locking eyes with her friend, and a small smile spread on her face.

"Yeah...?" Lexa said, feeling something in her stomach that felt an awful lot like hope.

"I think so," Margaret confirmed. Cosgrove shifted impatiently but both women ignored him.

"Okay, let's give it a whirl," Lexa suggested.

The scientist nodded, her smile widening, then turned back to her console and punched in a series of commands, glancing at the object on the table every few seconds. Finally, it stirred, eyelids and mouth opening.

"Where... am I?" it said.

"Hi, Alicia," Lexa responded, realizing that everything was changing in this moment, reveling in it. "It's very nice to meet you." She leaned in closer, her eyes narrowing, gleaming. "Now. I want you to tell me exactly how I can hack into the USM mainframe."

11

Chris watched his daughters playing with a half dozen other kids, running around like their lives depended on it, and smiled.

It was a beautiful weekend day, the sun shining in a clear blue digital sky, and he was sitting on a bench in the town center, the denizens of the OST milling about, going in and out of the stores, talking, laughing. The square was even more full than usual, and if Chris didn't know better, he would think he was back on Earth centuries earlier, when life seemed so much simpler. Then again, he knew the danger of nostalgia—nothing was ever as good as it seemed, especially since history was written by the winners.

Shaking away his cynical thoughts, Chris re-focused on the scene in front of him. Jane and Emma had taken to life on this colony much faster than he would have expected, especially his older girl, who shared his suspicious nature. But there she was, outrunning kids several years older and inches taller than her. She was in her element, there was no question about it. Their life back on Earth hadn't allowed for this kind of activity, not unless it was carefully planned and structured. This ability to just wake up, head out, find some other kids, and start playing was the thing that he didn't even realize was missing in his daughters' lives.

And then there was Emma. She was shyer, more cautious, more of a deep thinker. He could see her analyzing the nature of play, analyzing the tactics the others were employing during their game of tag, and then charging in, using everything she'd just learned to outplay the older kids. It was awesome to see.

Lexa had mentioned the idea of enrolling the girls in school here, and it seemed like a no-brainer at first. Then again, they would be hearing back from the USM shortly, perhaps with an alternate plan in terms of getting them to a residential colony.

He didn't like being in limbo, was a planner by nature, needed to know his precise steps forward at all times. It was one of the reasons he had been such a good soldier, and then commander, for so many years.

But perhaps he had earned this kind of indecision, as strange as that seemed. Maybe he didn't need to know the future right now—could just enjoy the present and the fact that his girls were laughing and smiling more than they had in years. Elizabeth would have loved to see them like this.

Rather than descending into sadness as his deceased wife rose in his mind, he was filled with gratitude that he had known her, that they had shared a life, that they had created these two amazing humans who were sprinting circles around the other kids in front of him. For the first time since Elizabeth had died, her memory brought him more happiness than pain. He recognized the breakthrough, and as much as it hurt, was thankful for it.

As if sensing his internal conflict and evolution, Jane divorced herself from the mass of kids and came sprinting towards her dad, stopping just in front of him, kicking up a cloud of dirt that billowed up into his face.

"Oops, sorry," she said, chagrined, while he coughed, waving his hand in front of his nose.

"No problem," he said, patting the seat next to him. "It's one of the dangers of being the dad of the fastest girl on the OST."

She rolled her eyes at him but smiled, sitting down and turning her eyes back to the tumult that was playing out in front of them. A few moments passed in relative silence.

"Jane, can I ask you something?"

She glanced over at him, clearly surprised. He had never asked her permission to pose a question before.

"Um. Sure?" she replied.

"Do you like it here?"

To his surprise, she considered his question rather than answering immediately. She looked around, at the kids and the stores, and even up at the sky. Then she turned back to her father.

"Yes," she said quietly, her forehead wrinkled.

"What's wrong?" he asked, confused.

"I wish Mom was here," she replied after a moment, staring down at the ground. "And Alicia. I feel guilty loving it so much when they're gone. I feel like... that makes me a bad person."

"Oh sweetie," Chris said, fighting back emotion, pulling his older daughter close to him. "You are the furthest thing from a bad person I've ever met in my life."

They sat together there for a long moment, watching the glorious chaos play out in front of them, until Emma finally staggered out of the crowd, dirt-streaked and beaming, and walked over to her family. She collapsed onto the bench on the other side of her dad.

"Whoo," she exclaimed, shaking her head at the maelstrom from which she had just escaped.

"You can say that again," Chris said.

"Whoo!" she said, louder, and all three of them laughed.

"I want to ask you both something," he stated after another moment, feeling butterflies in his stomach. Which was ridiculous. He was a hardened combat vet. Yet here he was, afraid to ask his daughters a straightforward question.

"Okay," his younger daughter answered, still distracted by the seemingly endless and exceedingly complex game.

"Of course," Jane said, her attention on her dad. She probably already knew what he was going to say. Or maybe not.

"Would you want to stay on the OST? I mean, for longer. Maybe forever?"

He felt Emma's entire body go tense next to him. She pulled her attention from the other kids and stared up at her dad.

"Really?" Barely more than a whisper.

"Yeah," he said, feeling more sure of the decision than before. The scene playing out in front of them, the kids playing and the adults chatting outside of stores—it felt like nothing less than a miracle. Too good to be true. But here they were. By dumb luck. It would be insane not to take advantage of it.

"I want to," Jane said simply. "Please."

"Me too!" Emma practically screamed, jumping up from her seat and shifting in front of her father, staring him directly in the eyes. "Pretty please."

"Pretty please, eh?" he said, grabbing and tickling her for a moment. She collapsed into his arms, laughing, and then he lifted her small frame and sat her down on his leg. Jane snuggled in even closer on his right side.

"Lexa offered me a job. I'm not sure if I'm going to take it. But it made me realize that maybe there's a place for us here. Even if the USM can find another civilian colony for us, is it really going to be better than this place?"

"I miss Alicia," Emma suddenly said, leaning into the crook between her dad's shoulder and neck, her entire mood shifting in a moment.

"I know," Chris said. "Me too."

A long moment passed as some of the other parents began to amble over and pull their kids away. It was lunchtime and the restaurant's doors had just been propped open. The town square began to quiet as the crowd dispersed.

"How about this?" he said, pulling both of his girls even closer. "We'll give it a try. A few months. See if we like it. Get you both back into school."

"Yuck," Jane said but her response was half-hearted, almost programmed. Glancing down, he saw a smile spreading on her face.

"Yuck," Emma repeated but he knew they would both love it. Plus, they needed a little structure in their lives.

"I know—yuck—but I'll give the job a chance if you'll give school a chance. Fair?"

Jane pulled back and studied her dad's face, scrutinizing the offer. Then she nodded.

"Fair."

"Emma?" he asked.

"Can I get a puppy?" she responded, her eyes growing wide, a hopeful smile emerging on her face.

"Well, let's not push it," he said, and laughed as she mock-frowned and dug her hands into his sides, finding the elusive tickle spot on his ribs, and then they were both tickling each other. Jane got in on the action, and soon all three of them were wrestling and laughing on the bench as the sun continued its journey across the arched dome above them.

John Wilkins closed the barn doors, yawning as he did so.

It was late. The animals had been acting weird in the hour or so before it was time to get them down for the night. The only other time he'd ever seen them like this was years earlier when one of the dogs had lost its damn mind and killed a baby cow. Wilkins himself had been forced to put the canine down, even though he had grown to love each and every one of his animals. Watching the light go out in that dog's eyes, even if it was a killer, had broken his heart.

Wilkins had been brought from Earth specifically for this job. *Like a latter-day Noah*, he often laughed to himself. He had been responsible for planning the number of embryonic animals to bring, forecasting future lineages, keeping a periodic eye on their progress while they hyper-slept during their journey to the OST. The survival and thriving of the animals were key to the colony's success. And what a success it had been—even considering recent events. The animals were doing better than anyone expected, resulting in plenty of food and companionship for everyone. More than enough.

But their current behavior was incredibly odd, as if something was silently stalking them from the perimeter of the property. But that was impossible. There were no predators on the OST. And all of his dogs were already hunkered down for the night.

Wilkins inhaled a deep breath and took in his property, lit by the moon that hung in the sky above him. *Sky*, he laughed to himself. It was so easy to fall into the delusion that he was on Earth, that he was bathed in actual moonlight—hell, even the fake stars that dotted the blackness above were a simulation of the ones seen from his homeworld.

He thought about the day he had arrived, how terrifying this planet was outside of the oasis that had been built here. He'd stared out of one of his transport ship's windows, jaw slack with amazement and terror at the storms that rocked the world in almost unending streams of rain and lightning and thunder. It seemed impossible that anyone could live here, let alone hundreds of people, a handful with families.

But it had been as good as promised. Better, in fact. Especially lately, despite some of his concerns about all the promises that had been made. And the suffering that had been required.

His mind cast back to his life on Earth. Despite loving his job as a veterinarian, he hadn't felt true happiness since his wife died shortly after their marriage. It had been a work-related shuttle accident—a freak situation, really. A million-to-one occurrence.

He had never fully recovered. Went about his job with a kind of rote mechanism, as if he was one of those androids he sometimes saw. He had considered just ending it all at times, late at night when the world was silent and dark. But when he heard that a mining expedition was looking for an animal expert, he realized that running away from his pain wasn't necessarily a bad thing. He had jumped at the chance.

And things felt so different now.

The OST had become his family, and he began to *feel* again, to care about other people in a way that he hadn't since the day his bride had perished—before they'd even had a chance to start their life together.

He threw himself into his work, caring for the animals upon which the entire community depended. In many ways, he was the most essential person in the entire colony. But even though he sensed that, he didn't allow the fact to invade his persona, didn't lord the fact over anyone. If anything, he was kinder than ever, to his animals and to the humans who surrounded him. He had found peace, at last. Here, in a small dome on a rock in the middle of the galaxy.

Until now.

In all the years he had been taking care of the animals on the OST, he had never seen them *this* spooked—not even when that poor baby cow had been slaughtered alive.

It made no damn sense. The only thing that had changed was the arrival of that ex-USM officer and his two girls. And the animals had loved them, especially the little one. Chris Temple seemed a little aloof, but Wilkins had already heard the rumors. He was apparently some kind of decorated vet, had seamlessly integrated into their small community, and Lexa herself seemed particularly interested in his future.

And who knows what else, the farmer laughed to himself, heading towards his small farmhouse. *Not that it's any of* my *business*.

A noise to his right halted him in his tracks. He peered into the shadows and caught a glimpse of something moving, but as he stared, he suspected that it was just the shifting light as the moon continued its journey across the curve of the dome overhead. If anything, maybe it was Tommy Travers or another one of the drunk miners, stumbling over to the farm to mess with the animals in their inebriated state. It wouldn't be the first time that Wilkins had been forced to shoo them away with a few choice words and his notoriously intimidating glare.

After a few moments of silence, he started back to his house, quietly reprimanding himself for being so paranoid. He must have been tired. Nothing a small glass of moonshine and a good eight hours of sleep couldn't cure.

A blur of motion in his peripheral vision surprised him and then he was hit with incredible force and speed, knocking him back towards the barn. He tumbled across the dirt, the wind knocked out of his lungs. He saw stars as his momentum finally slowed, arriving only a few feet from the barn doors, the animals within starting to shriek and cry, as if aware of the assault on their caretaker.

Looking up, Wilkins felt a shock of terror run across his entire body.

The creature was huge.

He couldn't even get a good look at it; his glasses had gone flying into the shadows when he'd been hit, and the monster's black exterior made it even harder to get a sense of its details, but there was enough light glinting off its angular frame that Wilkins knew he was in deep trouble.

He scrambled to his feet as fast as he could, unable to catch his breath, trying to keep his gaze on the thing in front of him, but his eyes were starting to water out of pure fear. The creature wasn't moving, and for a moment, Wilkins wondered if this was just some kind of elaborate prank. The miners were known for pulling mean-spirited stunts just to get a rise out of their victims and a guffaw out of their compatriots—a bizarre mix of humor and cruelty. If that was the case, he would laugh it off in the moment, admit that they got him good, but then he would plan some kind of revenge on them. Slip something into their food or drink when they weren't looking. See how they liked spending a day or two on the toilet, their insides betraying them the way these idiots turned on each other on any given night. Hope etched itself into his heart for the briefest instant, but then the monster took a step towards him, and he realized that this was no prank, no harmless joke.

A living nightmare was approaching him in the growing light of a false moon, claws outstretched, jaw opening, saliva dripping.

Wilkins opened his mouth to scream for help, but before he could even draw the breath into his lungs to make the cry a reality, the creature shot forward again, slamming into him with incredible force, pushing him back and then through the wooden door, several of his ribs breaking as they crashed through to the other side.

He blinked up at the dark ceiling of the barn as the monster clawed at him, ripping the skin from his body, blood gushing out onto the straw. The pain was shocking—he had never felt anything like it in his life, even when he'd accidentally smashed through a plate-glass window as a child and sustained serious cuts on multiple parts of his body.

Dizzy with agony, he laughed at the memory. It was so long ago—literally another world, and it almost seemed like a different lifetime. He still had the scars, though they had faded over time.

The creature bared its teeth again and somehow a second set of fangs emerged from the first, more saliva dripping onto his body. His vision had cleared somehow, though that seemed impossible—maybe he was imagining all of this and was tucked safely away in his bed back in the farmhouse.

The second, smaller set of teeth shot forward, unbelievably fast, and sunk into his body, and Wilkins screamed, not even sure how he had found the breath to do so, and the animals in the barn screamed along with him.

Blood filled his lungs and his lamentations turned into a watery whimper, the monster continuing to claw at him as its teeth sunk deeper and deeper into his chest. He couldn't draw any oxygen into his body anymore, could barely move at all, just kept staring up at the ceiling of the barn, a peaceful warmth now overtaking his entire body. There was no more pain, just a distant buzz, as if he was observing the situation from far away. For a moment, he thought he heard his deceased wife's voice, and he smiled at the sound.

Wilkins reached up with his right hand, his left arm not responding to his brain's commands anymore, and caressed the creature's head. It was shockingly smooth, and he admired it for a moment as darkness closed in around his vision. Even though this being was literally ripping him to shreds, some part of him admired its raw, simple beauty. He didn't know what it was, but he wanted to know everything about it.

As his consciousness began to fade for good, Wilkins' arm fell away from the creature and his head lolled to the side. He made eye contact with one of the horses. Luna. His favorite. It stared at him as if it knew what was happening, a look of compassion in its eyes. He knew that didn't make sense, but he took great comfort in it. He also knew it was the last thing he would ever see, and he decided that was okay. There was nothing he would rather be looking at as he passed from this existence into whatever came next—where he would hopefully be reunited with his wife.

He just hoped that this monster that was devouring him left the animals alone.

And then Wilkins was gone, and the animals grew silent, as if they sensed his departure, and the only sound that remained in the barn was the staccato slurping as the Xenomorph continued to feed on its very first meal.

1 2

Lexa handed Chris a cup of coffee.

He took a sip and marveled at how good it tasted. The coffee they served in the military was more like literal dishwater. Hot, yes, and full of caffeine—but when he took a second to savor it on his palette, he'd had to fight from puking it directly back up into the tin cup in which it had been served.

She turned away and the two of them began walking down the street, away from the town square, where they'd met up, and towards the colony's headquarters—a large building bifurcated by a low stone wall, located near the hospital where Chris had first awoken on this planet.

After a few minutes, they arrived, and Lexa strode to the front door. Casually shielding her hand from Chris, she punched a code into the security box next to the door and then held it open for him after it beeped, signaling that it had been unlocked. "After you," she said with a smile.

He walked past her, noting that this bureaucratic building looked like every other bureaucratic building he had ever visited in his entire life, no matter which planet he was on.

"Fancy," he said, glancing back at her. She laughed and shook her head, stepping closer to him as they approached a fork in the nondescript hallway.

"This way," Lexa said, taking a sudden left without looking back. He appreciated that she wasn't trying to handhold him on his pseudo-first day. He was a quick learner, and he suspected she knew that. Even though his file was mostly redacted, there was probably enough in there for her to have read his various test scores over the years.

"This is our communications room," she continued, pointing to her left at a large room. A few people sat at computer consoles, punching in data. They glanced up at Lexa and her guest, seemed unimpressed, and went back to work. "Still no word from USM on a potential new civilian colony for you. Although… that may be a moot point now?" She turned fully around and stared up into his eyes, placing both hands on her hips.

A younger man shimmied past their low-stakes standoff, mumbling, "Excuse me," as he went.

"Maybe," Chris replied with a grin. "Let's see how today goes."

"Yes, let's," she countered, and he could feel the tension between them. It was surreal, and he wasn't sure he completely understood exactly what was happening with her. He had to appraise this job opportunity as objectively as possible. A lot was riding on his decision.

After another moment, she turned and continued down the hallway, once again not bothering to check if he was following. Chris scanned every room they passed, every airduct, the face of every single person who passed them. He tried to stop himself, to fight against the instincts that had been hammered into him during years of training by the toughest women and men in the USM, but it was impossible. This kind of surveillance was as natural to him, and as necessary, as breathing.

He refocused on Lexa as she halted again in front of a door that looked like every other one that they had passed in this hallway. He joined her and looked inside. It was completely empty.

"Um… minimalist," he said.

"Don't be a dummy," she responded, hitting his shoulder gently with the back of her hand. "This will be your office. If you decide to grace us with your presence."

On some level, he had immediately known what this empty room was, or could be, but it still took him by surprise to hear her say it out loud. Despite all his years in the military, and his high-level rank, he had never had his own office—had never wanted one. He'd only spent time in ones that belonged to superior officers.

"Not bad," he said, feigning disinterest, but he couldn't stop the smile that began to spread across his face.

She noticed and opened her mouth to say something, but before she could, a noise down the hallway caught her attention. It was a voice, loud, then a second voice, even louder. An argument had broken out and was escalating quickly.

"Ugh. I'll be right back. Stay here," Lexa said and then hustled down the hallway, passing several doorways and then turning into one, her voice immediately joining the emotional chorus. Chris took another glance at the room that could potentially be his office while listening to the dispute that was raging down the hallway. Other than the drunken bar brawl, this was the first conflict Chris had witnessed since arriving. As he took a step down the hall towards the argument, trying to make out the words, someone within shut the door and the voices became muffled. He was tempted to walk down there and put his ear to the door but that was one step too far. Instead, he turned around and headed back in the direction he'd just come. He had seen something earlier that had caught his attention, and now that he was by himself, he wanted to check it out.

After a few moments, Chris turned down another hallway and stopped in front of the only door in this short, shadowy corridor. It was the only hall he'd seen in this complex that had just a single door, and the door was the only one with a security pad next to it. He tried the handle, but the door didn't open. He looked at its every detail, including the digital pad next to it, and was just about to reach out when a voice caused him to freeze.

"What the *hell* do you think you're doing?!"

Cosgrove was striding down the hall towards him, hands balled up into fists. This was a very different person than the guy who had suggested getting a drink outside of the warehouse a few nights earlier. Everything about the man in this moment implied violence. Chris readied himself.

"Just looking for a bathroom," Chris answered, forcing a smile. The lie sounded bad even in his own ears.

"Bullshit," the larger man said, closing the distance, his unpleasant breath curling out into Chris's face.

"I know you're just doing your job, but I suggest you back off. *Right* now," Chris instructed, his entire body suddenly flooded by that curious, calm feeling just before an explosion of savagery. It was a feeling he hated. And loved.

Cosgrove moved quickly, faster than Chris expected, and shoved him against the wall, an elated sneer spreading across his face. Chris shoved back, and his strength clearly surprised the bigger man. They went stumbling across the narrow hallway, slamming hard against the opposite wall. The breath burst from Cosgrove's mouth, but he still managed to swing a close-quarters uppercut towards Chris's jaw.

Chris took a half step back, watched as the meaty fist sped past his nose, and threw out his own punch at the same time, catching Cosgrove directly in the stomach. Already half out of breath, the larger man doubled over, and Chris immediately lashed out with his other fist, a nasty cross that connected solidly with Cosgrove's cheek. The man collapsed onto his knees, growling like an animal in an absolute pained rage.

Chris took several steps back, keeping his eyes on the other man as he got to his feet, wiping the blood onto his pants.

"Quit while you still can," Chris advised.

"You got lucky, Temple," Cosgrove said, his eyes practically glowing with hatred. "I'm gonna enjoy wiping the floor with your face."

"What the hell?!" a voice shouted, the sound filling the entire hall and causing both men to look over.

Lexa was stomping down the hallway towards them, looking even angrier than Cosgrove.

"What is going *on* here?!" she continued, her volume growing even though she was close enough to whisper at this point and they'd still hear her.

"He was trying to access the restricted section," Cosgrove said, his tone suddenly compliant. "He got aggressive with me when I told him to stop."

"Is that true?" Lexa asked, turning her eyes towards Chris.

"Partly," he answered. "But I'm not going to stand here and defend myself in front of this macho hothead. If he's representative of the kind of people you want working here, maybe this isn't the job for me. Or the colony."

"Let's not be hasty," Lexa answered quickly. "Cosgrove, go clean yourself up and get back to work. *Now*."

He opened his mouth to protest, but the look in her eyes stopped him cold. He spared a final, enraged glance for Chris, then stormed off, turning a corner in a huff, the sound of his footsteps finally fading. Lexa turned to Chris.

"Come on," she said.

Once they were outside the building, she finally spoke again, the anger dissipating.

"Did he start it?"

"That's not how I roll, Lexa. I'm not going to point fingers," Chris said. "I'll admit that I was checking things out, but I got bored and was just wandering."

"I get it," she said. "And I know he started it—you don't even have to confirm that." She let out a long sigh. "He's fundamentally a good guy, but he's got a bad temper. And we have a complicated history."

"That's none of my business," Chris replied.

"It kind of is," she said. "Or it could be."

The implication hung in the air between them, but Chris didn't know how to answer. Still didn't know how he felt about her. He nodded, and based on the look on her face, it was clearly not the response she wanted. But she nodded, too, and let out a long sigh. Then smiled.

"Do you want to go see how your girls are doing on their first day at school?" She glanced at her watch. "It's snack time, so they're probably outside on the playground."

"I would *love* that," he said, feeling his entire body relax at the prospect.

Lexa put her arm in his and led him away from the colony's headquarters. After a few moments, Chris glanced back towards the building they had just exited.

He couldn't be sure, but he could have sworn he saw Cosgrove watching them from one of the sun-glinted windows.

Chris jolted awake.

He found himself somewhat disoriented, and surprised by that fact. This was the deepest he'd slept since arriving on the OST. Part of him was glad—his body still needed to recover after everything it had been through in the past week.

He blinked against the shadows of his bedroom, immediately aware that it was the middle of the night, and then quickly stood up, padded silently down the hallway, and checked on his girls. They were both sound asleep. He took a few moments to stare at each of them, in awe of the contented looks on both of their faces. They had both seemed to have a great first day at their new school, and had fallen asleep right after dinner. Chris had crashed shortly thereafter.

They looked like their mother when they were asleep, and the resemblance filled his heart with an almost overwhelming combination of grief and gratitude.

As he headed back to his own room, a noise outside caught his attention.

Voices. Hushed but numerous. Strange for this time of night.

Heading to the front room, Chris crouched down and peeked out from the bottom of the window, pushing the curtains aside a fraction of an inch.

The part of him that had been trained by some of the best military minds on Earth surmised that whatever was happening outside, no matter how quiet, was the thing that had pulled him from his slumber. The low-level noise wouldn't wake up an average person, but Chris had been trained to sleep as lightly as possible, normally prepared to bolt awake at any given moment. He was already silently berating himself for clawing up out of unconsciousness so slowly minutes earlier.

Breathing evenly as his eyes adjusted to the mix of darkness and streetlights, Chris homed in on a small group of people who were walking down the sidewalk, already past his house and now heading down one of the OST's only side streets. Towards the farm. It was hard to tell who they were in the shadows of digital nighttime, but he definitely saw Lexa and Cosgrove. And three others. They were moving quickly. Clearly in a rush.

For a moment, he thought about following them, but there was something more important that he needed to do. He hadn't been sure when he'd have a chance, but it seemed like fate had now given him the perfect opportunity.

Hurrying back to his bedroom, Chris threw on a pair of jeans and a hoodie. It was surprising how easily he'd gotten used to wearing these clothes that Lexa had provided.

He headed to the front door, wrestling with his decision. He hated the idea of leaving the girls alone here again, asleep and vulnerable, but he promised himself he would be quick.

Slipping into his shoes, Chris exited the house as quietly as possible, shutting the door behind him in silence, locking it, and then headed towards the OST's headquarters once the group was fully out of sight, sticking to the shadows as he moved.

Lexa tried to keep her nerves calm.

From what she'd been told, the scene inside the barn was bad. *Very* bad. But she didn't want to make assumptions until she saw the evidence with her own eyes.

Even though Cosgrove and the others were trying to be quiet, it was the kind of whispering that was strained, emotional, but she didn't bother to shut them up. It was the middle of the night, after all. Everyone was asleep.

After a few minutes, the farm came into view, its outside lights all on, which seemed strange, and Lexa noticed that the barn door had been smashed apart, pieces of shattered wood splayed out on the ground in the unforgiving glare of phosphorescence.

As the group headed straight for the compromised structure, Milliken stepped out of the barn, a shocked look on his face. He was young, emotional, a total hothead, but Lexa had never seen him this shaken before.

"What the hell is going on?" Cosgrove demanded.

"You need to see it for yourself," was all Milliken could manage to get out.

Lexa looked at the other people in her small group. Fredericks. Connor. Baker. None of them had originally signed up for this, and the pale, wide-eyed looks on their faces betrayed that lack of experience.

"Let's go," she said, projecting the confidence they all needed.

The smell hit them first.

A strong iron odor, with undercurrents of animal feces. They all immediately put their hands to their noses, and then stopped in their tracks. The animals moved about restlessly in their stalls. Baker let out an audible gasp.

John Wilkins was splayed out on the ground, ripped to pieces, blood and organs spattered across the hay like an impressionistic painting.

"What the *fuck* happened?" Lexa whispered.

"It must have been one of his dogs, right?" Milliken said, pacing nervously. "You remember what one of them did to that baby cow."

"None of them have ever attacked a human on this colony," Cosgrove answered, his face a map of concern.

"First time for everything," Lexa said, squatting down, staring at what was left of John. She was deeply upset but pushed the emotions away—she had to be a leader right now, not a grieving friend.

"I don't buy it," Cosgrove said, moving next to Lexa.

She stood, stared up into his eyes. "What do you mean by that?"

"Wilkins just *happens* to die, horribly, a few days after a former USM colonel with a redacted file lands on our planet? You don't think that's a little suspicious, Lexa?"

"*Very* suspicious," Milliken confirmed, stepping next to Cosgrove. There were murmurs of assent from some of the others in the barn.

"You can't be serious," Lexa scoffed.

"*Dead* serious," Cosgrove responded. "Considering what's happening here… what we all did a few months ago… it would be idiotic not to consider all the angles."

"*How?* How could Chris have done *this*?" Lexa said, waving at the mess of a corpse on the floor. "Also, why would he kill Wilkins, of all people?"

"Lex," Cosgrove said quietly, taking a step closer to her. "Maybe… maybe you're too close to this."

"Answer the questions!" she barked.

Cosgrove visibly flinched, moved back to where he'd just been standing. Everyone in the room shifted awkwardly. They all knew about the history between these two people, even if they would never admit it. "Fine. Maybe he… maybe… I don't know. I'm just saying we need to consider that Mr Top Secret Military Man could be dangerous. Why are you defending him so much? Or maybe I don't *wanna* know why."

"*Watch* yourself, Cosgrove," Lexa whispered, her gaze and tone turning dark.

The two had a silent standoff while the others watched nervously. Even the animals had stilled. After a long moment, Cosgrove broke the stare first and moved off, began inspecting the rest of the barn.

"Whatever," he mumbled.

"Listen up," she said to the rest of her team. "We need to clean this up and get rid of the body," Lexa said. "Try to figure out if any of John's dogs are missing. Look for clues. And keep it *quiet*. The last thing we need is panic, especially with everything else going on."

"Luckily Wilkins doesn't have any family, so no one will ask too many questions," Francie Connor agreed. "We can say that he got drunk and fell on one of his pitchforks or something."

"Exactly," Lexa said. "Fredericks, I want you to go through personnel records in the morning—see if anyone else has any experience with animals. We need to keep our food and milk supply moving. I don't want *any* interruption."

Cosgrove mumbled something else and Lexa's face went even darker. She stepped towards him, menacing despite being so much smaller than him.

"*What* did you say?"

"I said, maybe your best friend Temple can do it," Cosgrove answered, louder. The other people in the group looked away, clearly uncomfortable at the continued exchange. "Even if he didn't kill Wilkins, we need to keep him as far away from HQ as possible."

"That's ridiculous," Lexa scoffed.

"Is it? He was snooping around today. Do you *really* think you can trust him?"

"That's none of your business," Lexa snapped, taking another half step towards him, getting increasingly annoyed by Cosgrove's insubordination. "But yes, I do. I've spent a lot of time with him, and I think he's a lot like us. I think he sees the world like we do. And I'm not going to waste someone as talented as him on a *fucking farm*! Do you understand me, Cosgrove?!"

The larger man seemed to physically shrink, and he mumbled, "Yes," then moved around her, walking to a nearby stall where a large horse blanket hung. "Help me clean up this mess, Milliken," he instructed, some fire back in his voice.

As the two men began to clean up the mess that had once been John Wilkins, Lexa stared into the distance. She just wished things would go smoothly. A perfect society was right within their grasp.

"You okay?" Connor asked, having appeared next to Lexa without her realizing it. She looked at the younger woman's kind face, felt her walls go back up. She had a job to do.

"Yes, I'm fine, Francie," she said, glancing over at Cosgrove, who was shoveling Wilkins' guts onto the blanket, a disgusted expression on his face. "Once we're done in here, everyone should get some sleep. We have a lot of work to do in the morning."

1 3

Chris observed the colony's headquarters from the shadows.

He was tired—exhausted, really. And felt a deep seed of worry about his daughters sprouting in the pit of his stomach. But an essential part of him, the part that had kept him alive in countless battle zones, told him that the answers to all his questions about the OST were hidden behind the door he had seen earlier.

The streets of the colony were silent. It was late, probably around 3:30am, and mercifully, a thick wall of clouds had finally covered the digital sky, making his mission that much easier. He wondered vaguely if the cloud cover had been programmed, or if it was completely random. Under better circumstances, he would ask Lexa—and maybe this was all a big misunderstanding, maybe his gut was wrong. He truly hoped that was the case.

Satisfied that no one was around, Chris moved towards the building with purpose, like he was reporting to work on a Monday morning. He had noticed earlier that there were no cameras outside of the building—no cameras anywhere in the colony, which struck him as odd. Perhaps the community had voted against it. He knew that privacy concerns had been part of the civil unrest that had erupted on Earth, particularly after the crash of the *Auriga* and everything that had transpired since.

When Chris arrived at the security pad, he smiled ruefully. Lexa had turned her back to him when she'd inputted the digits, but he was trained to see things that were supposedly impossible to witness, and had memorized the code as she punched it in. The numbers appeared behind his eyes as if they had been burned there, and he quickly punched them in. The pad beeped.

Chris entered the building.

It was dark inside, especially with the cloud cover, but he didn't turn on any lights. He waited several minutes as his eyes fully adjusted to the gloom. He was in a rush, yes, but there was a right way to infiltrate a location, and that usually required patience, even when waiting went against every instinct in a soldier's body.

Finally, the inside of the building became clearer and clearer, until he was sure that his eyes were as adjusted as possible, and he moved forward, cautious but quick. His mind went to his daughters, asleep in beds that were still new, in a home that wasn't truly theirs. A part of him wanted to leave this building at that exact moment, to go back, to keep them safe. But that was a short-term solution. If he really wanted to protect them, he needed more information about what was really happening on this colony. There were simply too many unanswered questions. And those kinds of unknowns were what got people killed in emergencies.

Chris sensed an emergency on the horizon. He just had no idea what kind it would be.

He had memorized the hallways of the HQ earlier that day, so he took the several turns as if he'd been working there for years, finally ending up in the hallway where he'd had the confrontation with Cosgrove. It was darker down here—very little of the muted light that was pushing through the other windows was able to reach this particular spot in the building.

But there was just enough luminescence for him to see the security pad. He punched in the same code, but it didn't work.

Swearing under his breath, he studied its contours. It was USM issue, the kind he had seen, and disabled, many times before.

Chris went to work.

Within minutes, he had disassembled the pad, disconnecting and reconnecting wires in the shadows. He barely needed to see. This kind of work had been drilled into him over and over again during his training. It had been years since the last time he'd bypassed this type of security system, but in his mind and for his hands, it seemed like yesterday.

The door clicked, quietly unlocking.

He opened it several inches, placing his foot between it and the wall, and then continued his work, putting the security pad back together. Part of breaking in without being caught was cleaning up immediately, not afterwards. God only knew what would happen in the next few minutes once he walked through this door.

The pad now reassembled, looking just as it had when he'd entered the hallway, Chris entered the other side of the restricted-access door.

He waited as it shut behind him and realized that this hidden hallway was lit by overhead lights every dozen or so feet, extending out and then unseen to the right.

Chris began walking, quickly. Now that he was within this inner part of the OST's headquarters, with no windows anywhere to be seen, he was free to go as fast as possible. He took the turn and was surprised to see a set of stairs that vanished into the darkness below.

He hesitated for the briefest moment, thought about the layout of the building. It became immediately obvious to him that he was entering an area that had been built underground. A basement, for lack of a better term.

What could they be hiding down here? What restricted materials would require subterranean lodging? Especially since they had the secret warehouse on the outskirts of town. It made no sense.

The descent down the stairs took several minutes. Lights had been embedded into the wall every now and then, but their glare only reached so far, and with the speed that he made his way down, the effect was almost strobe-like.

At length, he reached the bottom, where another hallway stretched out, with the lights appearing in the ceiling at similar intervals as above. He continued to make his way forward, quickly, when a noise caught his attention, and he stopped in his tracks, listening.

After a few moments, he realized that the sound was human voices. Whispering. Someone was down here with him.

Chris looked back towards the stairs, gauging the distance. He could make it back there in seconds, be out of the HQ in under a minute, back to the house and with his girls minutes after that. But no, he had come this far. He needed to know what the hell was going on here.

He pushed forward.

After a few moments, he approached a larger, open area with slightly brighter lights. He slowed his pace, moved closer to the wall as he continued. The whispering voices were growing louder. When he finally reached the end of the hall, he once again crouched and peeked out just enough to see what was within the large room. What he saw caused the breath to catch in his throat.

A row of cells adorned the far wall, running down the large room for several hundred yards. Within each cell sat or stood small groups of people, all looking pale and undernourished. Some stood by the bars, whispering to people in other cells; others sat or lay on the small beds that jutted out from either side of each holding area. The overhead lighting caused the prisoners' eyes to look like hollowed out shells.

Realizing that these people were no danger to him, Chris rose and stepped out into the open area. Several of the people gasped when they saw him, and anyone who had been sitting or lying down quickly rushed to the bars of their cells. Chris recognized one of them: the man with the red beard who Cosgrove had punched at the beginning of the bar brawl at Delilah's.

"You're… not exactly who I was expecting," a woman with shoulder-length black hair said as the rest of the prisoners grew immediately silent. "Who the hell are you?"

"I was just about to ask you the same thing," Chris responded, continuing to search the space, looking for cameras or any sign of a jailer.

His mind flashed to his girls. He needed to make this quick.

"My name is Jennifer Chu and I'm the leader of this colony. Or at least, I *was*," she said, bitterness tingeing her words.

"The… *leader*?" Chris asked, looking at the other people in the cells. One older man nodded, his eyes dark and serious. "The OST doesn't have a leader. It's run by an executive board."

Jennifer barked a laugh, a vocal eruption that had no mirth within it whatsoever.

"Is that what she told you?"

"She?" Chris asked, though he immediately knew the answer to his question.

"Lexa Phelan. One of my miners. She was a good worker for a while but then she started questioning the way I did things. Pushing back. Quoting bizarre Weyland-Yutani cult shit, getting other people on her side. We started to arrest some of them when they got violent, but there were more than I realized. They revolted, took out all the cameras so we couldn't track them... stole our weapons. Hurt a lot of people. And then threw anyone who still didn't agree with them down here."

"My God," Chris said, barely a whisper. He eyeballed the cells, couldn't see all the people in them, or how many there were. "Are there... *children* in here?"

"Thankfully, no," Jennifer responded. "All of the miners with kids joined her insane cause."

"How long ago did all of this happen?" Chris asked, mind spinning.

"I've lost track of time, but it's been a while. Weeks? Months? I don't know," Jennifer answered, looking him up and down again, her eyes narrowing in confusion. "I was able to get a distress call out to the USM just before they grabbed me... but you don't look exactly like a rescue squad. So, I'll ask again—who are you?"

Chris tried to gather his thoughts, but his mind clicked over into military mode and quickly sped through every memory since he'd woken up in the hospital. His brain settled on the five words he'd heard at Delilah's the night of the bar brawl, spoken by one of the men staring at him, the words that had echoed periodically in the back of Chris's mind ever since.

We shouldn't have done it.

He was an idiot. That clue and others had been there all along, like a map, and he had ignored—or buried—every single one. Had been increasingly blinded by the seemingly perfect nature of the colony, by the hope it represented for him, and especially for his daughters.

"My name is Chris Temple," he said, barely able to get the words out, fighting back a wave of self-disgust. He needed to stay focused on his mission, get back to his girls and figure out a way off this planet. He had no interest in getting caught up in the middle of a civil war. He stepped closer to Jennifer, looked into her eyes. "My daughters and I were on a transport ship to a civilian colony. We were… attacked, and we crash landed here. The three of us were the only survivors. The ship was completely destroyed, otherwise I would—"

"Completely destroyed?" the woman interrupted, a rueful smile appearing on her face. "You sure about that?"

"What do you mean?" Chris said, his face darkening. He didn't have time for games.

"The guards who come down to check on us and give us our shitty food aren't the brightest. They think we aren't listening when they whisper to each other, but we hear everything. We heard about the crashed transport ship—

though they never mentioned any survivors. They hauled what was left of it into the warehouse and are trying to pilfer it for weapons and any other technology that can help them."

"The ship is in the warehouse?" Chris practically yelled, taking another step closer to Jennifer. He knew he was being reckless, that she and her cellmates could grab him, assault him. But he needed to move as fast as possible. Everything had just changed.

"Jennifer," he whispered. "Please listen to me very carefully. I am a retired colonel of the United Systems Military." Her eyes went wide at his words, but she continued listening, her gaze locked on his. "A very dangerous creature was on board that ship. Lexa told me that *nothing* survived—but I don't know what to believe now. My two daughters are asleep in one of the miner houses, and I have to get back to them, protect them. *Right now.* After that, I'll figure out my next steps. But I'll figure out a way off this planet immediately, and I *will* come back for all of you. I won't leave you here to be slaughtered or to die of starvation. Is that understood?"

Jennifer opened her mouth to speak, but then simply nodded. Without bothering to see what she did next, Chris turned and sprinted back the way he had just come.

Normally, running up that many stairs would have winded him, especially since he hadn't been exercising regularly since quitting the USM, but his adrenaline must have been working overdrive because by the time he reached the main floor of the OST's headquarters, he was barely out of breath.

He made a quick detour into the room where Lexa had been fighting with the unseen people the last time Chris had been in this building. Sure enough, it was clearly their command center—or, it now seemed, had been Jennifer Chu's before the insurgency.

Chris ran his eyes over the room, memorizing as much as he could in the shadows, until they landed on a weapons locker that stood against one of the walls—locked. His mind raced and he weighed his options in a matter of seconds. It was essential that he ordered the facts in his mind before making his next decision. He suspected that this was a crucial moment in the survival of his family.

Lexa wasn't who she claimed to be—and neither was anyone else who had helped and befriended them on this colony.

The ship, or at least some of it, had survived—which meant that Alicia might be alive. It also meant the Xenomorph might still be alive, too.

Still, he didn't know for sure. Either way, Chris needed a weapon. For multiple reasons.

The weapons locker didn't have digital protection like the front door. The guns within were protected by an old-fashioned steel lock. Sure, he could get it off easily enough, but that would require breaking it, and he couldn't let Lexa and the other insurrectionists know that he was aware of what was actually going on. His knowledge of their true identities was one of the only advantages he had at this point.

Jane and Emma were at the house, alone, potentially with

a Xenomorph running around—though there had been no evidence that the creature had survived the crash. Not to mention a colony being run by traitors. His first priority was his daughters, and weapon or not, he needed to be with them for every single moment until they got off this damn planet. Nothing else mattered.

He would figure the rest out later.

Seconds later, he silently exited the building, slowly closing the door behind him, hearing the security pad beep as the locking mechanism clicked back into place. And then he raced towards the house, not caring at this point if anyone saw him.

"Good morning, sleepyheads," Chris said as his daughters both entered the kitchen in their pajamas, yawning, hair a mess, rubbing their eyes.

"What time is it?" Jane said, looking like she already suspected that something was off. Her eyes darted towards the window and Chris realized she was taking in the angle and amount of the sunlight. She was so bright, and the thought made his heart ache—they were all going to have to be very smart, and very lucky, to make it off this planet alive. After getting a couple hours of fitful sleep, he'd spent the morning looking out the window, watching for trouble, human or otherwise.

"It's ten," Chris answered. "I let you both sleep in. You're gonna skip school today, hang out with your old man."

"*What?* Why?" Jane demanded, clearly upset.

"Yay!" Emma yelled at almost the exact same time, running forward and climbing up onto her dad's lap.

"I just miss you," he said, and realized that it was true. Even though he had spent a lot of time with them, things had been so busy and hectic, even putting aside the mutiny. "I want to spend the entire day with you, just goofing off and having fun."

He realized he probably sounded too upbeat—he'd never been accused of being a good actor. Jane studied him. This wasn't going to be easy.

"But we *just* started," she said, continuing her interrogation. "And today's only a half day. You never let us miss school back on Earth. You'd get upset whenever we even suggested it."

"I know. And you'll get back to it, I promise. But things have been so crazy for us for so long. I just... *really* need a day with you, okay?" Her gaze didn't waver. "I need it," he said, a half-whisper. And it was true.

Jane's face narrowed and then her face softened, and she moved forward, a smile finally slipping onto her face. "Okay," she said. "Fine with me. Some of those kids are super annoying anyway."

"Oh yeah?" Chris responded, a feeling of relief washing over him. They were still in danger but at least he'd have his girls with him all day. He wasn't going to let them out of his sight. He stood up, letting Emma slide to the floor, and walked over to the refrigerator, realizing just how hungry he really was. "In what way?"

"They say some weird stuff," Jane replied, taking a seat at the table, stretching her arms over her head. "Like, it almost sounds like prayers...? And they all seem to know the words... like, they say them at the same time sometimes. They also whisper to each other a lot, like they're telling secrets, and then stop talking when I go up to them. I guess I'm kinda glad I don't have to go in today. I mean, I like being in school again, but I just hope I can find a couple of friends here."

"Ah, just kids being kids," Chris said, still looking at the interior of the fridge. He didn't want Jane to see his face— she would see right through his lie. This wasn't kids being kids. It sounded like kids reciting prayers from a religion.

Or a cult.

What had Jennifer Chu said?

Quoting bizarre Weyland-Yutani cult shit.

He'd had more than a few dealings with Weyland-Yutani separatists back on Earth, and that growing conflict had been a big part of the reason he'd quit the USM and left the planet. He had no interest in being part of a second civil war on Earth.

But maybe he had escaped one internal conflict only to find himself trapped in a more condensed version.

"How about scrambled eggs?" he asked, turning around with a fake smile plastered onto his face.

This was going to be a *very* interesting day.

1 4

The doorbell was loud, echoing through the house like the tolling of a funeral bell.

It was almost noon and Chris knew this was coming but he still jumped slightly at the sound. Part of him had hoped they'd be able to hide away in the house all day, safe—or at least relatively safe—until he could enact the first part of his potential escape plan later that night.

But that had been a pipe dream, and he had honestly known that fact all along.

"Who is it?" Jane said, running into the living room, followed closely by her little sister. They had been playing cards in Emma's bedroom, following a long argument with Chris about why they weren't allowed to go outside.

"It's a... work thing," he said, his stomach twisting. "I want you to go back to your room and keep playing cards. I'll be done in a minute, and then I'll play with you, too."

"It's *boring*," Jane insisted, her face darkening again. She didn't lose her temper often, but when she did, it was like a force of nature had been unleashed. Her mom had been like that, too.

"No, it isn't," Emma countered, looking up at her sister with a betrayed look on her face.

Chris quickly knelt in front of Jane. She was smart— smart enough to know that something was off, but Chris had to protect them, no matter what, even if it meant being momentarily brusque.

"Jane, I want you to go back into the bedroom *right now* and play cards with Emma. I don't want to hear another word about it. Do you understand me?"

It was the same tone that he'd used back on the transport ship, when they'd evacuated their quarters.

Jane's face was now the one that showcased betrayal, her father's sudden anger completely baffling her. Her chin trembled slightly, but she simply barked, "Fine!" and then whirled and headed back towards the bedroom. "Come on, Emma!"

The younger girl looked at her dad, confused too, but he didn't allow his face to soften. *I'm doing this for them*, he told himself.

"Go," was all he said.

Lowering her head, Emma walked off towards her bedroom, turning the corner just as the doorbell rang again. Chris willed his body to relax, forced a grin onto his face, and headed towards the front door.

Lexa stood on the porch, hands in her pockets, a look of pleasant surprise materializing on her face when Chris appeared in front of her.

"For a second, I thought maybe you weren't home," she said.

"Sorry, the girls are a little under the weather, so I was checking on them. They're just falling back asleep."

"Oh!" Lexa said. "That explains it. I was actually coming to check on them, too. I heard they weren't in school today."

Chris wondered vaguely if the teacher he'd met was even really a teacher—or a miner who had been 'promoted' after the insurrection.

"Yeah, sick day. Unfortunately," he said, trying to seem casual and uninviting at the same time.

"You don't seem like you've caught the bug," Lexa said, eyeing his face.

"Not yet. Knock on wood," he responded, tapping the doorframe with a knuckle.

A moment of awkward silence stretched out. He knew he was acting weird, wracked his brain for what he would have said if he hadn't known about all the lies and Lexa's violent takeover.

"Nice day," he said, and inwardly cringed. *You seem totally normal, Chris,* he berated himself.

Lexa squinted at him, then glanced at the sky—it looked pretty much exactly the same as every other day he'd been here. She turned her eyes back to him.

"It... is," she agreed.

Another moment passed. Chris tried to think of something else to say, something way less dumb, but came up blank. All he could think about was how this woman, who had kissed him, about whom he had very complicated feelings, wasn't at all who she said she was.

"Well, if they start to feel better, there's a mini carnival just getting going in town. The school has a half day, so we're getting set up now. I mean, it isn't anything fancy, but…"

"I wanna go!"

Jane pushed past her dad and beamed up at Lexa. Chris's heart sank, and he felt nauseous. He should have known that his oldest child was too headstrong to follow orders that didn't make any sense—hell, he had been guilty of that himself a few times during his time in the USM.

He glanced back. Emma was standing in the middle of the room, looking up at her father with huge, guilty eyes—clearly torn between guilt and a desire to attend the event. The mixed emotions on her face broke his heart all over again.

"It seems like you're feeling better!" Lexa said, ruffling the older girl's hair.

"I feel great!" Jane responded. "Me and Emma really, really wanna go to the carnival."

Emma appeared next to Chris, snuggling against his leg and looking up at him.

"Please, Daddy?"

His guilt and sympathy vanished and was instantly replaced with rage. At Lexa, for putting him in this position through her duplicity. At Jane, for disobeying him, even if he understood and maybe even respected her for it. And at himself, for allowing his daughters to once again be placed in danger.

His mind raced through potential scenarios in a matter of seconds.

He could put his foot down, order his girls back into their rooms, let them be disappointed and angry with him. It wouldn't be easy, and Jane would probably throw a fit, maybe even break stuff, but both of them would be safe. Or *safer*.

But if he did that, Lexa would be on to him. For all he knew, he'd been spotted breaking into the OST's headquarters the night before, and maybe she was just playing games as they figured out what to do with him—and with his daughters. Suspicion seemed to be playing in her eyes.

On the other hand, he could relent, let his girls attend the event in town. Stay close to them in case any trouble went down. It was possible he was just being paranoid about the Xenomorph. There hadn't been a single shred of evidence that the creature had survived the crash and made it into the dome. And if any danger *did* present itself, surely the OST's security forces would handle it, or contain it long enough for Chris to get his girls somewhere safe and figure out their next steps.

He didn't love either option but made a split-second decision based on all the factors that were rushing through his mind.

"Let's go to the carnival!" he said, forcing joy into his voice.

Emma squealed, hugging his legs, and Jane crashed into him as well, throwing her arms around his waist. Lexa smiled at him, the light in her eyes shifting slightly, softening. She reached out and placed her hand on his arm.

"They're going to love it," she said. "And I think you will, too."

Chris was not loving it.

Admittedly, his daughters were absolutely thrilled. The 'carnival' was nothing spectacular but after years of social dissolution on Earth, and months on a sterile spaceship, this was heaven for two young girls. The rides—if they could be called that—were cobbled together, and the games were only slightly better. But the delight in Jane's and Emma's eyes was undeniable.

Chris stood away from the other people, his posture clearly indicating that he wasn't particularly interested in small talk, and they eyed him like the outsider that he knew he was. His gaze fluctuated between his girls and the perimeter of the town square, alert for any potential danger.

But there was nothing. It was a beautiful afternoon, full of sunshine and the laughter of children. Picture perfect. Still, Chris was tense, and miserable, despite the fake half-smile he kept plastered to his face—as fake as the lazy white clouds slowly rolling across the sky.

Lexa appeared from one of the small crowds and approached him. He kept his breathing even, made a point of looking at her while also keeping his girls in his peripheral vision as best he could. It was peaceful now, but he'd found in his life that danger had a way of breaking out at a moment's notice.

"Having fun?" she said, sidling up next to him, turning around and taking in the scene from his vantage point.

"Absolutely," he lied.

"Good," she said. "And your girls clearly are as well."

They watched in silence for a moment.

"So, Lexa, when can I go see the scrapyard?"

He didn't know why he said it. He'd had no plans to do so, but that falsehood, in particular, had been bothering him all day. The idea that she would mislead him about where the remnants of the transport ship were—where Alicia's remains were. It made his vision go white-hot with rage when he thought about it. It wasn't the worst thing that Lexa and her fellow mutineers had done, not by far, but it felt personal to him. Still, he regretted the words as soon as he'd spoken them.

"The… scrapyard?" she asked, looking up at him, confusion wrinkling her forehead. "Why?"

The fact that she would even ask this made her guilt all the clearer, made Jennifer Chu's claim about the contents of the warehouse even more likely to be true in his mind. Lexa must have noticed the subtle shift in his expression because she rolled her eyes at herself, laughed self-deprecatingly.

"Oh! Of course. To look over the wreckage. Where is my mind?" She looked out into the crowd again, watched the small group of children as they screamed in joy.

"So... *when*?" he followed up. He was too far in at this point to let her off the hook. He was also curious to see how good of a liar she was when pushed.

"Sorry, I was just mentally going through the schedule. I keep all this stuff on my computer at HQ. We had to delay the last trip because of some more severe than usual storms outside the OST. It's easy to forget how awful the weather is on this planet outside of our little bubble!"

Okay, apparently a very good liar when pushed.

"Things have been a little crazy since the transport ship crashed and you and your girls arrived," she continued, looking at him, turning that admittedly disarming smile back on. "But I promise I'll figure out a time to get you out there. Not that there's much to see..."

He started to open his mouth, but she interrupted, putting her hand on his forearm.

"But I know how important it is to you, Chris."

He fought an impulse to pull his arm away from her, but he had a part to play, so he simply smiled, pretended that she'd said exactly what he wanted to hear.

"Thanks," he said, realizing that he still had Jane in his sights, but Emma was nowhere to be found. She could easily be on one of the makeshift rides, shielded from his vision, or caught in the middle of a cluster of kids, but his stomach sank, and he felt panic threatening to overwhelm him. Just as he started to move forward, however, a loud voice stopped him in his tracks.

"Lexa!" Cosgrove was approaching them, what looked like a permanent sneer etched onto his face.

She pulled her hand away from Chris's arm just in time for the taller man to insert himself between the two of them, knocking Chris out of the way as he did so—perhaps accidentally, perhaps not. He whispered something into Lexa's ear, harsh and insistent, but it was impossible to hear what he was saying.

Chris fought an urge to hit the man, to make it clear that he wasn't someone who could be pushed around, but he had more important things to handle. He still couldn't see Emma.

"Looks like you two are busy—I'll see you later," he said, hurrying off towards the throngs.

"Chris, wait!" Lexa shouted, but he was already several yards away from them, dodging people as he made a beeline for Jane. She tended to have an almost supernatural ability to find her younger sister.

"Dad!" she practically screamed as he approached her. She was soaking wet and held a water balloon in each hand, eyeballing an older kid who clearly had been at least partly responsible for her current state. Her smile was almost infectious. But Chris didn't have it in him to pretend anymore. His head swiveled as he desperately looked for his baby girl.

"Where's Emma?" he asked, doing this best to keep his voice calm.

"I think she's over on the merry-go-round type thing," Jane answered, peering around her dad, still in battle mode. In any other situation, he would have loved to see this kind of concentration on her face coupled with a look of joy that had been absent for far too long.

"Stay here. Do not move," he said, and headed off towards the ride Jane had described. He could hear her scoffing behind him, clearly annoyed, but he just hoped she would follow orders now better than she had earlier that morning. He was losing control of the situation. He just needed to get through this day, and then he would do everything in his power to change that.

He walked around the ride, avoiding people without even really being aware that they were there. A feeling overtook him that reminded him of being in a combat situation, when everything except the mission itself would go fuzzy. A comforting and highly unbearable sensation. The nonsensical dual edge of tranquility and panic.

Just as he felt his emotions about to overcome his calm, he spotted Emma several dozen feet past the ride, near the row of stores. A boy, slightly older and taller than Emma, had her shoved up against the wall, angrily shouting something, a fat finger pointed directly at her face. Huge tears glistened in her eyes—she looked terrified.

Chris's mind went from white to red. A deep-seeded part of himself knew he should approach this in a measured and reasonable manner. But the weight of everything—Elizabeth's death, quitting his job, the destruction of the transport ship, the loss of Alicia, the revelation that Lexa and her cohorts were violent insurrectionists—caused something to snap within him. He stormed over, grabbed the kid by the shoulder, and pulled him away from Emma.

"Back off," he growled.

The boy's eyes went wide—not with fear but shock. The kind of surprised expression a bully gets when their bad behavior is finally called out by someone bigger than them. Despite his surprise, the kid had a mean face, still wrinkled with rage towards Emma.

"Hey! Don't touch my fucking kid!" someone shouted, and Chris whirled, fingers balling up into fists. He was done pretending to be happy, to be nice. He was going to get his kids through this day, and then get the hell off this planet. Whatever it took.

Milliken was approaching, fast, flanked by several of his buddies. Each of them held an unmarked brown bottle, full of Delilah's moonshine, Chris assumed. Even though the upbeat, tinny music continued to play, the entire air of the mini carnival changed instantly, with every single set of eyes turning towards the confrontation that was playing out. Turning and settling on Chris. The outsider. He became more aware than ever that this was a group of people who had all willingly participated in a violent coup.

Every instinct in his body told Chris to meet Milliken head-on, the way he had with the drunk miner in the bar several nights earlier and with Cosgrove at HQ. He sized the four guys up in an instant—they were all big, strong, but their movements were careless, overconfident. Typical bullies, like the child Milliken had raised who didn't know any better. Chris was confident that he could take these men apart in less than two minutes.

But then he clocked Jane off to the right of the growing mob, heard Emma's quiet sobbing behind him. There was too much at stake here. Any momentary victory would derail his already bare-boned plan for later that night. Discretion was most certainly the better part of valor—as painful as that truth was right now.

He raised his open hands in supplication.

"I'm sorry," he said. "My daughter was scared, and I just wanted to separate them."

Cosgrove joined the men, eyes glowing. He was clearly loving every second of this.

"I haven't liked you since the moment you got here," Milliken hissed, spittle hitting Chris's face. It took every ounce of self-control to not knock this guy into next week. "And now you put your hands on my kid?!"

"I think everyone's pretty sick of you, Temple," Cosgrove said, quiet, but the words rang like a bell in Chris's ears. He knew that he was at an inflection point. He could blow it all up, or just take the abuse, stay focused on getting off this rock.

He reached behind himself without removing his eyes from Milliken's, his fingers finding Emma's shoulders. Slowly, he began to edge towards Jane, who looked terrified. She could clearly feel the shift in the crowd, too.

"Like I said, I'm sorry. I'll just take my girls home and we'll retire for the night."

"What if we don't *want* you to leave?" Milliken said, and several of his drunk buddies laughed. There was violence in their eyes—the kind of look Chris had seen on the battlefield, far more times than he cared to recall. Other colonists began to join Milliken's group. A few opponents were relatively easy to handle—a drunken, angry mob was a different story altogether. For the first time since crash landing on this godforsaken planet, Chris wondered if he'd actually be able to keep his daughters alive. "What if we wanna show you what we *really* think about you?"

"Enough!"

The voice was loud, full of anger. Lexa waded into the crowd, throwing a look of pure rage at Milliken and Cosgrove and the others, and the air shifted once again, the incensed crowd instantly cowing in the face of their secret leader's fury.

"This behavior is completely inappropriate," she continued, face apoplectic. "Especially in front of the children!"

Chris watched the fight go out of every single person that had joined Milliken, but he himself felt a sudden tinge of fear. Her tone and stance, not to mention the reaction of the crowd, conveyed a hidden but incredible power. Chris had seen this in his years of the military, particularly in the final few years when going up against Weyland-Yutani separatists. Normally, any given cult sect's goons were a tough fight but manageable. When they were in the presence of one of their leaders, however, their entire demeanor changed from violent to brainwashed—capable of doing horrible deeds in the name of a twisted ethos.

He saw that power on full display in front of him. And he was rattled by it.

Lexa turned to him, her expression immediately switching from irritated to pleasant, the once-angry mob melting back into the festivities just as quickly as it had formed. Chris realized that he'd been holding his breath.

Jane and Emma appeared on either side of their father, clutching him tightly, any joy they'd been experiencing a few minutes earlier completely gone now. He just wanted to get them away from this horror show of a carnival, but he had to play his part, couldn't reveal that he knew exactly who these people were.

Get home. Move forward with the plan.

"I'm so sorry," she said, her sympathetic grin slightly sad, but also encouraging—the perfect smile for this exact occasion. He marveled at how good an actor she was. He wondered what the real Lexa Phelan was really like. Was nervous he might find out.

"It's okay," he said, forcing a smile of his own once again. "I think the girls and I are just tired. They're still a little run down, I think, so we're gonna head home. But this has been great. Thank you."

He started to head towards the house, leading his girls along with him, but Lexa sidled up next to them, matched their pace.

"I'll go with you. Want to make sure you make it home safe. Some of these idiots got a little too drunk. Obviously."

"Great," he said, dreading the next few minutes. He just needed to get his girls settled down, then let them catch a few hours of sleep before he'd be forced to wake them up and explain what he was planning.

As the four of them headed away from the bustling town center and towards the tract of homes a quarter mile away, Lexa apologized again and then launched into a story about the early days of the OST, when they hadn't yet fully mastered the dome technology, and anyone could hack into the digital mainframe. All kinds of ridiculous, and sometimes hilarious, images were broadcast in the sky. Emma and Jane laughed genuinely at the story, and Chris faked a chuckle. He had to wonder if this story was even true. But it didn't matter. The house was getting closer and closer.

Finally, they reached it, and Chris hustled his girls inside, telling them to get ready for bed. They complied without a single word, clearly exhausted, both physically and emotionally. Chris could still detect the terror on the edges of Emma's eyes, and the fact that she had been bullied just a few minutes earlier filled him with a rage that he could barely conceal.

"You okay?" Lexa asked as Chris shut the front door, turning to her, trying to figure out how to make this goodbye as fast and innocuous as possible. There was a chance he would never see her again after this moment, and he was more than okay with that.

"Yeah, just tired," he answered, rubbing his face with a hand, feigning exhaustion. "Maybe I picked up what the girls had this morning after all."

"Maybe," she said, moving closer to him. "Or maybe Mister Big Tough War Hero actually got scared there for a second."

"Maybe," he repeated, slightly disconcerted that she was right.

"Good thing I was there to protect you, Chris Temple," she whispered, and then her lips were on his again, and he allowed her to kiss him for a few moments, allowed her to think whatever it was she needed to think, just to keep things smooth on what he hoped would be his last night on this planet.

She pulled away, placing her hands on top of his. Her eyes seemed to shine, like a predator's while eyeing its prey.

"We can take things slow, I promise," she said quietly. "Despite what those meatheads were saying, I really think you belong here, Chris. I can't wait to let you in... to everything. There is so much we can offer you. That *I* can offer you. You and your girls. We can run this place... and it can be anything we want it to be."

He blinked at her words, had no idea how to respond, and saw her face start to go slack with disappointment. He realized that he was losing her in the exact moment that he needed her to think he was all-in on this colony.

"That sounds amazing," he lied, then kissed her with a passion that he didn't actually feel, felt his stomach twist with regret as he did so. At length, he pulled away, and whispered, "Good night, Lexa."

A huge smile appeared on her face. "Good night, Chris," and then she turned away and walked down the porch steps and up the street, back towards the carnival, which was still blinking and blaring at full tilt.

From where he stood, the sound was warbled, almost threatening. The lights reminded him of the kind thrown off by emergency vehicles during his time with the military. His unease only deepened.

Lexa glanced back when she was a couple of blocks away, gave him a small wave, and then she disappeared into the distance. Chris clenched his jaw as he watched her go.

His night was just getting started.

1 5

Chris Temple sat by the window, waiting. Watching.

At last, after what felt like an eternity, the final group of miners drifted off from the remnants of the carnival, staggering into their homes, and the entire town went silent.

Good.

A large portion of the adult residents were drunk, which would make what Chris needed to do all that much easier. Not that 'easy' was really a word that could describe what he was planning. But his coming actions were absolutely necessary. Despite Lexa's intervention, he had seen the looks in those people's eyes earlier. The madness of a cult, empowered by recent victory. It was only a matter of time before they found a reason to throw him in a cell with the rightful leaders of this colony.

Or kill him.

It didn't matter whether the USM was coming to rescue

them or not—Chris couldn't wait. He had to save his daughters. Tonight.

He pulled himself away from the window and walked with purpose to Emma's room. She was completely passed out, curled up into a little ball like she always was a few hours after falling asleep, and he gently lifted her up and into his arms. She barely stirred.

He walked with his slumbering bundle to Jane's room and set his younger daughter down next to his oldest. Jane was sprawled out, the complete opposite of her sister, but the two girls sensed each other in their sleep and curled into one another, arms tangling up, eyelids fluttering.

Chris watched them for a few minutes, his heart melting and breaking at the exact same time. He wished he could leave them like this for longer, let them get all the rest they needed, but he required as much time as possible to enact his plan. He had no idea what was lying in wait for them. But he knew none of it would be good. The several hours of sleep they'd already gotten would have to be enough. Who knew when any of them would sleep again.

"Girls," he said quietly, shaking each of them. Jane sat bolt upright immediately, eyes wide, but he knew her brain was only half-functioning. Still, he admired her innate readiness—it was something that had taken him a long time to learn during basic training.

Emma, on the other hand, shoved his hand away, turned over, started snoring.

"What is it?" Jane said, sounding so much like Elizabeth.

His heart broke all over again, but he pushed the feelings down. There was still so much to do.

"Let's get your sister up and then I'll explain," he said, smiling grimly at his older girl. He could see the woman she would become, and he was so proud, and so devastated that her childhood was already slipping away from her. Friends in the military had told him about this, how fast it all went, and he had always disregarded it. But now he knew what they'd meant. And could hardly believe it.

Jane joined him in gently shaking Emma until the smaller girl finally sat up, rubbing her eyes, annoyed. "*What?*" she demanded, also like her mother. The righteous indignation would have made him laugh under different circumstances.

"Girls," he started, and they both sat up a little straighter at his tone, their eyes clearing, pushing exhaustion away. "I'm sorry to wake you up in the middle of the night. But I've found out some things. We need to get away from this colony as soon as possible."

"Daddy...?" Emma said, eyes huge and full of fear. It almost broke Chris, but he looked away, couldn't let himself be distracted. He was doing this for them. It would all be worth it. Eventually. He kept telling himself that.

"What kind of things?" Jane asked, immediately suspicious.

"I don't want to get into specifics," he answered, while proudly recognizing that it was a smart question, especially considering she wasn't even fully awake. "Not yet. But Lexa and the rest of the colonists aren't who they say they are. They took over this colony and hurt people. And I'm worried they might hurt us. So, we need to get out of here right away."

"Lexa wouldn't do that!" Emma nearly shouted. Her eyes were filling with confused tears.

"I know you both really like her," Chris said quickly, placing an errant strand of hair behind his little girl's ear, "but she's been lying to us. Trust me, I wish it wasn't true. I really wanted the OST to be our new home. I know how much you've been liking it here. And so have I. But it's not real. It's a mirage. And we need to get out of here, okay?"

"I understand," Jane said, then turned to her sister. "Dad is just trying to keep us safe. Okay, Emma? We need to listen to him."

The younger girl stared at her older sister and her face relaxed, the tears vanishing from her eyes as the two spoke to each other in complete silence. Chris had seen this before—his girls communicating the way he assumed only close siblings could. They both turned back to him, silent, waiting, ready to do whatever he told them.

His heart swelled, and then he told them exactly where they were heading next.

The small family made their way through the dark pockets of the colony.

Chris was in silent awe of how quiet his girls were being, how they stayed close to him, but not so close that they would hamper his movement, or their own. He had 'jokingly' taught them a few military tactics when they were little, more for Elizabeth's amusement than anything else, but some of those lessons must have burrowed deep into their minds, and were climbing out now, when they were unexpectedly needed.

They made their way around and behind the town square, and moved into the trees without missing a beat, their bodies fully engulfed by shadows, until the warehouse eventually came into view as they approached the edge of the woods.

"What's that?" Jane whispered, fully alert. Emma stayed close to her older sister, eyes wide but tired looking. Chris felt a pang of doubt at the sight but shoved it aside—she would have to be strong now. They all would.

"*That* is where they're hiding our transport ship. Or what's left of it," he responded, quiet, his eyes locked on the structure's entrance. After a moment, Milliken appeared out of the shadows of the warehouse.

"Is Alicia in there?" Emma whispered, her voice cracking on their android's name.

"I don't know," Chris answered truthfully. "I hope so. But we have to be prepared for the fact that she may not have made it, sweetie."

"I understand, Daddy," Emma said, and Jane took her sister's hand.

Chris led them to a particularly large tree and had them sit down, facing away from the warehouse. Their faces registered their confusion, but to their credit, they didn't say anything.

"First, and most importantly," he whispered, "I know I haven't said it enough since your mother died... but I love you. I'm sorry that I've had trouble saying it."

"We know you love us," Jane said back to him, quietly, her eyes shining. Emma nodded.

"I'm very, very happy to hear that," he responded. "Now. I want you to stay right here, exactly like this. I need to get us into the warehouse but in order to do that, I also need to do some unpleasant things. In fact, you may see a *lot* of unpleasant things before we get off this planet. And I'm sorry for that. But you're both going to have to grow up a little faster than I wanted. In fact, you already have. And it might get worse. I'm sorry about that, too."

Neither girl said anything, but after a moment, Jane reached out and placed her small hand on top of Chris's. "It's okay, Dad."

Those three words changed everything for him, and a calm overtook his senses, the kind of calm that he'd always felt in the seconds before he activated himself at the start of a mission. Those three words were the most powerful he may have ever heard as a soldier, and had come from the most unlikely of sources. He glanced at his older daughter, her eyes as deadly serious as his, and then gently cupped Emma's chubby cheek with his hand.

"Don't move. I'll be right back."

And then he was off, moving around the perimeter of

the trees, until he found the optimal route to approach the warehouse with as much stealth as possible.

The sucker punch he directed at Milliken was one of the hardest and fastest Chris had ever thrown, but to the younger man's credit, Milliken sensed it coming at the last second and moved his head slightly, causing the blow to land but not nearly as effectively as Chris had intended. Milliken stumbled back against the warehouse wall, fumbling for his firearm, eyes blazing when he realized who had assaulted him. Chris pressed his attack, slamming the man back into the wooden structure, the breath exploding from the guard's lungs even as his fingers wrapped around the gun's grip. While Chis landed a devastating uppercut with his right hand, his left battled Milliken's fingers for control of the weapon, which was already half-withdrawn from its holster.

Blood trickling from his mouth and down his chin, Milliken head-butted Chris with incredible speed, a direct hit to his nose, and stars danced before his eyes. He fell back, dazed, and lost his grip on the firearm, but blinked through the pain. He thought of his girls, several hundred feet away, and prayed they were obeying his commands. He didn't want them to see what he needed to do—or what might happen to him, if this younger man was able to outmaneuver him.

Milliken brought the weapon up, hatred blazing in his eyes.

"I'm going to fucking *kill* you," he said through gritted teeth, his trembling finger on the trigger. But Chris was already moving forward and ducking at the same time, and heard the discharge, saw the flash as the bullet left the chamber. He crashed into the man again and they went down to the ground, hard, the gun clattering into the darkness.

They wrestled for what felt like many minutes, but Chris knew it was probably more like seconds. Time had a way of distorting during life-or-death physical combat. The man was fast, but his moves were blunt, desperate. Chris let Milliken think he had the advantage, then used his burgeoning overconfidence against him. As the guard realized that he had made a fatal blunder, his attacks got wilder, and Chris quickly had Milliken in a vicious chokehold.

Soon, it was over. The man's body slumped, unconscious, and Chris got up and looked around for the gun. After a minute of fruitlessly searching the thick shadows, he cursed under his breath. He would have to do without it. He needed to retrieve his girls and get inside the warehouse.

But first, he had to deal with Milliken's unconscious body. Looking around, making a flash decision, he grabbed the man's arms and pulled him towards the back of the building, grunting as he did so. Milliken was extremely heavy.

Chris had used that specific chokehold before—only a few times, yes, but he knew that it knocked an opponent out for a considerable amount of time. Hopefully it would be enough for him and his girls to get into the warehouse and… do whatever it was Chris was hoping to do. His lack of a plan after this moment was deeply disquieting. But it was the best he had.

Already feeling physical exhaustion creeping in when he finally got Milliken to the back of the structure, where it was even darker, Chris grabbed the key card off Milliken's belt, pulling it violently away until the thin metal wire snapped. Then he sprinted back around the warehouse and towards the woods, where Jane and Emma waited.

He prayed they had kept their eyes averted, that the sounds of the two men fighting for their lives and the sound of a bullet discharging hadn't piqued their curiosity—or a fear for their father's life.

When he reached them, a flood of relief washed over him. They were in the exact same spot, still turned away from the warehouse. The only change was that Emma was nestled into her older sister, hands over her ears.

"Daddy!" Jane said, seeing their dad first, but it was Emma who leaped up, hugging her father, joined immediately by her older sister.

"Are you okay?" Jane half-whispered, emotion straining her voice.

"Yeah, I'm okay," he answered. "Did you… hear any of that?"

Jane didn't answer, just looked up into his eyes. She didn't have to answer.

"I'm sorry," he said but his older girl just shook her head. Emma clung to him like her life depended on it.

"What's next?" Jane asked.

"We go find out what's inside that warehouse."

* * *

Margaret Livingston had always been fascinated by androids.

She'd grown up in San Francisco, so she'd seen them on a regular basis throughout her life, had watched them with fascination over the years, and did research on them whenever she could find the time and resources. When Weyland-Yutani, in its waning years, had offered her a job, she considered taking it, but it would have been a desk job, running numbers—she wouldn't be working on the synthetics at all. So, she politely declined.

Instead, she dove into android research. Learned about the earliest Borgia Industries version, the Weyland Corp's David model, and Weyland-Yutani's eventual David-8 variant. She was particularly fascinated with the newer USM versions, the autons, which came about after corporations had been outlawed and the military organization had taken over multiple areas of technological research from the very companies they had helped run out of business.

Margaret didn't much care about who was in charge—Weyland-Yutani or the USM. As far as she was concerned, they were largely the same thing.

Or at least, that was the way she felt for much of her life.

After her parents died, one after the other within a week of each other, she decided that she wasn't bound to San Francisco, or to Earth, for that matter. After all, she wasn't married or interested in getting married, or in any romantic relationship whatsoever.

No, her first and only love was knowledge—particularly science. She'd always adored staring up into the stars as a child, had dreamed of someday going into outer space, of visiting another planet. So, the day after her mother's funeral, Margaret did everything in her power to find an opportunity to do just that.

The USM was planning its latest mining mission, and she went through a battery of interviews and tests, all of which she passed with flying colors. The people who tested her were shocked at her intelligence and knowledge of cybernetics, shocked that this genius had been living right under their noses for years. They offered her high-paying jobs on Earth, told her that she was too good to work on a mining colony in the middle of nowhere.

She thanked them for their kind words but told them that her mind was made up. The look of confusion and then disgust on their faces was burned into her memory.

She didn't care.

Those people would never understand someone like her. She didn't want or need money, or status, or to attend fancy parties with high-level dignitaries and politicians. She just wanted to touch the stars.

Shortly after blasting off, Margaret began to realize that this assignment might not be as simple or straightforward as she initially suspected. As many of the colonists began to enter the hypersleep chambers, she had a chance to meet Lexa Phelan, and the two took an instant liking to each other. Slipping into an easy but deep conversation, they both decided to delay their sleep and talked for hours on end.

Even though she was 'just' going to be a miner, Lexa had opened Margaret's mind.

Listening to the younger woman, the rational scientist came to realize that she had never truly allowed herself to understand the subtle but shocking differences between the USM and Weyland-Yutani. She had always conflated the two—and she couldn't have been more mistaken.

Lexa read to her from her favorite book, a massive biography, and Margaret realized that the corporation had perverted the true beliefs of Peter Weyland and Cullen Yutani. The company, in its insatiable growth and greed, had stripped the soul from the original creators' intentions, had replaced the fruit of an organic and important idea with a brittle husk that couldn't sustain or nourish a society.

Margaret realized, thanks to Lexa, that the USM was just repeating the same old mistakes, handed down century after century. Humans needed to get back to a more basic, more civilized way of existing. The way things used to be, a long time ago.

When they finally entered their hypersleep chambers a few days later, Margaret had vowed silently to herself that she would follow Lexa Phelan to the ends of the galaxy, or through the gates of Hell, if necessary.

And she was starting to realize that was exactly what she had done.

1 6

Chris and his girls made their way through the dark hallways, almost entirely silently.

He remained impressed by their ability to stay close to him and keep quiet, especially Emma, who had a habit of complaining, especially when she was tired. And the poor thing looked completely spent. But she soldiered on, gently touching her father's hand every now and then, as if confirming that he was still next to her in the deep shadows of the warehouse's corridors.

He had performed operations like this more times than he could remember, but never with the two most important people in his life trailing right behind him. He couldn't recall ever having butterflies like he did right now during his previous USM missions.

Luckily, the warehouse seemed to be completely empty. Which made sense. Who in their right mind would be working in the middle of the night after hours of drunken revelry?

They approached a large door at the end of the hallway and Chris slowed down, taking in every detail. He needed to make sure they weren't walking into some kind of trap—but everything looked innocuous. Another security panel was set into the wall to the right of the door, and he silently prayed that the code was the same as the one Lexa had punched in at HQ. He could bypass it, like he had at the headquarters, but it would take time, something of which he suspected they had very little.

Glancing at his girls for a moment, he then turned his attention back to the panel and punched in the code. After a nerve-wracking moment, the pad beeped, and a clicking sound reached his ears.

"Good job, Daddy," Emma whispered, and he winked at her, then opened the door. The three of them entered the cavernous space.

"Dad, is that…?" Jane started and Chris just nodded as they all stared up in awe.

The transport ship, or what was left of it, filled most of what was clearly the main chamber of the warehouse. It looked to Chris like a huge unfinished puzzle that a giant had given up on. Enormous beams of wood kept the hull propped up where key sections were missing, and nasty black scorch marks tattooed the ship in dozens of places. Significant segments were missing, but enough had survived that it was entirely recognizable. Whoever had piloted the ship to its fiery destiny had clearly tried their best. For this much of its shell to still be intact seemed like a minor miracle. He wondered if whatever was left of Alicia was somewhere inside this hulking monstrosity. Or perhaps she was scattered across the planet somewhere outside the OST's dome.

"Girls," he whispered, realizing that no one else was there. "Come on."

They made their way around, heading towards the back of the warehouse. Chris eyeballed a particular section of the ship, and then cursed silently to himself. The other escape pods hadn't survived the crash—and now his half-baked plan wasn't a plan at all. He just hoped that the colonists kept another interstellar vessel in here, even if it was just something basic in case of emergency.

And as far as he was concerned, his current situation qualified.

As they circled the desiccated hull, Chris's hope dimmed with each step, until he noticed a particular door set in the wall near the far corner. Unlike the other doors in the large space, a slight light emanated from the crack beneath it. He indicated it to his girls, who drew in even closer. After glancing back at the transport ship one more time, Chris swiped Milliken's ID and pulled the door open. He and his girls entered, heading deeper into the bowels of the warehouse.

During his time in the USM, Chris had visited a number of military laboratories, particularly after he'd been promoted to colonel. He'd seen an incredibly varied number of things—some that had shocked him, made him nauseous, even ashamed. But one thing that all those previous scientific spaces had in common was that they were immaculate. Clean beyond measure. The scientists who worked in those facilities took pride in the pristine condition of their surroundings.

This laboratory inside the OST's warehouse, however, did not share that trait. For a moment, Chris thought that perhaps a bomb had exploded inside the room, but he quickly disabused himself of that notion. It was just a mess. Like the room of a child, or someone who had lost their mind. Half-finished experiments were strewn across every visible surface, tubes and shards of metal and dog-eared books and batteries and syringes and microscopes and things he didn't even recognize cluttered tables and desks, an odd smell filling the entire room.

Chris moved forward, his girls staying close to him. He could almost feel the fear emanating off them, but there was nothing he could do about it other than protect them while they navigated this bizarre scientific maze. After a few moments, he heard something around the next corner, and he stopped, his girls halting milliseconds after he did. Their reaction time was highly impressive. He hoped he would have the opportunity to reward their incredible courage sometime very soon.

He breathed slowly, listened. Then he recognized the sound. Someone up ahead was humming.

He looked at his girls and held up his free palm, indicating that they should stay put. Jane wrapped her hand around her sister's forearm. Emma looked down and then back up, blinked at her father once. She understood her instructions.

Chris smiled slightly, tousled the hair on each of their heads for the briefest seconds, then set his jaw and moved forward, eyes narrowed in laser-like focus.

As he entered the main section of this bizarre laboratory, he was shocked to discover a mousy woman with gray hair sitting at a table, tongue stuck half out of her mouth, soldering something in front of her. She continued to hum, her eyes hidden by goggles which reflected the intermittent light that sparked in front of her. Chris made a point of avoiding direct eye contact with the sharp luminescence but looked over at what the woman was working on with such delighted concentration. What he saw made his stomach turn—with an equal amount of sorrow and elation.

It was Alicia. Or what was left of her.

"Drop it! Now!" he yelled, moving forward, fists balled, anger making his face go flush.

The woman screamed and ripped the goggles off her head, dropping the soldering iron as she did so. She blinked up at Chris as if he were a ghost, clearly shocked that someone had invaded her sanctuary at this ungodly hour.

"You... you're the survivor... the one from the transport ship..." she stuttered, trying to process what was happening.

"Step away from the table," Chris instructed in a clipped tone. He could see that her hands were trembling and might have felt bad in different circumstances, might have tamped down his aggression. But there was no time to be nice. She worked with or for Lexa, which meant she had taken part in a coup, even if it was indirectly. Chris had no sympathy for her.

He made his way closer to the table and looked down at Alicia.

For the most part, she was still intact, but her face had multiple cuts and burn marks, and one of her arms was completely missing. Her expression was peaceful but there were multiple holes throughout the rest of her body, and her tattered clothing was stained in multiple places with dried white android fluid.

"Alicia...?" he said, not even meaning to articulate her name, forgetting about the scientist for a moment.

In response, her eyes fluttered open, attempting to focus, head tilting slightly, awkwardly. Chris heard the scientist move and barked at her, grabbing a long piece of metal from one of the overflowing tables.

"I swear to God, I will kill you if you move again!" The older woman froze, terror filling her expression. He wasn't entirely sure if he meant the words he'd just spoken. Instead of trying to figure it out, he turned back to Alicia, whose eyes were now locked on his.

"Chris...?" she said, her voice not quite what he remembered, as if she was speaking to him from underwater.

"Yes," he said, and smiled. It was so good to see her again.

Before he realized what was happening, Jane and Emma were next to him, hugging Alicia, both crying. He realized he had tears in his eyes, too.

"It is not safe here," Alicia said. "These people are dangerous. You must leave immediately."

"We're not going anywhere without you!" Jane shouted, and Emma nodded, in complete agreement with her sister.

"Can you walk?" Chris asked.

Alicia tilted her head again, and he could hear machinery moving inside her body, something that had never happened before. It reminded him of when he'd first learned how to drive a loader—when he'd nearly stripped the engine.

"I believe so," Alicia said. "Though my gait may not be very impressive."

She smiled at him, and he grinned back. She was in rough shape, but there was something else different about her. The way she was looking at him, smiling at him. She almost seemed... *human*.

He shook his head, put the thought out of his mind, and turned back to the scientist, who hadn't moved a muscle since he'd threatened her moments earlier.

"Who the hell are you?" he demanded, jaw set, the piece of metal still gripped tightly in a fist. He didn't revel in the fear dancing in her eyes.

"I'm Margaret. Margaret Livingston. I'm just a scientist... I do what Lexa tells me."

"And what did Lexa tell you to do with this auton?" he asked, stepping closer to the terrified woman.

"I was…" she started and swallowed nervously, then soldiered on. "I was tasked with breaking through her mainframe, and then backchanneling and hacking into the USM communications systems."

"Why?"

"Lexa wanted to know if the USM was aware of… of what happened here. If they were on their way. She figured that a USM-constructed android might unwittingly have access to information and systems… that would help her defend against an attack."

"And were you able to get the information you needed?"

Margaret's eyes went wide, and she waffled a moment, and then spoke.

"The marines are on their way."

Chris nodded. It was smart. *Lexa* was smart. In fact, he would have done the same thing in her position. Use all the resources at your disposal to protect your people and your position. Perhaps if the USM realized that direct attacks were too costly, they would look to bargain. He had seen that kind of thing happen before. It was rare—but there was precedent. After all, the ore on this planet was very valuable.

But none of this was his problem. He wasn't going to wait around for a war to break out.

He glanced over and saw that his daughters were helping Alicia to her feet. It was a surreal sight, his emotionally damaged daughters helping their family's physically damaged android up—and he felt deeply grateful that Alicia was still alive.

She's not alive, he corrected himself, but even that notion didn't feel quite right in his mind.

"How do we get off of this planet?" he asked Margaret, his tone softening slightly. "The transport ship doesn't look operational."

Margaret laughed slightly, eyed him with what looked like respect. "You're correct, Colonel. That ship will never fly again. The damage it sustained when it made landfall was catastrophic. I'm genuinely surprised that your android was able to come out of it in one piece. Or mostly one piece. It must have actively worked to keep itself from being completely destroyed during the crash. Almost as if it passionately wanted to walk away from the impact, to live for something... or someone. But synthetics don't have human desires like that."

Chris ignored her comment, pressed her further.

"Could any living thing have survived that crash?" he asked.

"Absolutely not," Margaret scoffed. "Your nanny bot only survived because it isn't truly alive."

Chris let out a sigh of relief. That meant the Xenomorph must have died on impact. It didn't change the fact that he needed to get off this planet immediately, but it was one less thing for him to worry about.

"So how do we get out of here?" he asked again.

"About half a mile outside of the dome, southeast, there's a small structure that houses a ship. It wasn't built for long-term voyages—there are no hypersleep chambers. But it could certainly get you out of this planet's atmosphere. After that... well, your chances wouldn't be great."

"I like my chances better anywhere than here," he responded, though the ship she was describing was only a short-term solution. The idea of asphyxiating or freezing to death in space wasn't much better than his current choices, despite his words. He started to panic and then calmed down, reminded himself that he could only solve one problem at a time.

Chris glanced around and saw a spool of wire, then noticed a chair covered in papers. He walked over and shoved the papers to the ground, then indicated that Margaret should sit. She complied, and he dropped the metal bar onto the ground, then wrapped the wire around her securely.

"You don't need to do this," she said, a worried look in her eyes. "I won't tell anyone."

"You're right. You won't," he responded, making sure the wire was wrapped tightly around her, but not so tightly that she couldn't breathe. If she tried hard enough, she could eventually wiggle her way free. By then, he expected to be blasting off this planet. He'd deal with where they were going to go later. "If I get to that location and don't find a ship, I'm going to come back here and kill you myself. Do you understand?"

"I understand," she replied, staring directly into his eyes. "And I swear to you I'm not lying. I know that you're just trying to save your daughters, and I respect that."

He stared at her for a long moment, realized he believed her, then saw that Alicia and his daughters were watching him.

"It is so good to see you, Chris," the android said, her eyebrows lifting with seeming emotion.

"It's good to see you, too, Alicia," he responded, fighting an urge to rush over and hug her.

"So, what is next?" she inquired, tilting her head again, Jane and Emma on either side, clinging to her.

"Next?" he said, narrowing his eyes. "We get the hell off this planet."

PART 3

OCCLUSION

17

Lexa Phelan had always loved history.

The last of three girls, she grew up in a house that had bustled with seemingly unending activity. Her parents were both teachers, so their house was full of physical books, a remarkable situation considering that most learning was digital, and even that had been changing as she grew up, with implants and other technology changing the ways humans consumed information.

Her parents shunned those advances as much as possible. It made them unpopular at the university where they taught, but they took solace in each other, in their daughters. Dinners were a lively affair, with everyone talking about the book or books they had read that day, conversations overlapping as each person eagerly and earnestly tried to impress the rest with a fact or a story that had opened their mind just a little more.

It was during these early years, when Lexa was ten or eleven, that she came across a dual biography of Peter Weyland and Cullen Yutani in her parents' study. She knew she wasn't supposed to be in there, but one of her older sisters, Rebecca, had shown her where their parents kept the office key hidden. Whenever her parents weren't home, whether they were working late or heading out for a departmental function, Lexa would sneak in and dive into any number of books. And the day she came across that biography changed her life forever.

True, she didn't understand a lot of the words and most of the concepts—the true nature of humanity, the inherent power and dangers of technology, the complex potential of future evolution—but there was something more basic, more fundamental that resonated in her young mind.

Despite the industry that had risen around those two astounding people, Weyland and Yutani believed in the power of the human spirit to overcome any obstacle. They believed that technology, while helpful as a tool, was nothing without the purity of thought and meaning and emotion behind it. Technology did not enable the user—the user enabled the technology. The human mind, and all its various dependents, was the single most important element in the entire universe. When used in the correct manner, it could move mountains, thread stars, change entire planets. Everything else—self-serving desire, homogeny of belief, and especially corporate greed—were simply impediments to the greatness that human intellect and controlled, directed emotion could accomplish.

Her young mind missed a significant amount of nuance in the whole of the text, and she was constantly forced to scramble out of her parents' study before she could ever finish or truly understand the lengthy book, so her understanding of the words she was reading was limited. But what she got out of it, she applied to every facet of her existence for the rest of her life.

And the more she learned of those impediments to the human mind—especially corporate greed—the more she shunned them. She decided before she was even a teenager that she would dedicate her life to her warped understanding of Peter Weyland and Cullen Yutani.

A few years later, when she was still in school, but her older sisters had left to start careers of their own, Lexa's entire life changed with a single visit to the front door. She'd been home alone, attempting to finish her homework while scoffing at the ridiculously limited nature of the types of questions she was being asked by the obviously biased computer program, when a loud knock startled her, making her suddenly aware that it was much later than she'd realized. Her parents had been attending yet another mandated work function, but they were supposed to be home at least an hour earlier. It was unlike them to be this late. Especially her father, who followed schedules and rules to the letter. Both he and his wife cherished their time with their youngest child, knew that she would soon be leaving to start her own life, like their two older girls had done.

Lexa ran to the front of the house, assuring herself that her parents had simply left their key at home, even though she knew deep down that they had never done that, were both far too organized to *ever* do that, and threw open the door, an excited smile on her face that quickly faded as she stared at the USM officers who stood on her doorstep.

There had been a transport accident on the way down from Gateway Station. The other driver was injured but would survive. Her parents, however, had not.

And just like that, Lexa Phelan was an orphan.

The weeks after that were a blur. Her sisters came as quickly as they could, but the funeral planning was stressful and strained—for all their father's adherence to protocols, their parents had been academic to a fault, hadn't even bothered to draft a will. Maybe they thought they were immortal, Lexa mused on the day of the funeral.

The chaos of those days gave way to suffocating silence as Lexa's older sisters fought over who would take care of the youngest sibling. Both older women were in the middle of starting their own lives—including spouses and children—and neither felt equipped to take on a teenager with a growing chip on her shoulder.

So, Lexa made it easy on them. One night, she just slipped away with nothing more than a backpack full of the most important things in the world to her. Including, of course, the Weyland and Yutani biography.

She made a point of never looking her sisters up, and they either never searched for or couldn't find her. It didn't matter. She was no longer the person she had been in those moments before she'd opened the door and heard the news that the USM officers had murmured. Her promising academic career was a distant memory, and she threw herself into alcohol and manual labor—two things she was surprised to find that she genuinely enjoyed.

Her life soon devolved into a shapeless mess and the years passed in a boozy haze. She worked, she drank, and then she did it all again the next day. Week after week, year after year.

Until the day she came across a flyer that changed her life. It was for an upcoming speech that was being given at a local church—and it guaranteed that anyone who attended would have their mind opened. Half drunk, she laughed at the promise. She'd heard this kind of thing before, particularly from religious institutions, all of which she hated. But there was something about this flyer, or perhaps about the deep hole she'd fallen into since the loss of her parents all those years earlier, that made her decide to give this one a chance.

So, a few nights later, she hopped a shuttle to a run-down church on the outskirts of town and listened as a man talked about the sins of the modern world, and especially of the USM. She lost her breath when the man mentioned Peter Weyland and Cullen Yutani, mentioned aspects of their beliefs that she had only read about in her parents' book—as sacred a tome as she had ever possessed.

The man, who she considered nothing less than a priest by the end of the evening, spoke of Weyland and Yutani's true beliefs, not the perverted corporations that had ascended after their deaths, the greed and the immoral science and the sacrificing of human lives. No, he spoke of the exact opposite. Of the power of the human spirit, and how globalism and slavish lust for more and more advanced technology was actually grounding out what made humanity so unique and so special.

When she left that meeting, Lexa felt reborn. She never saw that particular man again, though she kept an eye out for him as she went to more and more meetings, even started going to some of the demonstrations and protests. She cursed at the brutal USM agents who dispersed them with extreme prejudice. She saw people get hurt. Even saw someone die, a casualty of an overzealous USM officer.

That was the night that she decided to get off Earth.

When she heard about a mining opportunity in a distant solar system, she jumped at the chance. There was nothing she wanted more than to get away from the planet that had killed her parents. There was nothing for her on Earth anymore.

At first, the OST was paradise. She could lose herself in her work—spend long days in the mines, working quadromite out of this strange planet's crust, bonding with her fellow miners. Especially Cosgrove, who was admittedly coarse and brutish, but could be surprisingly gentle and sensitive when they were alone together on long nights in the growing colony.

The original founders of the OST had attempted to create a community that would increase productivity, and they had succeeded in that, but they had also fostered an atmosphere that called back to a simpler time, a time that Peter Weyland and Cullen Yutani had celebrated in their earliest works. Yes, she knew that some critics of this particular biography had accused the author of twisting the two visionaries' words and message, but Lexa knew for a fact that her beloved tome captured the precise nuance that those two great thinkers had always intended. And she even saw a glimpse of their genius here, on this colony in the middle of the universe, millions of miles away from Earth.

And as she lay in her bed one night, mind racing with ideas, Cosgrove asleep next to her, Lexa realized that it was her destiny to take over this colony and transform it into the society that her idols truly envisioned, a paradise that had never really existed before—but finally could.

And she was confident that when people saw its success, her vision would spread to other colonies, and eventually to Earth itself.

Convincing the other miners had been shockingly easy. None of them liked Jennifer Chu—they felt that her managerial skills were blunt and cruel. The emotional abuse, the docked pay, the nights in the underground prison. The quaint little town that the original settlers had built, over many years, lay in disuse—a waste of time, Jennifer declared. They needed to focus on mining, on profit, and those distractions were costing the USM money. Resentment grew.

By the time Lexa was done whipping up her silent rebellion, the takeover was a foregone conclusion. The miners had the desire and the brute force to make it a reality. Yes, a few people died, on both sides, but within twenty-four hours after the siege had begun, Jennifer and her people were locked away beneath the headquarters, and Lexa was in charge.

Her first order of business was to take two days off from mining to get the town up and running again. She treated all her followers to a movie and then an extravagant meal at Delilah's. The hangover the next day had absolutely been worth it.

The months that followed weren't easy, there was no question about that. The damage done to the OST during the short-lived civil war hadn't been inconsequential. And a number of key personnel were now prisoners, so people had to step up. Discussions were had, conversations that lasted late into the night, about who would remain working outside the dome, mining the quadromite, and which would 'graduate' to leadership and infrastructure positions.

A decision was made to keep up a false pretense when the USM periodically contacted them. There was no reason any of the higher-ups had to know what was happening on the OST. As long as Lexa and her people kept delivering the ore, no one would ask too many questions.

And if they ever *did* find out... well, there were plans in place for that, too. Plans that were bolstered when Margaret hacked into Chris Temple's little pet robot.

Lexa found the mantle of leadership uncomfortable at first, but soon discovered that the position was growing on her. She took an interest in matters both large and small, learned every single person's name, and found that the people who were loyal to her also cared about her as a human. It was the first time she felt like she was part of a family since she'd lost her parents decades earlier. And while she wasn't in love with Cosgrove, she enjoyed his company, for the most part, even if he clearly liked her more than she did him.

Everything was going smoothly—until the transport ship unexpectedly crashed near the dome. And Chris Temple entered her life.

A loud noise pulled Lexa out of a troubled sleep.

She sat up immediately, eyes darting around the room, finally resting on the digital clock on the bedside table. 4am. Who the hell would be knocking at this hour? No, not knocking. Banging.

She quickly got to her feet and moved as fast as possible to the front door, throwing it open without bothering to look through the peephole, even though she was only wearing a t-shirt and underwear.

Cosgrove stood in her doorway, eyes dark and serious.

Before Chris Temple had arrived, it was more likely than not that Cosgrove would have been sharing Lexa's bed. But if she were being honest with herself, even before Chris had crash-landed on her planet, she was starting to tire of Cosgrove. His neediness, his possessiveness, his violence. It was unattractive, to say the least. When she met Chris, she finally realized that Cosgrove was not, and would never be, the man for her.

"What the hell is going on?" she demanded, her mind slowly clearing from the haze of slumber.

Cosgrove's eyes went up and down her body, only for the briefest moment. She felt violated by his gaze, even though they had once been very close, intimate on more than one occasion. But she didn't like the way he sized her up, the way his eyes went glassy as he did so. She would need to be cautious around this man going forward.

"It's time," he said, eyes now locked on hers. "They've entered orbit."

She was instantly wide awake. Even though she knew exactly what was happening, her mind still went through a mental check list.

The next quadromite pick-up wasn't due for at least three months. And there was no way a rescue vessel had already arrived for the downed transport ship. No one on Earth even knew about its destruction, despite what she told Chris. Lexa had never actually sent the message. No, she had no interest in bringing any additional USM attention to their colony. She didn't need some general to send an elite squad after one of their most highly decorated colonels. If all went according to plan, no one on Earth would *ever* know that Chris was there. And on some level, she was confident that Jennifer and her lackeys, rotting away beneath their headquarters, would see reason, and join them. Eventually.

"Thanks to Alicia, we knew this was coming. Have you finished implementing all the traps we've been planning?"

"Of course," he said, a slick smile appearing on his face. She nodded, didn't smile back. Didn't want to give him any false hope regarding their relationship, even in this crucial moment.

"Good. Meet me at HQ in five minutes," she ordered, then shut the door in his face.

Her mind raced while she quickly got dressed. She recalled the lessons her parents had taught her as a young girl, when she struggled with school. Even when you're up against your greatest challenges, be disciplined. Be smarter. Better equipped. The prepared underdog can not only win, but she can also use the element of surprise to crush anything that stands in her way.

As she threw her hair into a ponytail, her mind flashed to Chris, no doubt asleep in his house. She thought about the kiss he had placed on her lips earlier that night. The memory of it thrilled her, for so many reasons. It was proof that he was starting to come around—to her as a woman, and to her as a leader.

Based on their conversations, she knew he didn't love the USM, despite his many years working for them. He was disillusioned, just like she had been. As they entered this inevitable standoff with the most powerful military force in the known universe, she could use a man like Chris Temple at her side. She and her fellow Weyland-Yutani adherents had prepared for this day, and she was confident she could hold off the soldiers inside the orbiting ship.

But if she was working closely with Chris, in every way possible, she knew that they could not only fend off *anyone* who came after them, but fully, truly build the utopic society she had always dreamed about.

Moments later, she was sprinting the quarter mile from her house to the OST's headquarters.

Inside the command center, her inner circle was hard at work, analyzing data and talking with hushed voices. Cosgrove stood in the center of the room, arms crossed, surveying the situation like a displeased god.

"Report!" Lexa demanded.

"The USM ship is projected to land about two miles away in thirty minutes," Josie Fredericks shouted, her voice vibrating with nerves, long red hair tied back in her signature ponytail. She was a good kid, smart, but she'd been a newbie miner only a few months earlier. Her promotion had surprised everyone, especially her, but she'd stepped up when needed. This situation, however, was unlike anything Josie had ever experienced before. And it was showing.

Lexa pointed at two of her most trusted followers. "Malone! Shepard! Get down to the prison and keep an eye on Jennifer. I wouldn't be surprised to find out she's behind this. If she somehow gets out of that cell, put a bullet in her head. Got it?"

"Yes, ma'am!" they both shouted, and bolted out of the room. Lexa listened to them sprint down the hall, then turned back to her remaining team.

"Is everyone in position? Kids locked away with their parents in the safehouse?" she asked, keeping her voice calm. Even though her stomach was turning, she was the leader of this colony and she needed to project confidence. They would get through this. She was sure of it. But they had to execute their carefully laid plan down to the smallest detail.

"Everyone's in position, ready to go," Josie said, her voice mirroring her boss's confident tenor. "And it would take a nuke to get to those kids." Lexa liked her. She was young, like Milliken, but she had a certain ineffable grit that Lexa recognized and admired. It was possible that Josie would make an excellent third-in-command someday, working for Lexa and Chris. But that was a decision for later. Once this current crisis was handled. "They're scrambling their communications," Josie continued. "Even with the information that the auton provided, I can't hack it."

"That's fine," Lexa said. "Standard operating procedure for USM marines. They have no idea we know they're coming. They think this is just a routine operation."

"Anything but," Cosgrove said, leaning over a computer screen, his eyes glowing in its light, waiting for her command.

"Okay," Lexa said after a moment, every nerve in her body on fire. "We knew this was coming. Time to let everyone know that it's go time."

She glanced over at Cosgrove and saw the smile spreading across his face. Lexa shook her head at him. *Only an idiot welcomes war*, she thought. Regardless, he was a competent tactician and she needed him on her side.

"Do you want to do the honors?" she asked him quietly. As much as she had grown to dislike the man, they had planned this together.

"Damn right I do," he replied, staring at her with desire, mistaking her seriousness for attraction. He withdrew the walkie-talkie from his belt and hit the button. "The marines are on their way. You know what to do. Shoot to kill, watch your back, and protect each other. This is *our* colony, and no one is taking it from us," he said, savoring each word. He let go of the button and the room went silent after a quick burst of static.

After the slightest hesitation, the tension in the room almost palpable, Lexa's team got to work.

18

The USM warship landed in a fury of noise and fire.

The planet's unforgiving winds lashed the vessel, rocks slamming into its hull but doing no real damage. It sat for a moment, powering down, and then a hatch opened, a metal walkway extending and touching down on the rocky ground with a loud clang. A dozen USM marines went charging down, gripping assault rifles, eyes covered with high-tech goggles that connected to earpieces which would allow them to communicate amidst the howling winds and coming conflict.

Their battle uniforms were all black, the absolute latest design from USM engineers, and allowed for maximum protection in key areas, flexibility, and speed. Once they were all on the ground, they stood in a semi-circle and waited, completely silent. After a moment, their three commanding officers walked down the plank, eyeing the scene in front of them.

Beyond the wall of marines, the planet stretched out, a rocky, hostile wasteland. To their left, in the distance, they could see the jagged peaks of dark mountains—where the mining operation was based. That fairly innocuous topographical detail represented trillions of dollars for the United Systems Military. Hidden inside those mountains was literal tons of quadromite, a key factor in the USM's continued supremacy of the known universe.

It was true that at first, this was just another mining colony, like hundreds of others. They had detected quadromite in these mountains, yes, but the actual amount was initially inconclusive. It could have been a little, it could have been a lot.

After a year of almost non-stop preliminary mining, it turned out to be *a lot*.

Once the actual amount of the valuable ore had been reported back to USM headquarters, they immediately invested an obscene amount of money into the colony. When the earliest leaders requested material to build an old-fashioned town, no one in the upper echelons of the USM blinked. The cost was a drop in the bucket compared to the projected profit.

Eventually, however, some bean counter in USM accounting took note of the increased spending on the 'OST,' as the locals called it. He flagged it for his boss, who flagged it for her boss, and that's when the hammer came down. The idea that this colony had a bar, a glorified petting zoo, a goddamn movie theater—*that* was absolutely unacceptable.

They were there to do a job, not throw a fucking party.

So, the USM responded to this new accounting information by sending one of their top mining officials, Jennifer Chu, to oversee the outpost. Chu had always been a little too hard-nosed, but was highly efficient, two of the many reasons why the top brass left her alone once she was situated and had stripped the operation back down to acceptable levels.

Chu believed deeply in the USM ethos and hated everything that had preceded its ascension—especially the principles of Weyland-Yutani. As civil strife increased on Earth, it was good to know that they had someone they could trust running the OST—the profit generated there was also essential to keeping the separatists in their place.

When Chu's transmissions got a little odd, no one at USM headquarters thought much of it at first. She was mercurial, seemed to go through personality shifts every other day, depending on any given situation—it was part of what made her such an effective leader. She could be charming one day, brutal the next. Her mood swings kept everyone around her on their toes. USM brass loved that.

But the actual distress call from her, using a secure and secret channel—that was a very different matter. The USM/Weyland-Yutani division that was plaguing Earth had apparently traveled to one of their most important mining operations. Which, at this precarious moment, threatened the USM's very existence. A cultist uprising on Mining Outpost Omega Seven Tango was absolutely unacceptable.

As a result, they decided to quickly send an elite cadre of marines to the planet, strike these cultists before they even knew what had hit them. Yes, the marines were needed to deal with the strife on Earth, but if the USM lost one of their largest providers of quadromite, the ability to suppress Weyland-Yutani fanatics while also continuing key space exploration missions might be compromised. There was never a question about how they would proceed. The only question was—who would lead the mission. And that question was answered quickly.

Captain Taggert looked away from the mountains and over his right shoulder. In the distance, a couple of miles away, was a large silver dome, like a hunched giant attempting to protect itself from the elements.

The OST.

He had always thought it was a stupid acronym. Lazy and careless—just like the miners who had instigated the insurrection against Commander Chu. They were insane to think they were going to get away with it—but in his experience, fanaticism was never driven by intelligence. It was usually a slavish devotion to an ideal that had already run its course. *Of course* the past always seemed better than the present. Memory tended to wipe away the pain of what life had actually been like. Nostalgia was a dangerous drug.

"Okay, listen up!" he shouted, though he could have whispered and everyone standing near him would have heard his words as clear as a bell in their earpieces.

"I've worked with every single one of you before. You are the absolute best of the best. Now, the USM gives these mining colonies a lot of latitude, but that doesn't extend to armed insurrections. We may not know exactly what we're walking into inside that dome, but on the other hand, the insurgents don't know the shitstorm that is about to come crashing down on them."

"Goddamn right," Parsons said, nodding at his boss.

"Just remember the plan," Taggert continued. "Follow it to a T. We'll get in there, dust these Weyland-Yutani cult motherfuckers, put the good guys back in charge, and then get the hell back home. Easy peasy, no surprises. You all with me?"

"Sir, yes, sir!" they all shouted in perfect unison.

"Fall out!"

The marines moved instantly, running as fast as possible across the rocky terrain as the wind buffeted them, their weapons held tightly in their gloves. Taggert watched them with admiration, pride, and appreciation. Then he turned to Ashraf, who was studying her data pad.

"We good?"

"I'm seeing increased activity on the grid," she said, her voice tight, the way she always got right before an incursion. "It's possible they caught our signal, even though we came in hot and I scrambled our communications per protocol. It's also the middle of the night for them, like you instructed. Still… looks like a bunch of them are awake."

"Makes no difference," Taggert said. "Let's do this."

Ashraf nodded and started off towards the distant dome, Parsons following closely on her heels. Taggert watched his team as they moved with incredible efficiency towards an unknown set of dangers.

"Let's rock and fucking roll," he said quietly to himself, and then hustled off after the others.

The Xenomorphs' emergence into this world had been a violent, bloody affair and they'd been confused at first, pulling themselves from the rendered flesh of their hosts and finding a hiding spot in the shadows of the structure in which they'd been born.

Satisfied for the moment, realizing that it was dark outside of this structure, the twin aliens made their way through a window and moved through the darkness.

They molted in the forest, instinctually shedding their exterior in private, away from the loud, awkward creatures.

The larger of the two Xenomorphs made the first kill, surrounded by other strange creatures, but it had left those alone. The creature he'd killed, who had strangely caressed its head as it fed, would do. They had taken their next victim after a series of loud noises and bright lights, when the gangly organisms had dispersed and were heading away from where they had gathered. The larger waited for the perfect opportunity, when one of the smaller creatures was alone, stumbling along the road after all its compatriots had vanished.

The larger moved so fast that its victim didn't even have a chance to scream. The smaller Xenomorph joined in, clawing at the flesh of the weaker creature, tearing it to shreds alongside its twin.

After the awkward creature stopped twitching on the ground, the aliens began snapping at each other again—confused, frustrated. Angry.

The larger quickly got the better of his smaller sibling but stopped short of seriously hurting her. But the damage had been done and their short-lived relationship was already cooling. Hissing at her brother, the smaller began to move away.

And so they stalked off in opposite directions, more ready than ever to hunt.

Anthony Milliken sat up, grabbing for a weapon that was no longer in his possession.

"Fuck!" he spat, scrambling to his feet, trying to remember exactly what had happened. It took a second and then the memories came flooding back—that asshole Temple had sucker-punched him. The rest was blurry, but Milliken knew that he'd lost the fight. And that his gun was gone.

He looked around, tried to make sense of where he was, which was difficult with the heavy clouds covering the moon. He slowly realized that he was behind the warehouse, close to one of the dome's curved walls. His head was ringing, and he ached all over his body. Regardless, he was going to find Chris Temple and put a bullet in his head. And would smile as he did so.

Blinking several times to clear his vision, Milliken started heading around the warehouse towards the front of the building when a noise in the nearby trees caused him to stop in his tracks. Squinting, he could make out some movement but wasn't sure exactly what it was. Part of him hoped it was Temple, coming back for round two.

He stepped towards the trees and shouted, "Let's go!" when a black shape suddenly rushed towards him, its fangs and claws glinting in the false moonlight. His stomach dropped and goosebumps of terror erupted across his entire body.

The creature slammed into Milliken, who exhaled a brief, shocked scream, and fell to the ground beneath the monster's weight. The young man screamed as the monster began to eat him alive, his cries turning watery as the creature's second set of jaws exploded into his chest.

Overhead, the clouds rolled on.

Chris led Alicia, Jane, and Emma through the warehouse, back towards where they had entered.

"Any luck?" he asked Alicia as they made their way past the partially destroyed transport ship. Alicia took in its battered hull with interest—almost with emotion, it seemed to Chris.

"I am unable to reach the USM forces. I believe they are on their way, but I do not know how close."

"That's okay. Even if they're about to invade, we don't want to get caught in the crossfire. We need to proceed as if they're not coming," he responded, noticing her slight limp. "Are you okay?"

"I do not experience pain the way humans do," she responded, pulling her eyes away from the ship and looking at him. He was still trying to get used to seeing her damaged face and missing arm. He wished he had time to really look her over, try to help patch her up. He was shocked how upset seeing her like this had made him. Maybe if... *when* they made it safely away from this place, he could fix her. He'd taken some basic cybernetics courses during his years in the military. He was no expert, but he could try.

"Well, then you're lucky," he said, and forced a smile. She returned it, taking her hand in his, making his stomach turn slightly.

"But I have definitely changed, Chris," she said, quietly.

He tried to think of a response but couldn't find any words. There were so many questions he wanted to ask, so many things he needed to tell her, about everything he and his girls had been through since they'd last seen each other. But there was no time, and he didn't even know where to begin. Instead, he just nodded, and they continued on, quiet except for Jane and Emma's nervous breathing.

Minutes later, they burst out the door through which they had entered. Chris paused, thinking through their options.

Margaret had said there was a structure to the southeast of the OST with a small ship. It wasn't much of a chance, but it was something.

But he had no idea how to even get outside of the OST, or how his daughters would survive out there. He'd learned enough to know that the air was breathable, but the winds averaged three hundred miles an hour during the worst storms. Any trip outside the safety of the colony would be a challenge, especially with two young girls and a damaged android at his side.

He cleared his mind. First steps first. He had to figure out how the hell to get out of this dome. Making eye contact with each of them, he whispered, "Follow me," and the four of them moved forward and entered the line of trees.

As they approached the end of the forest on the other side, Chris noticed shadowy figures running around the town in the distance and held up a fist. Alicia and the girls stopped, and Chris sat down against a large trunk. "Let's take a quick break, figure out our next steps."

Jane and Emma collapsed into him and clung close but were silent. Chris wondered if they were starting to get used to this kind of trauma, and hated the fact that it might be the case.

"Alicia, can you hack into the OST's mainframe and find us a way out of here?"

"Negative," she responded, her eyes getting a distant look for a moment. "My systems were badly damaged, both by the crash and the experiments that Margaret Livingston was running on me to force her way into the USM's systems. I am sorry, Chris. For everything." She had never apologized to him before—he didn't realize that kind of sentiment was even within her operating protocols.

"You have *nothing* to apologize for," he said. "In fact, I need to thank you for saving us back on the ship. And as for getting out of here, we'll just have to do this the old-fashioned way." He kissed both of his girls on their foreheads. "Are you okay?"

"Yes," Jane said numbly, and he wished he could tell her everything was going to be okay. But lying wouldn't help any of them. And they needed to move fast. This place was a powder keg, ready to explode.

"I wanna get out of here, Daddy," Emma replied, fire in her eyes. The passion made him both proud and sickened. They were both being forced to grow up way too fast. But his absolute priority was escaping this hellhole, so they could grow up at all.

"Me too, baby."

"Perhaps the rightful leaders of this colony can help us," Alicia suggested and Chris nearly laughed at his own idiocy. It was the most obvious answer, and he had also promised Jennifer that he would save them.

Not to mention: the OST headquarters had weapons, and he was betting there were a *lot* of them.

Of course, the insurrectionists would have the same idea. Storming the HQ was a highly dangerous proposition, but they didn't have much choice. Besides, it was still nighttime, though morning wasn't far off. *If the digital projection continues its normal schedule,* he noted to himself.

"Good idea," he agreed, standing up, his daughters following suit. "Okay, let's go, and stay close. We need to move quiet but *fast*."

Both of his daughters took one of his hands and he squeezed their fingers reassuringly. He made brief eye contact with Alicia and realized just how correct her earlier words really were: she *had* changed.

"We can do this," she said, emotion seeming to tinge her voice.

He nodded, and then they were off.

Lexa stared at the screen, at the small green dots that were approaching the OST dome from two different points.

"Report!" she shouted.

"We've got a dozen people approaching, fast," Cosgrove sounded, his voice thick with tension. "Then there are three stragglers. Not sure what that's all about."

"The command team," Lexa said, looking up and around. Despite their careful plan, her people looked terrified. These were not seasoned warriors. But they were strong, and determined, and sick to death of the industrial-military complex. And they had access to some extremely dangerous weaponry.

"Okay," she said. "We can handle them. We know this place better than anyone else. Our ambush teams are in place throughout the colony. These marines are coming in here blind, overconfident, and they're in for a surprise. Just do what we've practiced. They are *not* taking our home away from us. Am I right?!"

"Yes, ma'am!" they all shouted, and the looks on their faces changed in an instant.

"Damn straight," she responded, eyes narrowing in determination, staring at the green dots getting closer. "Now. Let them come."

As his squad neared the 'back' of the dome, Parsons quickened his pace to join the half dozen marines under his command.

They slowed at the exact point they'd studied on the digital map—Parsons was still in awe, all these years into his tenure, about how accurate the USM's information could be. The wind and small rocks continually buffeted but the marines seemed unaffected by the planet's hostile conditions.

The next steps were straightforward. The grid for the entire colony was situated back here, though not easily accessed, and every mission always began with stripping away the most essential element of any enemy operation: power.

Parsons nodded, and his best marine—Moira Campbell—responded in kind, then moved forward, placing her hand on the metal dome, seeming to feel around in a chaotic manner, but he knew it was far from random. She was searching for an exact spot in the dome's hull—and then she found it.

She worked her gloved fingers under an unseen piece of metal, lifted it with an audible grunt, and a hatch came away, which she wrestled from its perch and then threw into the rocky distance once she was able to pry it from where it tenaciously clung. A command panel was revealed, a mishmash of wires and buttons, and a small digital screen that glowed red in the murky darkness of this planet's extended night.

Parsons smiled as Campbell began tapping data into the screen, bypassing security codes as if they'd been written by children. It was just too easy.

The bullets struck before the sound even registered.

Parsons felt them instantly pierce his battle uniform and enter his body at multiple impact points. Falling back, he marveled at the turrets that had emerged from the dome several dozen feet above them. These weapons hadn't been in the original schematics—the ones he and his team had studied for hours on the ship after they'd all awakened from their hyper-sleep—and he realized that these Weyland-Yutani cultists may have been a bit more clever than they had given them credit for.

As he collapsed onto LV-1213's rocky surface, and heard his marines screaming inside his earpiece, he kept his eyes on Campbell, who hadn't been hit, thankfully. She glanced back at him, and he could tell she was wavering—should she continue breaking into the separatists' defense systems, or should she help her boss? Maybe she even considered him a friend at this point.

"Do your job," he managed to say, and he realized in that moment that his lungs were filling with blood. Realized that he was dying.

As the bullets continued to rain down on them, he wondered how many of his marines had been hit—watched as they scrambled away from the tracer fire that seemed to be everywhere around them, like the fireworks he had enjoyed on vacations as a child. It was beautiful, he thought, the fireworks, then and now, and he found himself laughing, even as his vision started to go dim.

He blacked out for a second but fought back, clawed his way back into consciousness. One of his marines was lying nearby, a bloody mess, dead, but the others had found safety, hiding behind rocks or close up against the dome. He wished he knew which of his team members had paid the ultimate price, but suspected he would find out much sooner than he wanted.

He blinked against a sudden surge of pain, and then a surreal feeling of numbness, and focused his eyes on Campbell, who continued to work at the colony's security command console. He had personally selected her for this mission. She was young, and Taggert had questioned Parsons when he'd recommended her for a mission of this gravity, but he hadn't backed down. He knew there was something special about her—he had looked over her records closely, had watched in quiet awe while she took apart the USM's training modules, one by one. She matched previous records set by USM legends, and then surpassed them.

If anyone could knock out this colony's power, it was Moira Campbell.

And then, just as Parsons started to slip away, Campbell stopped working and looked over at him. The turret had stopped firing—out of ammo, most likely.

How much time has passed since it started? he wondered. Seconds? Minutes? It didn't matter. It had done its job. It had killed one of the commanding officers of the USS *Weaver*. But he needed to know before he gave up the ghost—had it been worth it? Had Moira completed her job?

They stared at each other, her eyes glimmering behind the goggles, and finally she nodded, her gentle voice filling his helmet as he began to fade away for good.

"Power is out inside the dome, sir," she said. Had her voice warbled with emotion? Unlikely, he realized—but possible. He wished he'd had the chance to get to know her better. There were so many things he would have asked, so many things in his life he'd left unfinished. He thought about his wife and three children, was filled with love for them, and regret that he would never see their faces again.

And then Campbell's voice sounded in his ears a final time. "You are authorized to let go, Doug."

"Thank you," he whispered, and then he was gone.

1 9

Chris watched the OST headquarters for a moment, trying to decide how to proceed.

He didn't want to bring his daughters into a potential firefight, but he wasn't about to leave them alone out here, even with Alicia. He had no choice—they all had to stay together.

They were hidden along the wall that ringed the HQ, the town sprawled out to their left. It was still dark out, but the digital sky was starting to lighten ever so slightly. The situation was bad—and every instinct told him it was about to get a lot worse.

"Alicia, I need you to listen to me very carefully. When I get us into that building, I want you to take the girls into an empty room, lock the door if possible, and keep them safe until I get back. Can you do that?"

"Daddy, no!" Jane insisted. "I want to stay with you!"

He knelt down quickly, then glanced over his shoulder,

back at the town, where sporadic figures appeared and disappeared just as quickly. Something was about to go down.

"I know you do. And you won't be in that room for long. I just need to talk to some people, so they can help us get out of here. Okay? I promise I'll be as fast I can. Lightning fast." He made a sound that sounded only vaguely like electricity, but she smiled anyway and hugged her dad. He hugged her back, and then Emma joined them. He felt something on his shoulder and looked up. It was Alicia's remaining hand, and she was staring at him intently.

"Alicia...?" he said.

"I will protect them... and you... with my life, Chris."

The words sent a chill down his body. No, not the words, the emotion behind them. He stood and stared Alicia in the eyes.

"I know you will," he said, looking at her face, at the perfectly imperfect cuts and burn marks. Then he blinked and set his jaw, turning back to the headquarters. "Okay. Stay close."

Just as he was about to take a step towards the structure, there was a high-pitched whining noise, and then all the power inside the entire dome went out. The digital nighttime sky glitched once, twice, and then was gone.

The four of them stared up and around in awe at the planet's real atmosphere. Three moons hung in the sky, covered and uncovered by racing gray clouds, lighting the scene in a strobing, muddy light. In the distance, rocky terrain spread out in every direction, high-velocity wind sending rocks flying, hitting harmlessly and soundlessly against the now-transparent domed roof.

Emma pressed her face against her father's leg. Jane moved closer, too.

"What happened?" his older daughter asked.

"I don't know," Chris responded. "But this actually makes what we're about to do a *lot* easier."

"Okay, everyone stay calm!" Lexa shouted as the emergency backup lights kicked in, covering the entire command center in an eerie red glow. "We knew this was coming."

"I can't wait to kill every single one of them," Cosgrove said, barely more than a whisper.

"Exactly," she answered, her mind ticking off imaginary boxes, all the plans she'd made in anticipation of this day. "Okay, let's do it. Get the weapons. Get into position. We take these fuckers out and go back to living our lives."

"And what about the next time someone from the USM shows up?" Cosgrove asked.

"We take them out, too," Lexa answered, eyes nothing more than black buttons in the scarlet-tinged darkness of the room.

Taggert and Ashraf watched as two of their marines cut through the thick steel of the OST dome.

It wasn't the fastest way in, but they weren't about to knock on the front door. For all they knew, the insurgents had figured out they'd arrived and were waiting with guns locked and loaded. They'd studied the manifests before they'd even left Earth. There were plenty of weapons in this colony—probably too many, if anyone asked Taggert. They were here to mine quadromite, after all, not fight in an intergalactic war.

Still, people got paranoid. And with good reason, it turned out. But the problem with having a lot of guns is that they can then be taken, and used against you.

"How much longer?" Taggert shouted, looking around. He was getting antsy. He didn't like sitting idle, even when his team was moving the mission forward. He had been in many battles in his career, had seen too many friends blown to pieces while they were waiting for the action to start.

"Two minutes, tops!" one of the marines shouted, not looking back, his attention completely on the job at hand, sparks flying in every direction as he leaned into his work. Taggert looked at Ashraf. She glanced back at him, but before he could say anything, several beeps sounded inside his earpiece. A long one and then three short bursts. A private message.

"Go," he said, calm, but he knew this couldn't be good news. Messages on the private comms rarely were.

"I managed to cut the power," the strained voice said. It was Campbell. One of their absolute best, and Parsons' favorite. They all knew she had a bright future in the USM. The way she sounded, however, made it clear that she'd only given him half the message.

"But...?"

"Lieutenant Parsons was killed by enemy fire. I'm sorry, sir."

Taggert felt his vision go hazy, the sound of his marines cutting into the metal falling away, his mind tunneling. Parsons had been one of his closest friends in the military, someone he had known since almost the beginning of his career. They had served on their earliest missions together, had always watched each other's backs. Taggert hadn't thought there would ever be a day when they wouldn't be there for each other.

He blinked away the fuzz in his head, focused on the task at hand.

"Did you take down the enemy combatant?" he asked, voice cold and hard.

"It was an automated turret, sir. But yes, I disabled it. We lost Bridgeman, too."

"Damn it," Taggert responded. Ashraf took a half step towards him, but he held up a hand, telling her wordlessly to wait. He knew she was going to be as gutted as him—but they had a job to do. They would mourn later.

"What should...?" Campbell started to say and then faltered, her voice cracking slightly. This type of behavior was very unlike her. He'd never seen her hesitate, even under intense enemy fire.

"Go ahead," he said, his tone softening. As a commanding officer, he knew when to push, and when to listen.

"What should we do with his body?" she asked.

Taggert ground his teeth, a wave of anger washing over his entire body. The image of Parsons' body sprawled across the rocks on this random planet filled his mind, but he pushed it away.

He was going to make these insurgents pay for what they had done.

"Leave it," he ordered, tone hardening again. "We'll retrieve when we're done. Proceed with your mission. Taggert out."

He tapped a button on his arm console and opened a private channel to Ashraf.

"What's up, boss?" she said, taking another half step towards him.

"Parsons is down."

"*What?*" Ashraf said, and started to say something else, but stopped herself. Then, as the two marines finished cutting through the metal hull of the dome: "What's the plan?"

"The plan?" Taggert said, raising up his massive weapon. "Let's go kill every last one of these motherfuckers."

Chris sped through the shadows, listening as Alicia and his daughters followed close behind.

The inside of the headquarters was mostly dark, but he could see a red glare through some of the windows.

Emergency backup lighting, he reasoned. He saw shadows, too, moving quickly. They were scrambling inside, trying to figure out what was going on. Hell, maybe they thought it was him. This entire colony was unraveling much faster than he could have anticipated. That was fine. Chaos would only help him get his family out of there.

Reaching the building, he suddenly realized that he wouldn't be able to hack the security pad, and his spirits fell, his shoulders literally sagging. He'd been so concerned with getting his girls out of the OST, so surprised by the sudden loss of power, that he hadn't thought to come up with a plan B. He silently cursed himself—he never would have made this kind of amateur mistake during his active military service.

Chris glanced at the windows again but they were no help—a little too high up and they looked like they were made out of thick plastic, not glass. There was no way he could break through them.

"I'm sorry," he said, turning back, looking Alicia in the eyes. "I was going to enter the security code, but with the power out, I can't get us in. I'll think of another way out of here. Maybe if we—"

Alicia stepped forward, gently nudging past him. She gripped the door handle with her one hand, and then stopped herself.

"Stand back," she instructed.

Chris took each of his daughters by the hand and moved several steps away. Knowing that the lack of power in the

OST would reduce the door's resistance, and rerouting a significant amount of her remaining power into her one arm, Alicia pulled in a single, swift motion, ripping the door off its frame with a loud metallic ripping sound. She dropped the mutilated metal slab on the ground with a clang.

"Shall we?" she said, smiling at the Temple family.

Chris stared at her with appreciation and awe. She was so different than she'd been before—it almost felt like he was looking at a totally different entity. And yet so familiar, too. It was an odd experience, one that he found himself enjoying despite everything that was happening.

"Let's go," he said and moved forward.

The four of them entered the darkened hallways of the OST's headquarters.

Lexa exploded out of the back emergency door of HQ, making a beeline for where her troops were hidden in pockets in and around the town square.

The automatic rifle felt good in her hands, and she was glad that she'd spent so much time refining her shooting skills at a makeshift shooting range on the farm—a daily routine she had instituted for her troops after she'd taken over. The image of John Wilkins' shredded body rose unbidden in her mind.

She wondered absently if the USM forces could be responsible for the man's death, but it made no sense. Why would they sneak in, murder a random OST citizen in a horrible manner, leave, and then wait several more days to attack?

And it wasn't Chris's doing. She already knew him too well. He was obviously capable of great violence, but there was no way he was responsible for that senseless death.

No, there was something else going on here. She'd get to the bottom of the mystery.

But first, she had to save the colony.

Her colony. The word just felt so right in her mind.

The OST wasn't the USM's and it certainly wasn't Jennifer Chu's. In fact, they were one and the same. All they cared about was funding their never-ending conflicts—on Earth and in the far reaches of space. Conquer and profit. Then repeat. Over and over again, until all individual thought and belief was stomped into nothingness.

Lexa was protecting a sacrosanct way of life. She was trying to save something that had been almost entirely crushed by the unfeeling wheels of 'progress.' This colony was proof that there was another way to exist. And she would die to preserve it. Or kill.

As she ran, she glanced momentarily up at the dome, half-expecting to see Earth's nighttime sky projected there. Instead, she was greeted with LV-1213's dark clouds and intermittent moonlight, wind-strewn rocks bouncing off the thick, oblong plastic that covered the colony. Biting down her anger at the invaders, she looked back down and continued sprinting forward.

Every single adult under her command had a gun of some kind or another, and she thanked her past self for making that very thing a priority. She had a small army at her disposal and would use it as and when necessary. These USM assholes were in for a rude awakening. They weren't coming up against a bunch of pasty bureaucrats like Jennifer Chu and her sycophants. Lexa and her team were hardened miners, the kind of people who had been scrapping and fighting and using weapons their entire lives.

As she approached the center of town, she stopped in her tracks, squinting through the intermittent light and darkness of the rapidly moving shadows overhead. Up ahead, on the side of the street, some kind of misshapen figure was hunched over, what looked like a tail jutting out of its backside, its long face—if it could be called that—pushed down into something lumpy and gyrating. If she was seeing correctly, the black arms ended in six-fingered claws, which intermittently ripped at whatever was in its grasp. Lexa took several slow steps forward, trying to make out what she was seeing.

No. Not *what*ever was it its grasp. *Who*ever.

It was Tom Sturben, who had greeted Chris Temple on his first morning in the OST—a miner who lived alone, a quiet man but a hard worker, with kind eyes. But right now, those eyes found Lexa's and widened, agonized hope rippling across his face as he realized that help might have arrived. The man opened his mouth and tried to speak as the creature burrowed its face farther into his stomach, but only wet rasps came out. Instead, he raised his hand towards Lexa, as if she could take hold of it and save him from what was happening.

The monster must have noticed the man's gesture because it withdrew its elongated head from the gory mess that had once been Tom's body and looked over towards Lexa. She gasped when she saw it, the clouds parting at that moment and the planet's three moons fully revealing the blood-spattered creature that crouched only a few yards away from her.

It was like every nightmare she'd ever had as a child come to life. The creature's long eyeless head tilted in her direction and what almost looked like a smile appeared amidst the shadows, a second set of terrifying jaws slowly retracting back into its bloody maw. Its long claws glinted in the moonlight, dripping red onto the carefully manicured grass where kids and their families had been running and playing only a dozen or so hours earlier.

Was this some kind of new weapon that the USM had created and unleashed on them? She'd heard rumors of unsavory genetic experiments that the military had been running but had dismissed them. Monsters that would be used for incursions…?

Ridiculous.

But as she tried to make sense of the gore-soaked scene in front of her, it suddenly seemed a lot less ridiculous. The

USM was clearly willing to do whatever it took to destroy Lexa and her groundbreaking Weyland-Yutani ideals.

All the more reason to kill every single one of the marines, and all of their 'pets.'

"Please… help…" Tom finally managed to utter. The words were weak, barely articulated, but somehow rang clear in Lexa's ears.

In response, the monster raised itself to its full height, its opaque, leathery skin glinting in the moonlight. It slashed at the dying miner's stomach, ripping it open in a spray of arterial blood. The man gurgled a final time, his body convulsing, and then he went silent and still.

Shocked by the creature's speed, Lexa began to raise her weapon, but the monster was already sprinting towards her, crossing the distance between them in a matter of seconds. Lexa managed to get a shot off, but the behemoth had already reached her, slamming into her with concussive force and causing the bullet to careen off towards the now-transparent dome ceiling. Lexa rolled with the blow, doing everything in her power to hold onto her gun. She knew that if she lost control of it, this would all be over very quickly.

Getting to her feet faster than even she could have anticipated, adrenaline pumping through her veins, she saw the creature's clawed hand heading directly towards her face. She took a half step back, raising her gun, and fired, feeling the comforting pressure of the recoil against her right shoulder.

This time, the bullet found its target, striking along its elongated skull. It was only a glancing blow, but the monster emitted a high-pitched scream and dull yellow and slightly green blood spurted out of the wound. Lexa smiled for a moment but then a few drops of the liquid hit her face and immediately began to sizzle. Pain erupted on her cheek where the blood had landed, and soon her scream joined the creature's.

Acid! This fucking thing has acid for blood, some distant part of her mind instructed her as she desperately wiped it away with gloved fingers. *Those USM scientists really are sick fucks.*

Despite the excruciating pain, she got off several more shots from her weapon, but the creature scampered off into the shadows, clearly not having enjoyed its first encounter with Lexa Phelan.

"That's right. Run, you piece of shit," she said, whipping off the compromised glove and holding her bare hand against her face, which pulsed with pain.

She staggered forward a few steps and looked down at the unlucky miner's corpse. His body and face were covered with so much blood that she wouldn't have recognized him if she hadn't seen him a few moments earlier.

"I'm sorry, Tom," she whispered, and then turned away. She would mourn later—for him, and for so much else that had gone wrong this night. But for right now, she had work to do.

20

Taggert and Ashraf entered the OST, silent, followed by six of the best-trained humans who had ever lived.

Ashraf could feel the rage radiating from her boss. She wanted so badly to talk with him, to tell him that she was hurting, too. They had shared many, many hours together over the years, and they were close, like siblings, but that would have to wait. The mission came first—everything else was secondary. Perhaps she would talk to Taggert on the way home, after the marines were tucked away in their hypersleep chambers, and she could express the pain that was roiling around in her brain.

She cleared her mind, scanned her surroundings. They had reached a concrete walkway surrounded on either side by small trees, and up ahead she could see squat buildings and what looked like a quaint town center. For a moment, she wondered if she was hallucinating, or looking at a digital projection.

She'd read that this colony was richer than most, had sunk a considerable amount of money into the esthetics of the place in an attempt to replicate late twentieth/early twenty-first-century Earth, but she hadn't really believed it. The idea seemed too fanciful, a waste of resources. But looking at it now as they moved forward in silence, she had to admit that the small town that had been created here was more than just charming. It felt like she had stepped back through time.

She glanced up at the ceiling, half-expecting to see Terran dawn breaking—she had also read about the digital roof. Instead, lightning danced from one dark mass to another, and streaks of moonlight appeared and disappeared over and over again as small breaks would appear, then vanish again in the cloud cover.

The six marines were spread out in front of her and Taggert in a semi-circle, moving quickly but cautiously, their weapons held at the ready. It was bizarrely quiet inside the dome. Outside, the sound of the wind and the flying rocks had been nearly overwhelming, but as they approached the fake town, there were no people, no sounds. It was like walking into the middle of a museum exhibit.

She re-opened the direct channel to Taggert.

"Weird," she said.

"Yep," he responded, glancing at her, the assault rifle held tight in his grasp. "I've never seen anything like this— except maybe in old movies."

She tried to imagine him sitting on a couch, spending a couple of hours watching entertainment from centuries earlier, and couldn't quite manage it. He seemed like the kind of man who only did two things: work and sleep.

"Weird... and quiet," she added.

At that precise moment, gunfire broke the silence, flashes of light appearing from multiple spots up ahead—from behind buildings and trees, from rooftops, from hidden spots along the ground.

Two of the marines collapsed and chatter erupted in their helmets as the other four went into action, spreading farther out and laying down return fire. Ashraf and Taggert sprinted forward and grabbed one injured marine each, dragging them behind a small copse of trees as the other jarheads took the fight to the unseen insurgents.

"Johnson!" Taggert shouted, his forehead nearly touching the marine's as he leaned down in concern. "Report!"

"I... I'm okay, sir," the young marine responded, already starting to get to his feet. "Just got the wind knocked out of me."

"Phillips?" Ashraf asked the soldier below her and he gave the same answer, was also up seconds later. Taggert eyeballed the dents in each man's battle uniform and silently thanked the USM engineers who had designed them. Still, there was only so much damage their suits could take, not to mention multiple vulnerable spots to allow for maximum flexibility and speed.

Rapid gunfire continued to sound as the four marines

at the front of the action coordinated their attack using the code words that had been drilled into them by their three commanding officers before they all went into hypersleep.

Taggert made eye contact with Ashraf, then the two battered marines.

"Let's go fuck these shit-bags up."

Chris stalked through the crimson-lit halls of the OST's headquarters.

They had found a small room that locked from within, and had instructed Alicia and his girls to stay inside, stay quiet, and not open the door unless they heard a specific series of knocks—a signal he'd made up in the moment.

He kissed Jane on the cheek, then Emma, and looked deep into Alicia's eyes. He couldn't believe the depth that he found there. Had it always been present and he just hadn't noticed it? Or was she actually evolving? He wished he had the time to sit down with her, talk with her, ask her questions. And he regretted that he had never really taken the opportunity to do so back on Earth.

She had vowed to protect them, again, and those few words filled him with a surprising amount of confidence in their safety. It didn't hurt that she was stronger than ten men, even with only one arm. She would let herself be destroyed before allowing anything to happen to Jane and Emma. She had already proven that, more than once.

Besides, he didn't have a choice. What he needed to do inside—and below—this building, he had to do alone.

As he turned down another hallway, he suddenly heard voices up ahead, and froze. He was close to the room with the weapons locker, but getting caught before he reached it wouldn't do anyone any good.

Hugging the shadows of the hallway, he waited for a moment, and listened. He couldn't hear Lexa's voice but there was one voice emanating from the nearby room that was hard to miss. Cosgrove. The man was quietly shouting enraged orders at whoever else was in the room, followed by fearful and slightly panicked murmurs of assent.

Chris thought back on his tour of the building a couple of days earlier, closing his eyes and reconstructing it as if he were looking down on it from the sky. This was another skill that had been hammered into him during his training. Even a casual glance at the inside of a building allowed for an almost-architectural rebuilding in his mind.

The voices were coming from the command center—and that was where he'd seen the weapons locker.

He thought about his options. He could easily avoid that room and make his way down into the prison, but it was the wrong order, and he knew it. His primary objective was to gain access to a weapon—or multiple weapons, if possible—and then effect the breakout. The good news was that everyone in the room was clearly preoccupied with something else—most likely the invasion from OST marines. His enemies' disarray was one of Chris's only advantages at this moment.

He took a silent, deep breath and prepared himself to assault every single person in the nearby room. It was unfortunate, of course, that he didn't even know exactly how many combatants were in there.

He thought about Alicia and his girls waiting for him in a dark room on the other side of the building, and then rushed forward, ready to take out anyone who got in his way.

Especially Cosgrove.

Lexa looked at the two dozen miners who stood in front of her, eyes full of anticipation and fear, and ignored the pain as it radiated across her face.

Despite the high-tech weapons they held, these were her weakest fighters, the ones who had shown the least natural skill or improvement in marksmanship, hand-to-hand combat, and tactical thinking. The rest of her makeshift army, her very best troops, had already engaged the enemy, springing the multiple traps they'd been formulating since the success of their insurrection against Jennifer Chu.

She listened to weapons fire in the distance, knew that her hidden troops were executing their plan against the USM interlopers. She was so proud of her people—the ones who were already fighting, and the ones who stood in front of her right now. Every single one of them had gone into this wide-eyed. She thought back to those early days after she had assumed command of this colony. Standing in the large communications room in the OST headquarters, warning them that this day would eventually come. She'd told them that it could be weeks, it could be months, or even years—but there was no avoiding it.

And now, here they were. She only hoped that her best fighters, who were currently up against what she assumed were marines, were holding their own. Then again, they had the advantage of knowing this colony like the backs of their hands.

"The time has come!" she shouted. "You are trained! You are ready! But be careful! They have not only weapons but also genetically altered creatures working on their behalf. But these monsters are vulnerable. Remember your training. Only pull that trigger when the enemy is in your sights. And most importantly: no mercy. They will kill you without a moment's hesitation. Are you with me?!"

"Yes ma'am!" they shouted back, confident but clearly still frightened—and yet no one bolted. They all stood, waiting for her orders.

"Positions," she finally said, and her inexperienced soldiers scattered in every direction. Lexa was filled with a surprising surge of emotion and appreciation for these people who had started as strangers on the transport ship all those years ago, and who were now her closest friends.

Her family.

One of them doubled back and approached her. A young woman, Francie, who had escaped an abusive marriage and come to LV-1213 all by herself, a miner who had been among the first to sign up when Lexa started the quiet whisper campaign against Jennifer.

Francie stopped in front of Lexa, concern wrinkling her forehead. The assault rifle looked awkward in her small hands.

"Your… your face," the younger woman said, raising her arm slightly as if she wanted to touch her boss's cheek but then clearly thinking better of it. "Are you okay?"

Lexa smiled, clapped her subordinate on the shoulder. "I'm fine, Francie. Thank you. But please… be careful out there."

"I will," the younger woman responded, her face hardening. "This is my home now… *our* home. And I'll kill anyone—or anything—that tries to take that away from us."

"That'a girl," Lexa responded, and then Francie sprinted off into the darkness, towards the increasing sound of gunfire.

Lexa pulled the walkie-talkie off her belt and radioed Cosgrove.

"How's it going?" she asked, keeping her breathing calm, even.

The radio spit a burst of static and then Cosgrove's voice came through, strong as ever. "Not bad at all. It sounds like the traps are working exactly like we planned. These USM assholes had no idea what they were walking into."

"Excellent," Lexa replied. "Shall we show them what we're really capable of?"

"Engaging Margaret's override," Cosgrove responded.

"Love it," Lexa said. "Phelan out."

After a moment, all the power in the OST came roaring back to life, but the lights and digital sky were modified in a specific manner, allowing Lexa's troops to hug the pre-arranged darkness while illuminating their enemies as much as possible. She could hear the gunfire increasing, more screams filling the air. All according to plan.

She looked around. That creature that she'd battled, whatever it was, was nowhere to be seen. As she checked her ammo, set her jaw and headed towards the fighting herself, she prayed there weren't any more of them. She already had too many enemies on this planet.

And she desperately hoped that Chris Temple wasn't one of them.

If he was even still alive.

Taggert wasn't amused.

Despite the last words he had spoken out loud to his troops, he and his team were not, in fact, fucking these shit-bags up. The traitors had been expecting this kind of assault. These uneducated miners had set a series of incredibly clever traps, and placed themselves in hiding spots that were not only difficult to see but also afforded the insurgents the ability to effectively press their attack on the surprised marines.

And now the goddamn power had been turned back on.

Taggert had never been one prone to overconfidence, but he now realized he had walked into this situation a little too sure of his own superiority—certain that the USM's training and weaponry would be more than enough. He cursed through clenched teeth as he hid behind a building, bullets ricocheting off the bricks around the corner from where he crouched.

He checked his weapon. Still plenty of ammo but it was meaningless if he couldn't get a clear shot or close enough to his enemy to engage. He wasn't even sure how many of his marines were still standing. The chatter in his earpiece had reached a fever pitch, and then gone silent altogether. It appeared that the insurrectionists had managed to hack their communications systems at the same time they turned the power back on, which shouldn't have been possible based on what he knew about these people—but they were proving to be a lot more resilient than he had expected.

A noise to his right caused him to turn and aim his weapon into the shadows but Ashraf came rushing out, collapsing next to him. She was bleeding from her shoulder but had applied a bandage—a rush job, but it was effective enough. The blood had soaked through but didn't look too serious. Still, he hated to see her like this.

"What's a soldier like you doing in a place like this?" she asked, smiling through obvious pain.

He laughed. In many ways, she was like the sister he'd never had. There were so many things he wanted to say but this wasn't the time. Instead, he resorted to command mode. "We need to take control of this situation. And to do that, we need to re-establish communication with our teams. If these assholes did hack our systems, they must have done it from their HQ."

"I think you're right," she agreed. "So, what's our next step?"

"You and me, we head over there and pay them a little social visit."

"I do like me a good social visit," she said, shifting her weapon, grimacing slightly as she did so.

"You sure you're up for it?" he asked, his voice softening for a moment.

"Pshh, this is nothing. I've had worse papercuts," she lied.

He kept his eyes locked on hers, fought back his feelings. "Okay. I'm going to lay down suppressing fire and then make a beeline for the HQ. I want you right on my heels, doing the same. We'll protect each other's backs, take out their central nervous system, and then close this shit out."

"Roger that," she responded.

"We'll be enjoying a frosty beverage on the ship before you know it," he added.

"Only if you're buying."

Taggert smiled at her, then stood, felt her weight against him as she stood as well. He hesitated a moment, surprised at how important this moment was to him, how important *she* was, then pushed away, out into the unnatural light and the danger, bullets exploding in the ground all around him. He fired back, aiming for the flashes of light from his attackers, and smiled when he heard one of them scream.

Ashraf was behind seconds later, firing her weapon as well, the two of them a well-oiled machine, this kind of high-intensity situation almost second nature to them after all these years. They could hear the remaing marines battling all across this strange little town, some hand-to-hand brawls beginning to break out as well, death struggles that were strangely muted. Taggert wished he could help every single one of his men and women, but he needed to cut off the head of this particular snake immediately. For now, his marines were on their own.

He and Ashraf continued their violent dance towards the OST's headquarters. Overhead, Earth's moon hung in the digital sky, oblivious to the battle below.

21

Chris burst in, going after Cosgrove first.

The lights had suddenly come on as he stormed the control room, which would normally have surprised him, but he was in battle mode, everything around him falling away.

Lights, no lights. It didn't matter. He needed to get his hands on those weapons, rescue Jennifer Chu and her people, and get back to his daughters.

His fist caught a surprised Cosgrove directly on the left cheek, a nasty cracking sound followed by the larger man collapsing in a heap on the floor at Chris's feet. He could feel the shock of the blow all the way up his arm, knew that he had split his knuckles on Cosgrove's face.

Whirling, Chris quickly took in the rest of the room. There were three other people here, all of whom he recognized, but no Lexa. In a way, he was relieved. He knew what he had to do in the next couple of minutes, and he wasn't entirely sure he would be able to unleash the way he needed to if she was here.

One of the younger colonists, Baker, a twenty-something kid who Chris liked, moved quicker than anticipated, bolting for the open weapons cabinet a few feet away. Chris glanced down at Cosgrove, who was struggling to regain his senses, considered going for the bigger man's pistol, holstered on his hip, but dismissed the idea—Cosgrove was strong, and it was possible he would recover and retaliate before Chris even got his hand on the weapon's grip. Instead, he lunged towards Baker, vaguely hearing the other two colonists shouting somewhere in a hazy distance— the kind of aural disassociation that was common for him during battles.

He hit Baker directly in the stomach just as the young man's fingers were wrapping around an assault rifle. They both slammed into the wall, Baker's body taking the brunt of the impact. Chris pressed his attack, landing two more lightning-fast blows into Baker's midsection. The young man slid down the wall, his eyes wide with shock at the savagery of the newcomer's attack, attempting to suck some oxygen into his now-depleted lungs.

Chris reached for the same assault rifle when a fist connected with his own left cheek, catching him completely by surprise. He rolled along the wall, barely avoiding a second blow, and looked up at his attacker. It was Josie, who had been kind and playful to his daughters. But right now, the fury in her eyes was anything but kind or playful. The blow that she had landed on his face was powerful, and he could feel the flesh burning from the impact. Her red hair was pulled back into a ponytail, like it always was, and her face was solemn, like she was doing a necessary job that she didn't particularly relish.

She threw several more punches at his face, which Chris barely parried. She was strong and fast.

Baker started to get up as well. Chris landed a brutal kick across the colonist's face, causing him to collapse once more onto the ground. Josie took advantage of the moment and landed a quick uppercut directly into Chris's solar plexus. His breath exploded out of his lungs, but he ignored the pain, ignored his body screaming at him to inhale. His mind went blank again. It didn't matter how much he liked these people, or at least the people they had been pretending to be. His daughters were waiting for him on the other side of this building, and nothing was going to stop him from getting back to them.

Across the room, he saw Cosgrove starting to get up and reaching for his pistol on his waist, so Chris grabbed Josie by both shoulders, an almost intimate maneuver, and her eyes went wide with confusion. Still out of breath, he shoved her forward, moving along with her awkwardly across the room, until they both smashed into Cosgrove, the three of them going down in an ungainly tangle.

The fourth colonist, an older woman named Janine, hesitated for a moment, watched the three people scuffling on the floor, and then glanced over at the unconscious form of Baker. She had never been a miner, had been hired as an engineer due to her aptitude with electricity, but somehow, she'd ended up as one of Lexa's most trusted advisers. Perhaps it was all the time they had spent together—sometimes with Margaret Livingston as well—getting this colony back up and running after the insurrection. She believed wholeheartedly in the core principles, the *real* principles of Weyland-Yutani. As far as Janine was concerned, however, those principles did not include violence. She stood there, frozen.

"Get a fucking weapon!" Cosgrove screamed from the floor, his voice tight, Chris's arm wrapped around his neck in a vicious headlock.

Janine started and then realized that he was right. Even if she trained a gun on Chris Temple, who she liked—and especially liked his sweet daughters—that didn't mean she would actually pull the trigger. She began making her way to the weapons cabinet.

Chris saw Janine moving towards the plethora of guns and knew his time was short. He didn't think she was a killer, but he had seen people do shocking things in the most intense of circumstances.

Keeping one arm locked around Cosgrove's neck, choking the breath out of the large man, who flailed wildly, landing several painful but ultimately ineffectual blows, Chris lashed out with his free elbow, which caught Josie directly in her nose as the woman brought up a fist of her own. Blood exploded in a violent spurt from the woman's face and she immediately collapsed to the floor, unconscious. He'd probably broken her nose, and he felt bad about it, but she would wake up alive and relatively none the worse for the wear.

Clocking Janine's movement in the corner of his eye, Chris increased the pressure on Cosgrove's neck and the large man went limp in his grasp. Chris didn't let up until he was convinced the man was actually unconscious. He had seen people feigning helplessness before, had seen friends die as a result—and there was far too much at stake for him to fall for anything like that.

Letting Cosgrove's unconscious form roll onto the floor in front of them, Chris quickly got to his feet but saw that he was staring down the barrel of a pistol in Janine's hands.

He raised his arms and took a step towards the final person keeping him from arming himself and heading down to the hidden prison level of the headquarters. In response to his movement towards her, Janine cocked the gun's hammer, her face visibly trembling.

"Don't," was all she said.

Chris took a single step closer, knew he was pressing his luck. But he had come face to face with killers his entire life. Janine wasn't one of them.

He hoped.

"Janine," he said quietly, feeling the sweat trickling down the back of his neck. For a moment, he realized how exhausted he was, but shoved the feeling away. It was essential that he focus on Janine. Nothing else mattered.

Neither of them said anything for a moment, and then they both jumped when they heard automatic gunfire in the distance. Her eyes somehow went even wider.

A wave of relief, and then concern swept across Chris. Based on what both Jennifer and Margaret had told him, the USM was on its way. And now, he surmised, they were here.

For a moment, he thought about abandoning his current plan and rendezvousing with whoever was leading this platoon. But he realized that approaching troops during a conflict, even if he was on their side, could be highly risky. He'd heard far too many reports of innocent bystanders getting caught in the crossfire.

No, he had to stick with what he had already decided. There was just too much at stake to change things midstream.

"Those are USM marines," Chris said, risking another step forward. He was now only a few feet away from her. If he made a surprise attack now, he could probably reach her before she got a shot off.

Probably.

"I know that because I used to be one. We don't have a lot of time. *You* don't have a lot of time."

"I'll kill you," she said, raising the gun a little higher, aiming it directly at his face. He didn't believe her, and he didn't think she believed herself either.

"I'm sure you would," Chris said, his voice calm despite the fear that raced across his entire body. "But think about it. You kill me and then... *what*? You fight the marines by yourself? If I were you, I would just get somewhere safe."

Janine's eyebrows beetled in confusion.

"Safe...?" she said, and at that moment, her voice sounded like one of Chris's daughters despite her age. Young. Terrified.

"Yes," he replied, his voice soft, soothing. "Is there someplace here you can go? Hide until some of this... craziness settles down?"

Her eyes flicked towards the other side of the room, focusing on a door set into the wall.

"Put down the gun, Janine, and I'll help keep you safe. Please."

She faltered, her hands trembling. He thought back on a short conversation he'd had with her at Delilah's on the night of the bar brawl, how kind she'd been to him when he didn't know anyone. Part of him wished he could take her with him—but no, he was going to have a hard enough time getting his daughters off this planet. He couldn't afford to feel bad for anyone, especially people who had gone along with Lexa's insurrection. He slowly took one more step forward, now an arm's reach away from her. But he didn't move another inch. He could already see the decision in her eyes.

And a moment later, she lowered the weapon, held it out to him.

"I'm sorry," she said, a tear running down her cheek.

"It's okay," he responded, gingerly taking the gun away from her. "And I'm sorry, too. I know you've been through a lot. Too much."

Her big eyes watched him, waiting for their next steps, and he hesitated for a moment, feeling a surge of sympathy for her, but the moment passed. He glanced over at the other three insurgents, still unconscious. For now.

"I don't want to kill you... *any* of you," Chris said, staring directly into Janine's eyes. "But I'm not sure what else to do. There are things I need to do, and I don't want Cosgrove jumping me while I'm doing them." He raised the gun she'd just been holding, pointing it at her, though he had no intention of pulling the trigger. "So, you see, Janine, I'm in a bit of a bind here."

"Wait!" she said immediately, raising her hand and pointing at the door she'd glanced at a minute ago. "That's a small office. Plenty of room for all four of us. I have a keycard... in my pocket... I can give it to you. You can lock us in. And once it's locked, you can't open it from the inside."

He kept the gun trained on her. "That works. Give me the card. Nice and slow."

Janine reached into her pocket, a little too fast, but he wasn't worried about her. He was more concerned that Cosgrove might wake up and immediately attack. Janine moving fast actually wasn't the worst thing in the world. Her fingers emerged with a small plastic card and Chris stepped forward, taking it from her.

He ushered her to the smaller office, instructed her to sit down in the chair on the other side of the room and keep her hands flat on the desk. She complied without saying another word. Placing the gun in his belt on the small of his back, Chris dragged the three unconscious insurgents into the office as quickly as he could, keeping his eyes on Janine as well. She wasn't going to make a move. She seemed elated that she was still breathing.

Moving the first two was relatively easy, but by the time he'd dragged Cosgrove across the room and into the smaller room, Chris was sucking wind. But it was done. He wouldn't need to worry about them and hadn't been forced to kill anyone. He thanked whatever god was watching, if any were, for small favors.

"Good luck," Janine said quietly as Chris swung the door shut.

"You too," he said, and then closed the door, swiping the card over the pad on the wall. It beeped and the small light turned red. He stared at it for a moment and had a vision of Cosgrove pulling an identical card out of his pocket. There was no way to know for sure that Janine was telling the truth.

Chris moved over to the weapons cabinet and got a better look at what was housed inside. His eyes widened as he made a mental inventory.

"That's what I'm talking about."

He had to move quick. He needed to get back to Alicia and his girls. But first things first. He grabbed one of the pulse rifles, a model he'd used more than once on missions back on Earth and on other planets as well. He knew this weapon inside and out.

Without even looking, he adjusted the settings and stepped back towards the sub-office. He'd have to be careful, make sure not to set the entire headquarters on fire. He pulled the trigger and a tight line of flame arced out of the gun's nozzle, hitting the metal doorhandle. After a moment, it melted into a deformed mass, and he released the trigger, inspecting his handiwork as smoke drifted up from the weapon's barrel. He swiped the card again and the small light turned green, then he pushed on the door, but it was still locked tight. No one was getting out of that room, or into it, without an axe or a battering ram.

Chris headed back to the weapons locker and exchanged the pulse rifle for a more traditional assault weapon and placed another handgun into his belt, mirroring the one pressed against his back. Those would have to do for now.

He moved quickly out into the hallway and headed for the door that would lead him down into the prison wing. And to the people who would hopefully help him get the hell off this planet.

Hands trembling, Francie fired back at the marines, bullets tracing above her head like lines of glowing string, an incessant barrage that filled her senses, culminating as a distant buzz in her ears, behind her eyes.

She was hunkered down behind the large rock at the center of town. Looking around her as she reloaded, she couldn't believe that she had been standing here a day earlier, celebrating with friends, playing games, and drinking a little too much moonshine.

Her hangover was long gone now, adrenaline wiping it away as if it had never existed. She could see a handful of her fellow rebels spread out across the town square. They continued firing at the marines, who they had pinned down inside Delilah's, where Francie had eaten so many meals, had made so many memories.

A handful of the USM forces had attempted to sneak through the restaurant to ambush them, but the rebels knew this town too well, knew every nook and cranny of the place, so the 'surprise' was anything but. And now the rebels had these soldiers surrounded, their guns pointed at both entrances, front and back. They also knew secret ways into the building, so one by one, they were working on their own sneak attack. Up and around the soldiers. It was going to be a blood bath. But for now, they needed to keep them inside the building. Squeeze them until they bled out and died.

And then they could go back to living the life they had worked so hard to build here. Despite the Originals.

That's what they called the people rotting away in the prison beneath the headquarters, though no one had told Lexa or Cosgrove that. It was a term that only the lower-level colonists, like Francie, used. They liked having their own language, their own terms. It drew their rough-edged army even closer. Their leaders didn't need to know about all the nights they stayed up, talking about the depths and beauty of the Weyland-Yutani philosophy. Francie loved all her fellow Rebels. Every single one of them. Would kill for her comrades. Would die for them.

Her weapon fully loaded again, Francie peeked over the bullet-riddled rock and unleashed another barrage towards the line of buildings she had grown to love so much. When all of this was over, they would rebuild—just like they had done before, when they'd ousted the Originals. It might take weeks, or months, or even years, but they would put this place back together, piece by piece.

As she fired towards the shadows inside the restaurant, Francie thought about her parents, God rest their souls, glad that they weren't here to see this. They'd been part of the very first group of settlers, the ones who had worked so hard to terraform this barren rock into something resembling a home. They had been instrumental in putting the dome together, and then the town within it. She had only been a baby then, but she watched, year after year as she grew, in awe, as her amazing parents worked to make the OST into what it was today. Or, at least, yesterday.

Today was very different.

As Francie continued to fire, feeling like she was going deaf from the proximity of her assault rifle, she thought back to the last time she'd seen her parents. She was sixteen, almost done with school, looking forward to a life of mining and maybe even eventual management. But every kid, no matter whose, had to start with mining. The true Weyland-Yutani philosophy had already started to sneak in, even back then. No one was better than anyone else, and no one was born more privileged than another. Each person had to make their own decisions, work hard, and write their own fate.

The night her parents never came home was etched into her memory. She had tried excising it, blotting it out, with alcohol or other extreme experiences, most of which she now regretted. But there was no escaping the moment that Jennifer Chu knocked on the door to her childhood home. There'd been an accident in the mine her parents were inspecting. It was just bad timing, nothing more, and it was a tragedy.

Francie remembered crying into Jennifer's shoulder, but also blaming the woman who held her that night. It was *her* fault. As the OST's leader, why hadn't *she* been there? Why had she sent her parents for the inspection? She'd heard the three of them arguing at night, downstairs, while Francie pretended to be asleep.

They'd always had different philosophies, but the gulf between their beliefs had only grown wider in recent years. The last fight between her parents and Jennifer had been particularly bad. And Francie had always wondered, vaguely, if perhaps it hadn't been an 'accident' at all. Jennifer Chu could be brutal, vengeful. But there was no proof, just an itch at the back of the young woman's mind.

So, when Lexa approached Francie a few months later, talking about losing her own parents, and murmuring quietly about a revolution against Jennifer, against the USM itself, and its self-serving, inhumane ways, Francie was all ears.

Lexa had become something of a mother to Francie in the days after her parents' passing, and in the days since. This fact made her hold the weapon even tighter in her grasp, take even more careful aim at the soldiers hidden inside the building across the street.

As she paused to reload yet again, she heard a crackling— at first she thought it was a result of the damage to hear ears—but realized it was her walkie-talkie, strapped to her belt. She quickly reached down and grabbed it, hitting the button on its side and shouting into its face.

"Say again!"

"Francie! We've taken out multiple targets inside the restaurant!" It was Lexa. The sound of her strong voice filled Francie with her own surge of confidence. "I want you to make your way through the alley between Delilah's and the movie theater. Stay in the shadows as much as possible. The rear guard needs backup, and you're the closest. Do you copy?"

"Roger that, Commander," Francie responded, shoving the new clip into her weapon, realizing that the battleground had gone quiet for a moment. The silence felt wrong after so much chaos. She peered up over the rock. She couldn't see any figures inside the restaurant now, and couldn't see any of her fellow rebels anywhere either. It looked like everyone was on the move. Which was fine with her. She could use the break from dodging—and firing—bullets.

Tensing her body, allowing her mind to go blank, like Lexa had been teaching her at the firing range on the farm, Francie suddenly burst forward, keeping her weapon close to her chest. She half-expected to get hit by a bullet as she sprinted for the alleyway, but she didn't hear a single shot, much to her relief. Seconds later, she reached the row of buildings and slipped into the fluctuating darkness of the alley.

She stopped, allowing herself a moment, and decided to briefly catch her breath before heading towards the back of the building. Even though it had been a short run, she'd gone as fast as she could, and her lungs burned. She wondered how much was actual fatigue and how much was just the stress of being in her first real firefight. Once again, she wished her parents were there. She hoped they were proud of her, if they could even see her from wherever they were. In an autonomic response to her thoughts, she glanced up at the sky, and was met with large dark clouds, which mostly covered the digital projection of the Earth's moon. The light fought to escape, and the darkness of the sky made her stomach drop, the thoughts of her loving parents falling away, replaced by a gnawing fear.

Francie set her jaw, looked back down, squinted into the deep shadows in front of her. She'd passed through this alley more times than she could remember, since she was a kid, but it looked virtually unrecognizable now, a dark hole inside which anything could be hiding.

She shook these defeatist thoughts away and moved forward, slightly crouched, her gun held out in front of her. She'd seen the suits that the USM soldiers were wearing. There was no doubt in her mind that those outfits were bullet resistant and helped protect them from LV-1213's elements, but they were also bulky and probably not optimal in a confined space like Delilah's.

Francie moved forward silently, her eyes and ears straining for the slightest noise. None of her compatriots would be in this alley—Lexa had told her, and her alone, to cut through here. So, if anyone appeared, if anyone made a noise...?

Francie would blast the hell out of them and ask questions later.

Halfway down the alley, suddenly bathed completely in darkness, Francie heard a slight noise up ahead and froze. Her finger found the trigger, but she didn't fire despite her thoughts only moments earlier. She did, however, crouch even farther down when the noise repeated. She began to squeeze the trigger when an image flashed in her mind: killing one of her friends who was cutting through this same alley despite not being instructed to by Lexa. Emotions were running high—was it so implausible that someone would sneak through here in an attempt to get away from a bad situation?

No. She couldn't take that chance. They'd all had Lexa's rules hammered into their brains: if the USM shows up, follow orders. Do not ask questions. Kill or be killed.

If Francie heard the noise one more time, she would fire. A single shot. The burst from the gun would illuminate whoever was in here with her, if anyone even was.

She waited. She knew that only seconds passed, but they felt like hours.

Then, just as she stood up straight and was about to move forward, telling herself that she'd only imagined the sound, she heard it again. Without hesitating, Francie pulled the trigger, and sure enough, the flash from the bullet leaving the barrel lit up the scene for the briefest moment. And what she saw sent a wave of terror running through her entire body.

There wasn't another person in the alley with her, but she wasn't alone.

A massive creature stood only a foot or two in front of her, long claws glinting in the momentary light from her weapon's discharge, oblong head staring down at her, what looked like a serrated tail rising up behind it like some kind of nightmarish scorpion.

In the brief moment between the initial shock of light and pulling the trigger again, Francie screamed, a sound of pure terror, and she could hear the creature scrabbling through the darkness towards her. Before her finger could fully engage the weapon, something raked across her forearm—those horrible claws, she assumed—and the gun went flying out of her grasp. She screamed again, in pain now, feeling the blood erupt out of her rendered flesh. She still couldn't see anything but got down to her knees, arm throbbing, and started to feel around for the weapon. If she could only get her hands on it, get off a volley of shots, she might be able to get out of this damn alley, get some help.

Just as her fingers found the rifle, something connected with her shoulder and she felt another stab of incredible pain. Whatever had just hit her sunk in and through the skin, exploding out through the area next to her shoulder blade. She tried to scream again but couldn't catch her breath. As she was lifted off the ground, she wished desperately she could at least see what was happening. The complete darkness was almost as bad as the intense pain that she felt in her shoulder and arm.

"Please..." she finally managed to say, the tips of her booted feet still touching the ground, trying futilely to find purchase.

The claws gently wrapped around her face. She was surprised by the tenderness of the touch. For a moment, she wondered if the creature had suddenly had a change of heart. Perhaps it had just been scared, too, and now it was going to let her go. Her wounds were bad, yes, but she suspected she could survive them. She just wanted to live. She would gladly give herself up to the USM if it meant surviving this horrible experience.

"Please," she said again, more urgently.

Above, the clouds parted momentarily, false moonlight reaching the alley. Blinking against the sudden illumination, Francie wished it had stayed dark.

The monster's face was directly in front of her, its fangs parted, drool dripping down onto the ground. She could see a second, smaller pair of jagged teeth inside the creature's jaw.

"Oh please…" she said a final time.

Overhead, the moon fell victim to the incessant cloud cover, bathing the alley in complete blackness once again.

22

Chris made his way down the stairs that led to the underground prison.

He moved as fast as possible while also attempting to make no noise whatsoever. He had no idea if any of Lexa's troops were down here. He'd gotten lucky last time, it was the middle of the night, and the colony wasn't under attack by the USM.

When he finally reached the bottom, he took hold of the assault rifle in both hands once again and moved forward through the corridor. The shadows felt especially deep down here, and he ignored the sweat that was already rolling down his face. He didn't remember it being quite so hot during his last impromptu visit.

When he reached the corner that led to the cells, Chris slowed down, crouching just as he'd done the previous time, and peered into the larger area. Just as he'd feared, two of Lexa's guards were there, holding their own weapons, one of them standing near the bars, the other a few feet behind his comrade. Jennifer was saying something quietly to the guard closest to her, but he cut her off with a shout.

"Shut the fuck up!" he yelled, bringing his gun closer to her face. "I don't want to hear your goddamn USM propaganda!"

Chris didn't want to engage in a firefight, especially with so many unarmed prisoners standing close to the guards, but he was also painfully aware that his daughters were somewhere above, waiting for him to return.

He moved forward, ready to do whatever it took to complete his mission. This was a feeling he'd felt so many times before—probably too many times. If they made it off this planet, he hoped to never feel it again.

"Drop your weapons!" he shouted. "Now!"

The man near the cells turned and immediately brought his weapon to bear on Chris.

You idiot, Chris thought ruefully while pulling the trigger of his weapon, putting a bullet between the man's eyes, which went wide in silent surprise before he slumped to the ground, dead before his body had even ceased its downward trajectory.

In a smooth motion, Chris turned his gun on the other guard, who had his own weapon half-raised, a look of abject terror on his face. He was young—so damn young.

"Please," Chris pleaded. "Drop it. I don't want to kill you, too."

The kid thought about it for a moment that seemed to stretch out forever. His eyes flicked over to his dead comrade, to the prisoners, and back to Chris. Silence filled the room, each person's eyes little more than dark holes in the weak lighting. For a moment, Chris was certain that the young colonist was going to relinquish his weapon. Maybe he'd even help get the prisoners out of there and they could all leave this planet together, figure out a better place to go.

But then the kid's eyes hardened, and his muscles tensed. Chris knew exactly how the next few seconds would play out. He knew, and he hated that he knew.

The guard began to raise his weapon, screaming something that Chris couldn't even hear as his own mind went combat fuzzy once again. The man's scream was cut off as a bullet entered his head before he even had the time to aim the gun at his enemy. Chris watched the second body fall, wracked with guilt and regret but already moving forward, refusing to stall his mission because of this poor brainwashed kid. Later, maybe in a few hours, or days, weeks or even years, he would wrestle with the choices he'd been forced to make in order to save his family.

Ignoring the blood that was already pooling along the floor, Chris checked both men but couldn't find a set of keys on either of them. He stood and stepped towards the prison cells. Jennifer watched him from under a furrowed brow.

"I know that wasn't easy, but it was the right thing to do," she said quietly.

"Get back," was all he offered by way of a response.

She and the other prisoners did as he ordered, and once they were pressed against the back wall, he fired into the locking mechanism, then kicked at the door, which swung open, its hinges creaking as it went. He repeated the process several times, as fast as he could.

The prisoners poured out.

"We need to get upstairs before Lexa can retaliate," Jennifer said. "The USM marines should be here any time now."

"They're here," Chris corrected. "And it sounds like there's a full-blown war brewing out there."

"Good," Chu responded.

Chris shook his head, always suspicious of people who welcomed conflict into their lives. But he said nothing, simply finished firing on the last of the locking mechanisms for each section of cells. Soon all of the prisoners were free and running for the stairs that led up to the OST's headquarters.

Chris closed the two guards' eyes before following the prisoners up and out of the underground holding facility.

The looks on each of their faces were burned into his mind, but he shoved them back, compartmentalized them with the faces of all the other enemies he had been forced to kill during his many years in the USM. He could remember every single one of them.

As he followed the other people up the stairs that led to the headquarters, he realized that hatred was starting to take seed in his heart. Hatred for the United Systems Military, and for the Weyland-Yutani cult, and for every organization, military or otherwise, that forced its members to kill in its name. He wanted to be done with it, to put violence behind him, and just be a dad. He knew how unrealistic this thought was, but he desperately yearned for it anyway.

Reaching the top of the stairs, hearing the excited shouts of the people he'd just freed, Chris glanced into the room where he'd just battled Cosgrove and the others. The door to the small office was still welded shut, and now Jennifer and her people were ransacking the weapons locker, stripping it bare in a matter of minutes. Chris wondered if Cosgrove was awake by now, seething at the sound of his former bosses taking control of the headquarters once again.

Whatever. Not his problem.

"What are you doing?" he asked Jennifer. "The marines can handle this. Let's focus on getting out of here, getting safe."

"Not happening," Jennifer said, gripping a weapon as if it were her child, a smile spreading across her face. "Lexa and her little idiots are going to pay. This is *my* colony."

Chris started to say something, to tell her she was being an idiot herself, but he recognized the look in her eyes. She *wanted* to fight, and nothing he could say was going to change that.

Instead, he turned and sprinted back towards the room on the other side of the building, where Alicia, Jane, and

Emma were waiting. He'd been gone for fifteen or twenty minutes, but it felt like hours. He couldn't wait to hug his daughters, to tell them he loved them and that he was going to get them out of there, and to tell Alicia...

Tell her *what*?

Some part of his mind knew the answer but held it back from conscious thought. Instead, he ran faster, turning a final corner and seeing the door at the end.

When he reached it, his stomach dropped. The small inset window was cracked, the glass spider-webbed from a recent impact, and the room was full of smoke. He tried the door, but it was locked—just like he'd instructed Alicia. He pounded on it, shouting, his mind going red.

"Alicia! Open the door!"

But there was no movement within, other than the roiling gray and black smoke. Without even thinking, Chris slammed his shoulder into the wood, hearing it crack against the impact. Then he repeated the movement a second time, shouting loudly as he did so. On the third try, the door shattered open and Chris tumbled into the room, losing his balance and falling to the ground. The smoke was even thicker than it had appeared, and he immediately started coughing, blinking against the stinging air.

"Jane! Emma!"

There was no response, but he found the source of the smoke a moment later. A small fire blazed on the far side of the room, where an explosive device had clearly blasted into the building. His eyes calculated the projectile's trajectory and he walked towards the far wall, the smoke dissipating slightly as he moved. When he reached the other side of the room, he stopped in his tracks, stomach dropping with fear.

A large, jagged hole was etched into the wall, obviously a result of the fighting that was escalating out across the OST. And splayed across the broken brick and concrete beneath the hole was a blood-soaked man still holding a gun, eyes lifeless.

Something had happened here. Something very bad. But there was no sign of Alicia and his girls. Chris wracked his brain, trying to imagine where they could be, looking around desperately. As the smoke in the room began to clear slightly, he noticed something on one of the walls. Writing. A single word, written in red.

No, not just red. It was written in blood.

MOVIE

It most certainly had not been there when he'd left the room earlier. Someone had written it, most likely after the explosion that had carved that uneven hole in the wall. He wondered who had killed the colonist on the floor. Ultimately it didn't matter.

Although the bloody word on the wall was an odd sight, Chris knew exactly what it meant. Knew exactly where he needed to go next.

Taking his assault rifle into his hands once again, he jumped down onto the ground, setting his jaw against the increasing gunfire in the distance. Squinting at the increasing amount of smoke that hovered over the entire OST, he could see figures running, screaming, firing weapons at each other, the civil war raging.

Chris Temple began running as fast as possible towards the center of town.

Or what was left of it.

Taggert and Ashraf moved among the shadows that led up to the OST's headquarters.

The sounds of battle all around them were only increasing but their eyes were locked on their target. If they could gain tactical control of the HQ and then take control of not only their comms but also the outpost's power, they could coordinate the next phase of their assault from a stronger position. Right now, running around in the dark against a surprisingly well-trained enemy, they were struggling to regain the upper hand. They needed an advantage.

Taggert held up his fist and Ashraf immediately halted, crouching down close to the ground next to her CO. He nodded towards the windows of the headquarters and her eyes followed, spotting an increasing number of individuals inside. There was no weapons fire within the building, at least not right now, but there was no way of telling who was actually in there, or which side they were on. Rushing inside, even if they had superior firepower, seemed ill-advised.

"What next?" Ashraf asked, her voice hushed.

Bullets exploded against the ground near them and whizzed past their heads. They both hit the ground and shimmied forward, taking refuge behind a section of wall that bifurcated the building off from the rest of the colony.

"Goddamn it!" Taggert shouted. "How the hell did they creep up on us like that?"

"They're better prepared than we... than we..." Ashraf stuttered, then went quiet.

Taggert pulled his gaze from around the wall and looked at his XO. Blood pooled out of her side, just below her ribs on the right side.

"No," he said, barely a whisper. Then: "Talk to me," more confident, as if he was willing her to be okay.

"I can't feel my legs," she responded, tears filling her eyes, reaching up and touching his cheek. He was only a few years older than her, but she looked so young right now. He fought back tears of his own. There was no time for that. Bullets were hitting the wall but not going through. For now.

"You're just in shock," he said, though he knew it was more than that. "I'm gonna get you out of here, get you patched up. As soon as I kill these motherfuckers. Just stay with me, okay?"

Taggert withdrew his pistol and fired blindly around the corner of the wall and the counterfire stopped for a moment. It was unlikely that their attackers knew that one of them was hit. They wouldn't risk coming around the wall. At least not immediately. But their caution wouldn't last forever.

When he looked back down, Ashraf's eyes had gone glassy. It was a look he had seen too many times before. He knew what it meant.

"No," he said again, and now the tears fell. "Riya, please..."

"It's okay, Jim," she responded, a sad smile arcing onto her face. She still had her fingers on his cheek. They were so warm, so soft there. He placed his free hand on top of hers.

"I don't want you to leave," he said.

"I know," she whispered, her eyelids closing. "I'm sorry."

Her body went slack, her hand falling away from his face. Taggert looked down and saw just how much blood had flowed out of the relatively small hole in her side. She was gone. It didn't seem real.

He laid her down as gently as possible, a wave of rage rushing across his entire body, his vision blurring. Taking a moment to close her eyelids completely and say a short prayer, he then re-holstered his pistol and took hold of his assault rifle again. Whoever had done this was going to pay. He didn't give a fuck about the politics of this backwater colony, or who was fighting who—he was going to find out who put a bullet into Ashraf and execute them himself.

Taggert came around the corner, spraying bullets as he did so, screaming. He saw dark figures retreating through the shadows.

"Come on, you motherfuckers!" he yelled. "Let's end this!"

* * *

Tracer fire filled the air above and around Chris as he sprinted in the general direction of the movie theater.

It was hard to get a clear sense of where he was. The amount of smoke had only increased since he'd left the headquarters. Keeping as low as possible, he still breathed in some of the toxic air and fought from coughing. His long-ago training echoed in his mind: *Do not make yourself a target.*

A dark figure erupted out of a nearby shadow, making a beeline for him. Chris whirled, aimed his gun at the figure, finger on the trigger. A USM marine appeared as the intermittent moonlight washed across parts of the colony. The man had apparently lost his gun, and quite possibly his mind as well. His face was almost completely covered in blood—a head wound most likely. Even when not severe, they were the injuries that bled the most. He held a nasty-looking knife in his hand and his eyes were locked on Chris, a murderous look glowing from beneath the streaked crimson flesh.

Chris wrestled with the idea of firing on the man but couldn't bring himself to do it, even though he knew his life was in immediate jeopardy Even injured, a marine was a highly dangerous individual. Chris knew this better than most, knew the kind of training they went through, and how deadly they were with a knife in hand.

"Drop it!" Chris shouted. "I don't want to—"

But the man didn't stop, didn't even slow, just lunged

blindly. He was big, but clumsy in his pain, and Chris sidestepped the attack easily, using the marine's momentum against him. The man hit the ground face first but turned over almost immediately. However, before he could register what was happening, Chris connected a massive punch to his face, delivering him into instant unconsciousness. The knife fell from his suddenly slack fingers.

"Sorry," Chris said, kicking the weapon away, and then continued his hasty trip to the movie theater, which vanished from view once again as the cloud cover increased.

Lexa sprinted away from the HQ.

She had hoped to get inside, to take control of the situation again, but had been surprised to find two of the USM officers heading there, too, attempting to hide within the deep shadows she'd programmed to keep her own people safe.

Lexa had a couple of the better-trained miners with her and when she saw the two marines, she quietly instructed her subordinates to spread out, count to ten, and then open fire on the enemy.

The plan had worked perfectly, and based on the reaction of the man who came out gun blazing moments later, they had succeeded in taking out the other one, the woman. The man—a captain, based on the stripes on his arm—looked supremely pissed at losing his comrade.

Well, Lexa thought, *I'm pretty pissed, too.*

She had lost sight of her two soldiers but that was fine. They knew what to do. And she preferred working alone anyway. She circled around to the back of the HQ but then hugged the shadows as she saw a line of people streaming out.

Shit.

It was Jennifer, leading her own troops out of the headquarters—and they were holding all of Lexa's weapons. It was painful to see them back in the hands of these USM sycophants.

"Heads up," she whispered into her walkie-talkie. "We've got OG forces on the ground. They escaped somehow. Hunker down and take these fuckers out. All of 'em. And then we go back to our lives."

A chorus of Yes ma'ams came back to her and she nodded, proud of her troops.

As difficult as it was, Lexa waited until the last of Jennifer's forces left the building. And then waited another full minute, just in case there were any stragglers.

Finally, she moved forward and slipped inside the OST's headquarters. Her headquarters.

Taggert fired as he ran.

It was hard to make sense of what was going on amidst all the smoke, but he could hear screams coming from almost every single direction. He cursed himself for what felt like the thousandth time that night.

He'd led too many easy missions lately against soft Weyland-Yutani cultists back on Earth. Those battles had been straightforward, and he had lost only two soldiers in the past couple of years—though each of those losses had hurt him deeply. They'd come into this situation thinking they had the upper hand, but they had been wrong. *He* had been wrong.

Now, on this mission out here on a rock floating in the middle of outer space, he was losing to a bunch of hick miners. And losing badly.

Then again, maybe they weren't such hicks after all. They had pulled off a successful insurrection and now were holding their own—*more* than holding their own—against some of the best-trained marines Taggert had ever had the privilege of leading.

Regardless, his mission hadn't changed: kill every last one of them.

Or as many as he could before they took *him* out.

2 3

Chris made his way around the squat collection of buildings, hugging the shadows as much as possible.

The sounds of battle still echoed throughout the night but back here, right now, there was no one to be seen. He did notice a few bodies strewn across the ground in the distance, over by the trees that led to the warehouse in the distance. Part of him wanted to head over there, see if any of those people were alive—regardless of which 'side' they were on—see if he could help them.

But he turned away. Looking at the back doors to the establishments he'd been frequenting, and enjoying, for the past several days, he did a quick mental calculation. He'd memorized the layout of the buildings' fronts, back when Lexa had given him the initial tour—which felt like a million years ago. But he'd never really taken the time to focus on the back of them, a mistake in retrospect.

Zeroing in on one of the doors close to the center, he hustled forward and tried the handle.

Locked.

Chris grimaced as he heard movement coming from the colony's one alleyway, followed by hushed but strained voices. He didn't have time to think it through. He kicked the door with all his strength, and it splintered off of its lock, swinging open into darkness like an unhinged jaw.

He ducked inside as fast as possible and then slowly closed the door behind him, attempting to shut it completely, though it was impossible due to the damage he'd just done to it. Still, it stayed in place—for the most part. Someone would have to look closely to notice that it had been smashed open.

Chris made his way down a short hallway, gun brandished in front of him, but it was quiet inside, and fairly dark. The lights in here were older, not new and bright like the ones at the headquarters, which made sense. This theater was a luxury—a luxury that seemed ridiculous and indulgent now that the colony was engulfed in war.

He walked up three steps, which led him into a small office, still barely lit, and he moved slowly past a small, cluttered desk and into a second hallway, which led into a larger foyer. Across the shadows, he could see the glint of glass—the front doors, through which intermittent flash of gunfire could be seen, and then heard a half second later.

Most of the light came from the theater itself, which was off to his right through still-open doors. A movie was playing, though there was no sound.

Gripping the assault rifle tightly in his hands, Chris entered.

On the big screen, a black-and-white movie he didn't recognize played, actors' mouths moving wordlessly. The theater was completely empty, and his stomach sank. Had he misunderstood the message in that room back at HQ? Had Alicia or one of his girls even written it? If he'd been wrong, that meant he had *no* idea where they were. Or if they were even still alive.

He pushed those thoughts out of his mind.

No.

He had to believe they were here. It made the most sense, and he relied on logic to keep him, and his loved ones, alive. If he were them, he would stay out of sight, stay safe until help arrived. Until *he* arrived.

"Jane!" he called out in a frantic whisper. "Emma!"

Seconds later, two heads popped up from between the first and second rows of seats, and a wave of relief washed over Chris.

"Dad!" Emma practically screamed, followed by Jane shushing her with just as much fervor.

Chris sprinted down the aisle, throwing the rifle's strap over his shoulder. He was aware that it was bouncing unceremoniously against his body and didn't care. He rushed down the row between seats and grabbed both of his girls in a massive hug, holding their bodies close to his, tears filling his eyes. They were sweaty and dirty, and it was the best thing he had ever smelled in his entire life.

"Oh my god," he whispered. "You're okay."

Behind them, Alicia stood up as well, a smile on her scarred face. Letting his girls go for a moment, Chris reached up, placed his hand on the android's cheek.

"I was hoping you got the message," she said, her voice soft. "I was hoping you would come for us."

"I got it," he answered, stepping closer to her, his girls still clinging to his sides. "And I will always come for you. For all of you."

Alicia took a step closer to him but at that moment, a sound at the back of the theater made them all freeze. Crouching down, with the other three following his lead, Chris looked over, a huge lump filling his throat.

A Xenomorph was stalking into the theater, dragging a body along. Chris couldn't believe what he was seeing, cursed himself for assuming the thing had died.

"Get down," Chris whispered. "*Now*."

The flickering light continued to fill the massive space as the four of them hugged the floor.

"How did that thing survive the crash?!" Chris whispered to Alicia.

"It is not the same Xenomorph," the android responded, just as quietly.

"Not the same…?" Chris murmured, his mind swimming. "How did it get here?"

"I do not know."

As the creature's footsteps filled the otherwise empty and cavernous space, Chris berated himself silently. He should have fired at the monster the moment he'd seen it, but his protective dad brain had kicked in, shoving the soldier part of his mind away for a moment. He was exhausted, not thinking straight, but that was no excuse.

Locking eyes with Jane and then Emma, he tried to formulate a plan but his mind had gone gray and fuzzy. He held up a single finger to his lips. It was essential that they all remain absolutely quiet. Perhaps the creature would turn around and leave after doing... whatever the hell it had come in here to do.

But no, he couldn't sit and wait. He'd been trained to take action when in danger. He'd seen the consequences when fellow soldiers sat back and hoped for the best. It rarely ended well.

The creature had stopped moving but a new sound followed—a wet stretching. Chris glanced over at Alicia, gave her a quizzical stare, but she just shook her head. She didn't know what was happening either. He looked her over. She looked so vulnerable with her scarred face and body, and with her one arm, which he now noticed was wrapped around Emma, outstretched fingers touching Jane's shoulder as well. Even after all she'd been through, she was still protecting his girls.

Slowly, painstakingly, Chris arched his neck up, an awkward maneuver that strained his legs as he attempted to see over the line of chairs without revealing anything lower than his eyes. He couldn't see the Xenomorph at all, and despite the strange, liquid sound still emanating from somewhere, a part of him grew elated by the idea that perhaps the monster had already left. But that was ridiculous, and he knew it.

His eyes searched the stark shadows of the theater, moving his neck as little as possible, until he realized that the creature was standing very near to them, close to the wall, its body camouflaged almost perfectly in the black and white flickering from the film.

The movie had cut to a nighttime scene, so the theater was even darker than it had been moments earlier. Chris squinted, trying to make out what the Xenomorph was doing—and then he realized that it had somehow created what looked like a chrysalis against the wall, the corpse wrapped up in it like a fly caught by a spider.

Wait. No. Not a corpse.

The person's eyes fluttered open, then closed again. Whoever it was, she was still alive.

Chris clenched his jaw, sat back down on his haunches. He couldn't wait any longer, had to take action. There was still a chance he could save that poor girl. He ran through his choices, none of them good.

He couldn't get his assault rifle off his shoulder without making the kind of noise that would alert the creature. He knew from extensive research in his previous life, and from the experience on their transport ship, that these monsters were incredibly fast. He needed as much time on his side as possible. Once it became aware of him, he would only have seconds to act.

Slowly, he reached down and withdrew the pistol from where it was housed against his stomach.

Alicia noticed and tilted her head as if calculating his thought processes. She started to pull her arm away from Emma and move to get up, but Chris leaned forward as fast as he dared and gently pushed her back down, shaking his head as he did so.

No, his eyes told her. *You've already done enough. Sacrificed enough.*

He took a long, deep breath—touched both of his girls' cheeks gently with his free hand, and then exploded into action, freeing himself of the rifle at the same time, which clattered to the ground as he moved.

He fired the handgun as he moved, not even fully upright before the first bullet hit the Xenomorph's stomach. The creature screamed as its acid blood shot out, hitting the floor and bubbling, smoking, hissing. He wished he could have started with a headshot, but he feared that a blow at that height might result in the deadly blood hitting the already hurt woman who was currently wrapped up in the creature's cocoon. Not for the first time, he cursed the lack of good options at his disposal.

The creature screamed again—or was it Chris's daughters screaming—or maybe everyone was screaming—and rushed towards him, its fangs and claws glinting in the light from the movie rolling along oblivious next to and above them. The monster now clear of its victim—or clear enough, Chris hoped—he fired again, aiming for its head, but just as he feared, it was too fast. The bullet merely glanced off its elongated skull, barely doing any damage at all.

Now in the aisle, he stopped moving and fired a third shot that hit the Xenomorph in its shoulder, spraying more lethal blood, and then the creature was upon him, its claws streaking across his face, drawing an instant gush of blood that got into his eyes. He crashed into the alien with his full momentum, and they collapsed onto the floor, rolling unceremoniously towards the front of the room, drops of the creature's blood hitting him and instantly burning through to his skin.

Chris screamed and rolled away, feeling waves of pain wash across his body, whipping off the long-sleeved shirt. He'd lost track of how many bullets he'd fired—a rookie move—and hoped he had enough to finish this monster off. Continuing to shimmy backwards, he blinked through the pain and pulled the trigger, but nothing happened—just an empty click. The Xenomorph seemed to recognize what this meant and lunged towards him, an otherworldly scream emitting from deep in its throat.

Chris tossed the gun away as he scrambled backwards, closer and closer to the large wall that housed the movie screen. He reached back, grasping for the pistol on the small of his back as the creature's fangs grew nearer.

The alien's imminent arrival appeared as surreal flashes in the flickering light, almost like a movie scene itself. Chris got his hand on the gun and swung it around, but he knew the spatial realities of this moment. Get his finger on the trigger, aim and pull. That would take a second, maybe two. He'd be dead before then.

He just hoped that Alicia was already shepherding his girls out of the theater. He hoped they weren't even inside the building anymore.

Still, he wouldn't give up. Even if he got off a single shot with his dying breath, it would be worth it.

Just as the Xenomorph's claws were about to latch on his face, its momentum suddenly halted, and it even stumbled back a step. It made no sense. Chris didn't care. He put his finger on the trigger. As he tensed to fire, he noticed something behind the monster, and the alien turned its head too.

Alicia held the creature by the end of its tail with her one hand, her face showing the strain as she held the incredibly powerful organism back from Chris.

"Do it," she managed to get out as the monster turned to face her, raising its claw up, screaming again—a sound of pure rage.

A direct shot would have put Alicia in danger and Chris refused to do that, not again, so he hurled himself forward, crashing painfully along the ground, knocking the wind out of himself, and pointed the gun up, pulling the trigger over and over again as fast as he could, rolling away as he fired.

An arc of bullets sprayed out, several hitting the creature in the head, the blood splattering away, hitting neither Alicia nor Chris, and the creature collapsed to the ground, a final whimper emitting from its double jaws.

Dead.

Letting go of the empty gun, letting it clatter to the ground, Chris crawled forward, avoiding pools of alien blood that still hissed and smoked as they burned through the concrete. Alicia had fallen back down onto the ground and blinked at him, looking surprised but happy.

"Is it...?" she asked.

"Yes. We're safe," he said. "For now."

He reached her and took her in his arms, hugging her. He had never done this before, couldn't remember ever even touching her, but it felt so right. She wrapped her one arm around him and said something, though the words were too quiet for him to hear.

"What?" he said, pulling back.

"I said..." she began, looking down, and then up again, holding his gaze with certainty. "I care about you, Chris. So much."

He opened his mouth, then shut it. He suspected what she was really trying to say but it made no sense—her programming should have made those kinds of feelings impossible, but there was no doubt in his mind that she was experiencing them. His mind raced for answers, but no logical collection of words came together, other than the ones he then spoke without consciously decided to utter them.

"I care about you, too, Alicia."

His own admission surprised him, as much as hers had, but what surprised him even more is that he knew they were absolutely true.

Before he knew what he was doing, he kissed her, and the sensation wasn't what he expected, not warm or particularly soft, but not unpleasant either. He felt emotion welling up in his chest, then gently pulled away from her.

"I'm sorry," he said.

She shook her head gently. "Please don't be."

Chris laughed gently. On top of everything else, it was the first time he'd ever heard her use a contraction.

At that moment, two forms collapsed onto Chris—Jane and Emma, tears running down their faces. The four of them embraced for a moment, the movie ending on the screen above them. After a few seconds, Chris disengaged.

"We need to help that poor girl. And then get the hell out of here."

Alicia helped Jane and Emma up while Chris stood and headed towards the woman, avoiding the acid pools on the floor. She was still wrapped in the chrysalis—face pale, eyes closed—and she looked so young. Not all that much older than Jane, really.

"I'm gonna get you out of here," he whispered and started to grab at the sticky material that held her to the wall. She wasn't moving, at all. He reached out and placed his fingers on her neck.

Nothing. She was gone.

"Goddamn it," he said, then turned away from her, glancing at the Xenomorph corpse on the ground. How many people had died because of these creatures? First it had been Weyland-Yutani's fault. And now the USM's. Two armies were out there murdering each other in the names of those organizations, but they were the same thing, one just as bad as the other.

But at least the monster was dead. One less thing to worry about while he worked to get his family out of this hellhole.

He walked back over between the chairs, collected the assault rifle, and then joined Alicia, who once again had her arm wrapped around the girls. Jane and Emma looked shellshocked, but they weren't crying anymore. Chris fought the urge to take them into his arms as well. He needed them to be strong right now, therefore he needed to be strong, too. Dispassionate. Survival was all that mattered. They could grieve later, when they were safe.

"Come on," he said quietly. Behind him, the credits began to roll on the film. Names of people who had died centuries earlier. "We still need to figure out a way off this planet."

"Now that the power is back on," Alicia responded as they walked back up the aisle towards the door, "I may be able to access the colony's mainframe and find out exactly where that ship is located. I would just need to find a port."

"Roger that," he said, putting his arm around her for a moment, enjoying the feeling of her proximity. His mind went back to all the time they had spent together in the past several years, how close they had been to each other without it ever really registering for him. She had become a friend over the years, a close friend—his closest, really. And he realized that these larger feelings for her hadn't come out of nowhere, weren't a result of the pressure cooker they were all currently inhabiting. No, these feelings had been developing for some time now. He had been ignoring them because part of him had still thought of her as 'just' a machine.

But now, he only thought of her as the person he loved.

2 4

"Step back from the door!" Lexa shouted.

She heard muffled responses from within, waited another five seconds, and then fired at the melted door handle. Within another couple of seconds, she managed to break through enough of the deformed metal and the door fell open with a pained creak. Cosgrove, Baker, Josie, and Janine came running out. Bruised and bloodied but alive.

"Where are Malone and Shepard?" she asked, heading over the computers at the front of the room.

"Dead, I assume," Cosgrove growled, rage filling his voice. "I heard Jennifer and her sycophants rummaging around in here, stealing all the weapons."

"We have plenty of weapons stashed all over the OST, you know that," she responded, attempting to access the system.

"Yeah, and I'm gonna use them to wipe out every single one of these motherfuckers."

Lexa punched uselessly at the keyboard, but the screen continued to ask for a password. "Why can't I get in?!" She shoved the monitor and it fell off the back of the desk and shattered on the floor, sparks arcing out in multiple directions.

"Chu must have hacked back in and locked us out," Cosgrove surmised. "It doesn't matter. They have no idea what's waiting for them. A lot has changed since they were in charge."

"Goddamn right," Lexa agreed, taking hold of her gun again. "Let's go get all of you armed, and then get reacquainted with Jennifer."

"Music to my ears, boss," Cosgrove said, and followed her out into the night.

Chris watched Alicia, wrestling with his admiration for her and his desperation to get his girls out of this hellish situation. His many wounds had stopped bleeding for the most part, and he worked to ignore the pain in multiple parts of his body.

They were hidden inside the small pharmacy next to the theater, which was mercifully empty—ignored by both the OST faction and the USM marines, all of whom were out in the middle of the colony, engaged in a bloody, bullet-fueled battle. Chris had been in the middle of countless wars, but he couldn't remember ever seeing one more savage than this—or one that felt more personal.

Shaking his head at the senselessness, he turned back to Alicia, who had opened a small hatch in her arm, withdrawn a thin wire, and plugged it into a port behind the counter. Jane and Emma clung to him, quiet, waiting for him to tell them what to do, where to go. He put his arms around them and thanked them silently for being so strong. Again.

"Well?" he asked quietly. Alicia had a far-away look in her eyes, her head tilted. He knew that particular tic was just an offshoot of her programming—probably a flaw—but he loved it. Wondered how many times she had done it in front of him and he hadn't even noticed. He would never take her small eccentricities for granted ever again.

"The colony's grid is severely compromised," she answered, her eyes focusing on him, a serious look on her scarred face. "Multiple factions are battling for control of it. But the USM ship is currently unattended. Approximately two miles west of the colony." Her voice lowered to a whisper. "But we're surrounded by massive firefights. There's no clear path to any exit."

Chris nodded as Alicia disconnected from the port, then took her hand. The four of them huddled close together on the floor of the shattered innards of the store. He kissed his daughters' foreheads.

"We're getting out of here," he said quietly but with conviction. He had never believed a spoken sentence more in his entire life. "I don't care what it takes. I'm getting all three of you off this planet. I'm not sure where we're going but I will find us a home. Okay?"

"Okay, Daddy," Jane said.

"Okay," Emma echoed, looking up at her dad, her eyes shimmering with emotion.

"Let's get the hell out of here," Alicia said.

Chris smiled at her, then stood and turned towards the front door.

"As soon as the time is right, we're gonna head out of here in single file. Jane, you stay as close to me as humanly possible. Emma, you stay that close to your sister. Be her shadow. Alicia, you have rear flank. Protect our girls at any cost."

"Roger that, Colonel," she responded.

Chris glanced back, caught the mischievous twinkle in Alicia's eye. He couldn't believe how different she was—or how differently he saw her.

"You might make a good officer yourself," he said, a small smile playing on his face.

She winked at Chris, eliciting a surprised but gentle laugh from him, and then he turned back towards the front door and the battle that raged outside. He gripped the assault rifle tightly in his hands, hoping he didn't need to kill again to get his family to safety.

But deep down he knew how unlikely that wish truly was.

* * *

Taggert put a bullet into another insurgent, smiling as he did so.

The entire mission was FUBAR, but most of his brain had shut off at this point and he found himself running on autopilot. The feeling reminded him of his earliest days in the military, when he'd been let loose by his commanding officers, allowed to do what he did best: take out the USM's enemies and not ask any questions. His bosses had joked that he was a one-man killing machine, and he reveled in the perceived compliment, felt emboldened to work even harder to impress them.

There was a freedom in those early days, a freedom that had been stripped away, little by little, with every promotion he got, every set of eyes that looked up to him for approval, for orders. And now, all this time later, he suspected that he was the last marine standing on this godforsaken planet. He didn't know how it had come to this, and truth be told, didn't want to think about it too hard.

Still, he had to grudgingly give these insurgents credit. They had known the USM was coming, and they had prepared.

Now it was Taggert against the world, and that was just fine with him. He thought back again to some of those earliest missions—in jungles, in deserts, on distant planets. He'd faced worse odds than these before.

The power on LV-1213 was now cutting in and out—either because different factions were wrestling for control of it, or the system was overloaded and attempting to self-correct. Regardless of the reason, the intermittent surges were creating an almost strobe-like effect, a beautiful stretch of Terran stars glitching in and out of existence, momentarily replaced with the dark clouds of this hellish planet, then back to the serene beauty of an Earth that didn't exist anymore. The streetlights kept popping on and off as well—the ones that hadn't already blown out or been blown up—adding to the surreal visuals.

At this moment, as Taggert stalked the streets of the colony, firing at any movement, it was dark, almost completely black within the dome, and he squinted against the deep shadows, willing himself to find his enemies and kill every single one of them.

As he passed a row of houses, he spotted a figure approaching, clearly armed with a weapon that didn't look particularly dissimilar to the one Taggert was holding. They saw each other at the exact same time.

They took aim and some distant part of Taggert's brain was impressed with this person's speed. Despite having killed so many enemies over the decades, he always recognized talent when he saw it, and respected it.

He pulled the trigger, a smooth, easy motion he had effected thousands of times before, and saw his bullet find its target just as pain exploded in his own thigh. He grunted against the agony, refused to allow a scream to pass his lips, and half-collapsed, breathing hard against his suffering. His counterpart's aim had been good—but not good enough, and not as good as his. He knew based on the way the person's body had snapped back that he had landed a headshot.

Propping himself back up on his feet using his gun as makeshift crutch, he staggered forward, hearing gunfire and yelling in the distance. The fighting was continuing unabated—if anything, it was getting louder, more intense.

Taggert limped forward and felt his mind start to swim. He looked down at his leg, something he should have done immediately, but his training was a distant chorus in the back of his mind. In a way, he didn't even know who he was anymore. He was pure emotion, pure rage. Riya's face—still alive, smiling—flashed in his mind and the anger overpowered the pain in his leg for a moment.

Blood was pumping out of the wound in time with his heartbeat. Taggert realized that his opponent had displayed better aim than he had thought—or had pure dumb luck.

His femoral artery had been punctured. He had seen wounds like this before. There was no coming back from it, not in the middle of a war zone. Even if he tied it off, it was too late. He was a dead man walking.

Swearing, he limped forward, determined to see the face of his killer.

Stars dancing in front his eyes, Taggert finally reached the body on the ground, and he slumped down next to it. The power suddenly turned back on, glitching for a second and then remaining on, at least for the moment. A surreal bright blue sky above, dotted with large white clouds, revealed the scene in clearer detail.

His shot had been incredibly clean, a single red-black hole etched into the person's forehead. It was a woman, her long hair covering her face.

Reaching out with trembling fingers, he pushed it back, revealing the features underneath. As his vision started to go dark, he realized that he recognized this woman. Had been looking at her picture, on and off, for months.

Commander Jennifer Chu. The rightful leader of Mining Outpost Omega Seven Tango.

In his anger, his blindness to his own training, he had killed an ally, the woman he had been sent to rescue, and protect. What a waste. What a stupid, pointless waste. All of it.

"Damn it," he whispered, turning over onto his back next to her, almost as if they were intimate partners retiring to bed for the night. He blinked up at the beautiful sky, thought about days like this back when he was a kid, before he had given all of himself to the military. Part of him wished he could go back and do it all over again, maybe take his life in a different direction. But he shook that away, fought against the fuzziness in his tired mind. He was a soldier. Period.

He thought of Doug and Riya, of all the time they had spent together, and a small smile played on his pale face.

"See you soon, lieutenants," he whispered, and then the darkness fully engulfed his mind, and his eyes closed one final time.

* * *

Chris and his family waited for the false daylight to vanish once again.

They'd been watching the sky, looking for any kind of pattern, but it was clear now that there was none. Alicia confirmed that multiple individuals were trying to override an already taxed system, and it was a miracle that there was any power at all within the OST. Despite the irregularity of the intermittent blue sky, there was no question that it was appearing less and less frequently—a good thing for a family of four who were trying to abscond unnoticed while the fighting raged on around them.

After a few more minutes, the gorgeous fake sky blinked out again, replaced by the dark clouds of the long LV-1213 night. Chris squinted at the darkness above for a full minute, then turned to Alicia and his daughters.

"It's time," he intoned quietly.

The small family headed out into the raging civil war.

Chris moved away from the town square and around the row of houses, towards the hospital and then hopefully the front exit. He listened intently to the sounds of gunfire as they moved. During some of his earliest missions, he had been instructed by his superiors to infiltrate a location, steal an item or save a comrade, and sneak back out undetected. There was an art to it, something that was part instinct and part training, and Chris Temple was one of the best his bosses within the USM had ever seen.

As far as he was concerned, however, all those earlier operations were just field tests for this one: the most important he had ever carried out.

After several minutes, as they got closer and closer to the exit, the clouds overhead got even thicker, and the darkness became almost absolute. Without realizing it, Chris slowed slightly, and Jane bumped into him, her arms wrapping around his waist, the trembling of her body immediately palpable.

"Dad…?" she asked, and he could hear her terror. She was always so tough, but right now she sounded like the baby girl he could still picture so clearly in his mind.

"It's okay," he said, though he wasn't sure if that was actually true. He wanted very badly to put this horrible place behind them—and they were so close. But he also knew that this was the most dangerous part of a mission, when you could see the exit ahead and you started to breathe a little easier. "It'll clear up in a second."

He stared up at the sky, as if he could somehow force the moons to appear again with sheer will alone. As if in response to his silent direction, the clouds parted and two of the planet's three moons revealed themselves, their light shining down. Chris looked down at Jane and smiled.

"See? What did I tell you?"

"Look out!" Alicia yelled but it was too late. The butt of a rifle connected with Chris's forehead, sending him sprawling, his own gun falling from his fingers and landing on the ground nearby. He felt the blood start running down his face and blinked against the pain and the dizziness of this latest wound. Fighting through both, he stood, staring at the figure who faced them.

Lexa.

Chris noticed her face—badly injured, just like his and Alicia's. He realized how much the three of them mirrored each other at this moment. So damaged. In another world, he would try to talk to Lexa, perhaps even to understand everything that she had done—was still doing. But right now, he just wanted to get his girls off this rock. And Lexa was standing in his way.

"I'm sorry," she said, training her weapon on him. In his peripheral vision, Chris saw Alicia step in front of Jane and Emma. "I just needed to knock some sense into you."

Chris glanced down. His gun was nearby, but it was too far for him to grab in time. He saw the look in Lexa's eye—desperate, murderous. Splotches of blood were sprayed across her body, though she didn't seem to be injured, other than her face. He wondered how many people she had killed tonight.

He needed to keep her talking, figure out a plan. He raised his hands, managed a half-smile.

"It's okay, I understand," he said. "This situation has gotten really bad. I just want to take my girls and get out of here. Okay? You can do whatever you want, but please just let us go."

"*Let you go?*" she said, then laughed, a bizarre sound punctuated by more gunfire in the distance. "I need you here, Chris. I thought you knew that."

"I can't stay, Lexa," he responded, taking the smallest half-step possible towards his weapon. If she noticed, she made no indication of it.

"Where are you even gonna go?" she scoffed, laughing again. "It's a wasteland out there. Trust me, I know! I went out there every goddamn day, climbed underground and worked my fingers to the bone, trying to get quadromite for the stupid fucking USM! Trust me, there is *nothing* out there for you and your girls. Or that worthless one-armed piece of junk you're still carting around."

He felt anger rising in his chest at her words but breathed deeply, calmed himself. He needed to keep his wits if he was going to get past Lexa.

"We can turn everything around, Chris. Can't you see that? The marines are *all* dead. We knew they were coming, and we were prepared. And Jennifer? Yes, her troops are tough—but we can beat them. But I need you by my side in order to do that, Chris. I... I love you."

The declaration surprised him, and for a moment, he felt pity for her because he knew she meant it.

He knew he should keep his mouth shut, perhaps should lie, tell her what she wanted to hear. But he couldn't— especially not in front of Alicia and his daughters. Instead, he told her the truth.

"Lexa, you don't even know me."

For a moment, she looked completely shocked at his words, and then her eyes narrowed, face darkening. She took aim at Chris's forehead. He raised his hands slightly higher, realizing that he should have lied—but still glad that he'd said what was in his heart.

"Don't worry, I'll take care of your girls," Lexa said, barely more than a whisper, and tightened her finger on the trigger.

A blur of motion appeared near Lexa and a large, dark form connected with her as her gun fired, the bullet whizzing past Chris's head. Splayed out on the ground, Lexa screamed as the Xenomorph's claws dug into her stomach.

Chris's mouth fell open as he backed up, trying to make sense of what he was seeing. He had just killed the Xenomorph in the movie theater. Had he been wrong? Had the monster somehow survived?

He quickly realized that this creature was smaller than the one he had just dispatched but seemed even more vicious than the previous one.

Lexa's scream was cut off as the monster's jaws sank into her throat, its serrated and jagged tail glinting in the moonlight. Blood arced out and splattered its black skin. Lexa's body shuddered and then went still.

But Chris wasn't watching. He had picked up his weapon and was already running, Jane clutched to his chest with his free arm, seemingly weightless in his panic.

Alicia held Emma in her one arm and ran next to Chris.

She could easily have run faster, outpaced him twice

over, but she took comfort in having Chris by her side, their girls grasped tightly.

Their girls.

Part of her felt confusion at these thoughts. When they escaped this planet—*if* they escaped this planet—she would try to understand exactly what was happening to her.

And she knew that Chris would help.

The main exit loomed ahead, a dark mouth beckoning them forward. She could hear skittering behind them but neither of them looked back, and both girls had their eyes shut and shoved against the crook of their respective adult's shoulder.

They sprinted through a corridor that led to the large metal doors, Alicia cocking her head slightly to the side as she attempted to make her way through the white noise of the OST's overwhelmed operating system. It was close to shutting down completely—which was fine with her. She just needed to remotely hack into the system one last time, something she'd been struggling to do after Margaret's experiments on her.

"Can you…" Chris started to say, breathless.

"I'm trying," she responded, locking eyes with him. A strange feeling erupted in her stomach, and she couldn't believe how much she felt for this man. This human.

Just as she started to get nervous that she would fail, she pushed through and connected with the OST's system and gave it one final order. The door started to open, the raging winds of LV-1213 already pushing against them.

* * *

Chris lowered his head against the elements and plunged outside the dome, the first time he'd been outside in far too long. It was difficult to breathe in this atmosphere but not impossible.

The USM ship was two miles away—not a terribly daunting distance if they'd been back on Earth. But here, with this dangerous terrain and holding Jane in his arms, it would take time to get there—time they didn't have. Slowing but continuing to move forward, he dropped his older daughter to the ground. Her eyes popped open, and she looked up at him with a mixture of terror and resolve.

"I need you to make it the rest of the way on your own, okay?" he said. "I need you to do this one last thing, and then we can relax."

She began running as fast as possible next to her dad, both of them careful not to twist an ankle as they made their way towards the distant, unseen ship. Alicia, still holding Emma, followed close behind, the OST slowly receding behind them.

"Is it still behind us?" Chris shouted, knowing he should look back, search for the Xenomorph, but focusing instead on keeping Jane's hand in his, eyes peeled for the USM ship.

"I don't think s—"

Alicia's words were cut off by a pained grunt and Chris whirled, Jane's hand falling from his. The monster had tackled Alicia, pinned her to the ground, its claws digging into her arm, jaws already beginning to extend towards her face.

"No!" Chris shouted and rushed forward, raising his assault rifle and trying to aim for a spot that wouldn't result in acid pouring down onto Alicia.

Just as he found a headshot that he thought would spare her, Chris watched helplessly as the creature's tail whipped towards him, lightning fast. He had never seen an appendage move that quickly. Before he could even react, it struck his head, sending him to the ground, the gun falling from his hands and clattering down amongst the rocks.

His forehead made contact with something sharp, and he felt fresh blood flowing down his face, stinging his eyes. Breathing heavily, once again ignoring the pain like he'd been trained to do, he wiped his eyes clear and was shocked to see the Xenomorph charging towards him.

Why did it abandon Alicia? he wondered. It could have easily killed her, ripped her to pieces. Perhaps, Chris thought, as the monster bore down on him, it knew on some level that he'd been the one who had killed its sibling. Perhaps this was fitting—could he really blame this monster for hating him? How many people had Chris killed during his years as a USM soldier? As he scrambled back, the rocks scraping his palms, knowing that he couldn't move fast enough to get away from the Xenomorph, he thought maybe he deserved what was about to happen. He just hoped Alicia could get Jane and Emma away while he struggled with and ultimately succumbed to this killing machine.

Just as the Xenomorph was about to reach him, Chris shut his eyes—an instinct, really. He had always thought he would meet his death with eyes wide open, but his brain didn't agree with that assessment, and his world turned black a second before death descended upon him.

The sound of Jane's voice rose above the howling wind.

"Dad! Catch!"

Chris opened his eyes, rolling out of the way as he did so. The monster crashed into a large rock, which exploded into a barrage of shrapnel, several pieces entering Chris's body—more pain, more blood.

He didn't feel it, didn't even notice. He blinked through the gore on his face and saw that Jane was holding the assault rifle, ready to throw it to him. He smiled, an insane bloody grin, and held out his hand, pleading with his eyes for her to move fast.

In the corner of his eye, Chris could see the creature getting to its feet, letting out an enraged scream as it did so. But he didn't look away, kept his gaze focused on his daughter as she threw the weapon with all her strength, falling to the ground as she did so, her own hands splitting open, blood gushing out immediately. But she didn't cry, didn't make a sound, just watched as the weapon sailed through the air towards her father.

Despite the screams, human and otherwise, and the increasing winds, the entire scene went silent for Chris, almost devolved into slow motion. He watched as the gun spun through the air towards him, knew that he needed to keep his eyes on it, needed to time his catch perfectly, despite the fact that the Xenomorph was already scrabbling across the rocks towards him.

Jane's throw was perfect. Chris's hand wrapped around the grip and he fumbled the weapon only slightly as he turned at the same time, hoping there was enough time to get his finger on the trigger and fire on the alien.

There wasn't.

The monster crashed into him, its smaller but no less deadly set of teeth tearing into his shoulder. Chris grit his teeth, didn't scream, and fired the weapon. The resulting acid might kill him, but it would be a death on his terms.

The bullets went wide, missing the creature's skull by millimeters. The Xenomorph removed its teeth from Chris's shoulder, clawed at him and readied its razor-like teeth for a killing blow, drool dripping from its jaws.

Through the pain, Chris tried to adjust the rifle, to get a clear shot, but the monster had him pinned. There was nothing more he could do.

A large rock suddenly connected with the monster's head, snapping it back and loosening its grasp on Chris, though not enough for a clear shot. Both combatants looked over and saw that Alicia and the two girls had picked up rocks and were throwing them at the Xenomorph.

"Get off my daddy!" Emma screamed, throwing a rock that didn't come anywhere near hitting the monster.

Chris almost laughed, probably due to the blood loss, he surmised, but continued to push back against the creature, which still had him pinned.

He and Alicia made eye contact and his stomach twisted all over again. This couldn't be it. There was still so much he had to say to her.

The auton picked up another rock from the ground and threw it at the alien with incredible speed and accuracy, hitting the Xenomorph directly in the head again, causing it to rock back farther, just enough to loosen its grip further on Chris.

"Dad!" Jane screamed, holding a rock but watching the struggle with huge tears in her eyes.

Chris smashed the Xenomorph across its jaw with the weapon and it slashed at him with its tail, but he rolled away, fresh wounds crisscrossing his body. He got to his feet as the alien charged again, indefatigable, but Chris was ready. He aimed directly at its mouth.

War will always find a man like you.

"No more," he whispered, and squeezed the trigger.

The bullet hit exactly where Chris had been aiming, exploding out the back of the monster's head. It collapsed a few feet away from him, claws still outstretched. The twitching Xenomorph writhed as it attempted to reach its enemy, acid blood pouring from its ruptured skull and melting the rocks around it.

Alicia and his girls reached him instead, and he held them, unaware of his many wounds or the pain, reveling in the feeling of the people he loved in such close proximity to him after all that they'd suffered.

The creature let out a final pained sigh, and then stopped moving, the thick drool still dripping from its half-open mouth.

"Come on," Chris said, scanning the distance for the USM ship as the wind continued to pick up. "It isn't that much farther."

The four of them continued on, moving as fast as possible as the dark clouds rumbled past overhead, the light of the three moons playing over their bodies, then vanishing, then appearing again, over and over until the small, exhausted family finally reached the ship.

2 5

Covered in bandages after a quick stop at the ship's medical bay, an exhausted Chris Temple settled into the captain's chair, the controls laid out in front of him.

He'd been on this kind of USM ship more times than he could count. It was a newer model, but the mechanics were fundamentally the same. He just hoped his personal passcode would still work.

"Here goes nothing," he said to Alicia and the girls, who had all taken various seats on the bridge. He laughed silently, without mirth—this was easily the strangest crew he had ever commanded.

He punched in the code and for a second, but nothing happened. *Goddamn it*, he thought, but then the computer powered up, the engines humming to life.

"You did it, Daddy!" Emma yelled, bouncing up and down in her seat. Chris smiled at her, glanced at Jane, whose hands were also wrapped in bandages. Her eyes were already starting to droop. Once they got out of orbit, he would check out the hypersleep chambers.

Chris inputted a series of instructions, the steps coming back to him in a rush. As the vessel rose up off the ground, the thrusters melting the rocks beneath them, Chris let out a long sigh. They had done it. Jane and Emma were safe. That was all that mattered.

The winds were strong, and even through the incredibly well-crafted nature of this marine ship, they could feel those forces pushing against its hull. Chris punched in another series of commands to compensate, and then turned on the viewscreen as well, positioning it so that they could see the OST as they passed over it.

The power was completely out, at least at this moment, but the moons of LV-1213 were unobscured, so the four of them had a clear view of the colony that had been their home for the past several days.

In the middle of the ruined town square, people were fighting, using guns and other weapons, as well as multiple instances of hand-to-hand combat. From this height, Chris couldn't tell who was who—they all looked the same.

Emma appeared next to him, eyes glued to the screen, and Chris picked her up, depositing him onto his lap as they both continued to watch the conflict.

"Why are they still fighting, Daddy?" she asked, barely more than a whisper.

He thought about it for a moment as they made their way past Mining Outpost Omega Seven Tango, and then it was gone from the viewscreen, lost forever behind them.

"I think that's the only thing they know how to do," he responded, tapping the computer again, changing the view to the stars above as they ascended towards them.

"There's another outpost approximately five hundred trillion miles away, Chris," Alicia told him. "If we maintain optimal hyperdrive speed, we can be there in approximately two months."

"Sounds like the perfect amount of time to eat a big meal and then take a nice, long nap," he answered. "What do you think, Jane?"

His older daughter, looking exhausted and grumpy, trudged over and climbed up into his lap, too, curling into him like the baby she had once been. Chris thought about Elizabeth, missed her so much, but he had kept his promise—their girls were safe.

Once they were out of orbit and their course laid in, Alicia walked over and stood next to Chris, slowly putting his arm around his shoulder. Jane and Emma were both asleep in his lap and his eyes were feeling pretty heavy, too. He smiled up at Alicia and leaned back against her arm.

"Hey," he said.

"Hello," she responded, smiling.

Chris turned back to the viewscreen, and the two of them gazed out at the distant stars, at their unknown but beckoning future, silent, man and machine—safe and together, at last.

AUTHOR'S NOTE

Alien debuted in theaters on June 22, 1979. I was seven years old, so perhaps it's not entirely surprising that I didn't see it on the big screen during its initial run (though I *had* seen *Star Wars* two years earlier when it finally hit our local dollar theater—at least according to my sister, and I am inclined to believe her, mostly because I *want* it to be true).

I'm not sure when I first saw *Alien,* but it must have been during my VHS obsession in the mid and late 1980s. Luckily, the clerks working at our local mom-and-pop video store didn't sweat renting R-rated movies to underaged kids, so I was lucky to watch such sci-fi classics as *Blade Runner, The Terminator,* and of course, *Alien.*

Ridley Scott's perfect blend of science fiction and horror will make an impression on anyone, but even more on a young person who had no idea that a monster would—you know—burst out of someone's chest, or that several of the characters would literally knock one of their co-workers' heads off and the guy *would keep coming after them*. (I mean, how cool is Ash?)

As I mentioned in my dedication, while every frame of *Alien* is cinematic perfection, the film contains three essential elements that have allowed this franchise to grow into multiple movies, comic books, video games, and (as you are very aware) novels. These three elements are:

The Corporation

The Monster

The Android

Any *one* of these would be cool, but there's something very special about all three of them together. At the heart of each, there is an inherent coldness that is at fundamental odds with the humanity of the protagonists in each *Alien* story. That's part of the reason why it was so fun to create an android, Alicia, who would buck that trend. I'm fascinated with AI (and terrified by it, to be honest), so it was a true pleasure to explore the concepts of identity and humanity.

Like almost every *Alien* fan, I also loved James Cameron's *Aliens* (also seen before I was 'supposed to' on VHS), which revealed even more about 'The Company,' calling it Weyland-Yutani for the first time (and even showcasing its now famous—or infamous—logo). It is one of those rare sequels that is as good as its predecessor, if for different reasons. I particularly loved Ripley's expanded story, and the addition of Hicks, Bishop, and Newt. It's a propulsive, heart-pounding film with fantastic character moments throughout.

Alien³ was the first of the franchise that I actually saw in the theater. I was twenty years old and had just finished my sophomore year of college. I remember being excited to finally see an *Alien* film on the big screen, but within the first few minutes, I knew that I was probably not going to enjoy myself.

Not only did they kill off Hicks and Bishop, two characters that I loved, but they killed off Newt! The little girl that Ripley had fought like hell to save during the better part of *Aliens*. It honestly felt like a kick in the teeth (at least to me), even though I recognized that it was an incredibly well-made film.

Before I discuss *Alien: Resurrection*, an important film in terms of the novel you've just read, it's important that I talk a little more about *Alien³*—because it's my personal distaste for that film's opening scene that led to the creation of this very book.

A few years ago, I became aware that a graphic novel version of William Gibson's *Alien³* screenplay had been published, so I quickly bought a copy. Finally! An *Alien³* that didn't kill off three of my favorite sci-fi characters of all time (at least, I hoped).

But when I read this 'alternate universe' *Alien³*, I still felt highly unsatisfied. Yes, Gibson is a fantastic, legendary writer. Yes, the art was great. But it wasn't the *Alien³* story that I wanted.

So, I did what any normal person would do: I wrote a treatment for my *own Alien³*! In *my* version, Ripley, Hicks, and Newt crash land on a planet, forming a family unit, only to discover themselves in the middle of a very dangerous conflict, and with a Xenomorph thrown into the mix as well, of course. I didn't write the treatment for any other reason than I just wanted this version to exist. Even if it was only fan fiction.

As fate would have it, however, I was already in business with the publisher who had the rights to do *Alien* novels, Titan Books. They were just about to publish my original *Morbius* novel, *Blood Ties*, and would later hire me to write a *Guardians of the Galaxy* novel as well.

So, realizing it was a longshot, I sent my *Alien³* treatment to my *Morbius* editor, Steve Saffel. To my utter lack of surprise, he told me pretty much immediately that they were decidedly not interested in publishing yet another version of *Alien³*. Which was fine. I had expected that. And I was still glad that I'd written it. I filed it away with all of my other dream prequel/sequel pitches that had never come to fruition (*Blade Runner*, *Tron*, etc.).

Then, a year and a half later, Steve reached back out to me and asked if we could discuss *Alien* again. He wanted me to pitch an original novel, taking what I'd already written (which he liked) and tweaking it so that it had no connection to any previous iterations, other than it taking place within the larger *Alien* universe. I politely accepted his invitation. (I believe what I actually said was *HELL YES, I'D LIKE TO DO THAT!!!*)

Sure enough, I took my *Alien³* concept and modified the

concept, and I was over the moon when Steve told me that Titan wanted to publish the book. Now I just had to write it!

The first question was *when* it would take place during the lengthy *Alien* timeline. As mentioned, there are movies, comics, video games, and novels—the franchise literally covers centuries.

I was put in touch with Clara Čarija, Titan's resident *Alien* expert. We had a lovely conversation (on opposite sides of the world, which seemed somehow appropriate) and she suggested that I set the book shortly after the events of *Alien: Resurrection*.

This gave me a chance to watch the fourth *Alien* film for the first time since I had seen it in the theater in 1997. At the time, I had just moved to New York City and remember being underwhelmed by the film.

Revisiting it recently, however, I found it to be highly enjoyable and I took notes as I watched, realizing that setting my novel in this section of the *Alien* timeline opened up all kinds of cool possibilities.

And then I dove into writing, and you are now holding the end result of that process.

To say writing an original *Alien* novel is an honor would be a huge understatement. I *love* this franchise. I mean, who doesn't love building better worlds?!

ACKNOWLEDGEMENTS

First and foremost, I want to deeply thank Steve Saffel. I explained in detail how he came to hire me to write *Morbius: Blood Ties* in the Author's Note section of that novel, but suffice it to say that a general publishing meeting with Steve several years ago changed my life for the better. He is a great editor and an even better human.

I would like to thank my previous agents and editors, all of whom helped me in my writing career. Each win leads to the next, and I'm incredibly appreciative of all of these people: Richard Pine, Charlie Olsen, Anthony Ziccardi, Melissa Singer, and Fenton Coulthurst.

I also want to thank all teachers everywhere. You are underappreciated and underpaid, and the best teachers in my life made it possible for me to not only pursue my dreams, but also to attain them.

Two other dream supporters include my parents, Irene Murray and Rich Deneen, to whom I dedicated my

Guardians of the Galaxy novel.

I'd also like to thank Daft Punk. I always listen to a single album when writing a novel, and for this one, I listened to the *Tron: Legacy* soundtrack. It was the perfect backdrop for Xenomorphs, evil corporations, unexpected love, and a dad who just wants to keep his girls safe.

Huge thanks to Daquan Cadogan, who worked hard to help get this novel into its finest form possible. We spent a lot of time emailing about every aspect of the book, and he is a joy to work with. As a professional editor myself, I know what he does for Titan is no small feat—and it is deeply appreciated.

Finally, thank you to my amazing wife, Kim, and our two daughters, Eloise and Charlotte. Your continued support means the world (and universe) to me.

ABOUT THE AUTHOR

Brendan Deneen is the author of the award-winning coming-of-age novel *The Ninth Circle*, as well as the critically acclaimed horror novels *The Chrysalis* and *Morbius: Blood Ties*. He's also the author of the four volume *Rocket And Groot* picture book series for Marvel/Disney, and *Green Arrow: Stranded*, an original middle grade graphic novel for DC Comics. His other graphic novel work includes multiple volumes of *Flash Gordon*, an original *Island of Misfit Toys* book, and the dark superhero tale *Scatterbrain*. Upcoming graphic novels include *The Bones of the Gods* and *Mortimer The Lazy Bird*. His short stories and essays have been published by St. Martin's Press, Reader's Digest Books, 13Thirty Press, and Necro Publications.

ALIENS™

BISHOP

T. R. NAPPER

Massively damaged in *Aliens* and *Alien 3*, the synthetic
Bishop asked to be shut down forever. His creator,
Michael Bishop, has other plans. He seeks the Xenomorph
knowledge stored in the android's mind, and brings Bishop
back to life—but for what reason? No longer an employee
of the Weyland-Yutani Corporation, Michael tells his
creation that he seeks to advance medical research for the
benefit of humanity. Yet where does he get the resources
needed to advance his work. With whom do his new
allegiances lie?

Bishop is pursued by Colonial Marines Captain Marcel
Apone, commander of the *Il Conde* and younger brother of
Master Sergeant Alexander Apone, one of the casualties of
the doomed mission to LV-426. Also on his trail are the "Dog
Catchers," commandos employed by Weyland-Yutani.

Who else might benefit from Bishop's intimate knowledge
of the deadliest creatures in the galaxy?

TITANBOOKS.COM

For more fantastic fiction, author events,
exclusive excerpts, competitions, limited editions and more

VISIT OUR WEBSITE
titanbooks.com

LIKE US ON FACEBOOK
facebook.com/titanbooks

FOLLOW US ON TWITTER AND INSTAGRAM
@TitanBooks

EMAIL US
readerfeedback@titanemail.com